— Book 2 —

VERITY CHRONICLES

DIVIDED LOYALTIES

T S VALMOND

A K DUBOFF

Published by Dawnrunner Press
Cover Copyright © 2020 A.K. Duboff

ISBN-10: 1954344066
ISBN-13: 978-1954344068

0 9 8 7 6 5 4 3 2

Produced in the United States of America

TABLE OF CONTENTS

KEY TERMS, CAST, & LOCATIONS

KEY TERMS

Taran – The race of all people in the Taran Empire; synonymous with human

Tararian Guard – The primary military force for the Taran Empire

Tararian Selective Service (TSS) – A quasi-military organization with Agents specializing in telekinesis; a complement to the Tararian Guard

Jump – Faster-than-light travel through subspace

Beacon Network – The navigation method for subspace jumps, maintained by SiNavTech

High Dynasties – The seven ruling families of the Taran Empire, collectively a governing council

Lower Dynasties – Influential families throughout the Taran worlds, second only in power to the High Dynasties

CAST

Verity **Crew and Passengers**
Iza Sundari – Captain of the Verity
Trix – Lynaedan android companion of Iza
Joe Anderson (AKA 'Jovani Saletas') – Undercover TSS Agent
Braedon Valtteri (AKA 'Devon Arvonen') – Pilot and VR gamer with a gambling problem
Cierra Quetzali – Healer and Braedon's ex-girlfriend

Apex Enterprises
Karter Hyttinen – Lower Dynasty heir and starship salesman
Becca Drejas – Karter's right-hand and assistant

Iron Dog Crew
Marten Douketis – Captain of the *Iron Dog* hauling freighter
Sydney Reis – Second-in-command of the *Iron Dog*

Additional Key Characters
Desirae Hyttinen – Failed TSS Agent turned Enforcer; cousin to Karter
Victor Arvonen – Head of Arvonen Dynasty; father to Devon
Viper – Competitive gamer and engineering genius
Yeaga – Leader of the miner revolt on Hubyria
Ian Mandren – TSS Sacon Agent Division Lead; Joe's direct supervisor

LOCATIONS
Tararia – The central planet of the Taran Empire

Lynaeda – Technologically advanced central world, specializing in AI and cybernetics
Beurias – Middle world with significant shipping industry, including headquarters of Apex Enterprises
Galminus – Dusty outer colony world; transit hub
Hubyria – Outer colony planet specializing in ore mining
Leveckis – Outer colony planet; home to Cierra
Phiris – Prosperous middle world
Sarduvis – Asteroid housing the Sarduvis Penitentiary

1

FOR THE FIFTH time that morning, Iza wondered why she'd allowed so many people on her ship. All she needed were a couple of non-sentient androids to help Trix carry heavy loads when the time came. What she had instead were complications, expenses, and liabilities.

She tried to block out Braedon's and Cierra's bickering as she scooped up more hay to toss around the makeshift pen in the back corner of the cargo deck. "Can we get there any faster?" Her question echoed off the large domed room as she called out to Trix working on the opposite side of the room.

Trix's pale skin hid her non-organic components, her brunette hair hanging past her shoulders in neat waves as she bent over to move more bales of hay into the cargo hold in preparation for their next job. The Lynaedan android could pass for any woman delivering news in the Sensationals, but her artificial frame could lift five times her body weight and her advanced processing core could complete computations impossible for anyone of flesh and blood. Of all Iza's crew members, Trix was the one she could trust to be drama-free and focused on the task at hand.

Trix scrutinized Iza. "We are almost to our destination now, and the route was plotted in accordance with your instructions to minimize transit fees. Specifically, you said," she switched into an exact copy of Iza's voice, " 'We're not made of money, so get us there on the cheap. This boat is already costing me too much as it is. I refuse to give those bomaxed officials another credit.' "

"Yeah, yeah." Iza's mouth twitched as she held back a smile. Trix had no idea she was so funny.

Owning a starship meant having the credits to take care of minor things like repairs and transit fees, so she needed to be smart about her expenditures. In some cases, taking a little longer was worth the savings gained by traveling through normal space rather than using the SiNavTech beacon navigation network for subspace jumps. At least her next job was a done deal; she only had to pick up the haul and drop it off on a nearby colony. It was so easy she could do it in her sleep. Too bad she wasn't getting any.

Strange dreams continued to disrupt Iza's rest. She blamed the mysterious artifact she'd found under the stairs in the cargo hold a month and a half prior. The metal sphere remained in its box within her nightstand, humming. Whatever its origins and purpose she couldn't blame the sphere for her annoying guests. Nor was it the cause of her current dilemma with Jovani Saletas or her fake engagement to Karter Hyttinen.

Above, Braedon and Cierra erupted into another round of shouting about natural cooking and Braedon's unappreciation for holistic living.

Iza sighed. "I miss it being just the two of us," she said to Trix.

The android shook her head. "You do not mean that. You

are happier now than you have been in the many years I've known you."

Maybe I am, but for how long? Iza didn't reply out loud. She hadn't even been able to tell Trix about the true nature of her arrangement with Karter. When Jovani learned about the engagement, she had no doubt it would devastate him. She'd tried to keep her distance, but she could only make so many excuses.

She vented her frustration through the hay-tossing. As if the interpersonal drama wasn't enough, she could never escape the mysterious sphere's infernal humming emanating from the nightstand drawer in her cabin decks above. It didn't matter where it was, the hum followed her everywhere. Iza still found it strange that no one else heard it. Other people would probably laugh and assume she was crazy if she told them the truth about what she'd found in that hidden little box.

Iza and Trix completed the preparations for receiving their cargo, and they headed for the flight deck. She wasn't keen about their pickup from Galminus, but it paid well. The last time she'd been on the planet, the local Enforcers had falsely accused her of transporting stolen goods. This time around, she didn't want to risk any delays or complications.

Jobs never came easy. Iza had to haggle, debate, and persuade the people she worked with that she had the capacity and honesty to get products delivered on time. With all the underhanded dealings and disreputable crews out there, the Taran Empire needed sharp-witted and honest haulers. She was up for the challenge, provided the universe was willing to give her a chance.

The *Verity* dropped out from subspace shortly after Iza arrived on the flight deck. She stared out the viewport at the world's familiar green and red landmasses where the dry northern hemisphere met the wet southern one.

"How are we on timing?" Iza asked.

"We are on schedule for the pickup," Trix replied from where she stood at the center of the flight deck. "I should note, however, that there was a slight hesitation during our last entry to subspace. I will run a diagnostic on the jump drive."

"Thanks, Trix. I want to stay ahead of any problems. No more getting stranded due to poor maintenance."

Along the port side of the room, Jovani was at the tactical station. Iza couldn't recall offering him an official place on the crew, but she couldn't argue with the skills of the former TSS Agent. "Just a heads up, there's a chance that we'll have trouble at the border."

"Why?" Iza asked. Jovani had a knack for sensing potential issues; that's why she liked him at tactical, even though his presence tended to cloud her head. "Aren't the clearance codes working? Our documentation is legitimate."

"No, it's something else." His eyes narrowed as he pored over information on his console. "All ships are being stopped at the border and questioned. It appears there was an incident earlier today."

"Why bother with the inbound ships?" she asked.

"In case they're arriving to aid an escape, I suppose." Jovani shrugged.

Iza made a tsk of annoyance. It was the last thing she needed today, but she remained calm and put on what she hoped was her most charming smile. Enforcers loved a friendly smile.

"Trix, open a comms channel to border patrol."

"Channel open."

The holodisplay went black and then white as the vid displayed the Enforcer sitting in front of a white background.

"This is Captain Sundari of the *Verity*. We're here on a standard haul."

"Just checking your credentials, Captain. We had some trouble this morning." The local Enforcer seemed annoyed to have to repeat his story.

"What kind of trouble?" Iza asked. Despite his annoyance, she wasn't going to miss the opportunity to get as much information out of him as she could.

"It's all over the local news. Several of our top scientists went missing from the lab in the Upper West End at the start of the workday. It seems they were just going about their business when someone snatched them."

"Is there a shortage of scientists in the colonies?" Iza asked in an attempt to lighten his mood.

"Not that I'm aware of," he replied, missing her intended humor. "All of them were average folk with families. If you hear or see anything out of the ordinary, we're asking that you report it to the Guard immediately."

"Will do," Iza acknowledged with a small salute. "Any leads yet on who took them?"

"No, but if you've got a scientist on board, I suggest you keep an eye on 'em." His image disappeared, and the viewport once again showed the stars with the planet in front of them.

"Was that his idea of a joke?" Iza asked, but neither Trix nor Jovani responded.

Missing people weren't altogether uncommon in the outer reaches of the Taran colonies. The authorities didn't like to admit that more and more criminal elements were taking root throughout the border worlds. Though those organizations weren't new, the recent shift in governance on Tararia had provided a prime opportunity for power-plays. She hated to think what might be in the works if scientists were being abducted. No doubt, it was to craft tools of war rather than for anything altruistic.

While Iza was trying to think of another witty comment, Braedon entered. He sat down in the pilot's seat, his shoulders slumped forward in defeat. His last bout with Cierra hadn't gone his way, it seemed. Anyone with eyes saw the connection between them, but their differences seemed to outweigh everything else. Braedon started mumbling to himself.

"Something wrong?" Jovani asked.

"I don't get it. I do everything I can to make her happy, but it's never enough. How am I supposed to improve when she runs away from me or shuts down?"

Jovani gave Iza a significant glance that made her pulse quicken before turning back to Braedon. "Women are a mystery and we may never fully understand them, but trying and getting it right five times out of ten makes it all worthwhile," he said.

"Braedon, run a check on the local broadcasts to see what we can find out about the scientists that were abducted."

"Abducted scientists?" Braedon's fingers tapped the smooth screen of the console for a moment before he turned back to Iza. "Ah, looks like there was an official statement from a local governor about the abductions and the information in that is just being repeated everywhere else. The governor didn't seem overly concerned about the kidnappings. He must not be into science." Braedon shrugged. "I'll keep checking, maybe dive into the Sensationals for more news."

"You're not going to find any real news there, don't waste your time," Iza said with a wave of one hand. "Trix, once we have the all-clear, put us back on course for the pickup coordinates, and let's get our haul."

"Yes, Captain."

—

They parked the *Verity* on the outskirts of town. It was still a remote, dusty area that hadn't yet been developed beyond a rudimentary ship port and related services.

"What are we picking up today?" Braedon asked, standing up from his seat.

"Sheep."

"Sheep?" Jovani tilted his head. "I guess that explains the hay."

"Yes, there's a breeder on Beurias who needs good stock. The sheep will be quite the haul, since they'll be live cargo. That's extra credits for the crew. Once the sheep are on board, it's going to be noisy and messy down there. So watch your step."

"Got it. And will there be some time to handle necessary business while we're here?" Braedon rubbed his hands together in anticipation.

"I won't stop you if you've got stuff to do. Trix and I can handle the sheep for now, but stay out of trouble. If you get yourself arrested by Enforcers and thrown onto Sarduvis again, I promise I won't be waiting around."

"It was just the one time. When are you going to let that go?" Braedon shouted and then grabbed Jovani by the arm. "Don't leave without us. Jovani's cute to look at, but what would you do without me?"

"We do not need another pilot," Trix said. She seemed annoyed he would imply they needed him at all.

Iza rolled her eyes and smiled back at Jovani, who grinned at her.

"Bye," Iza sang as Braedon dragged Jovani off the flight

deck. "Trix, adjust the temperature controls. I swear Braedon has been playing with them again lately; it's blazing hot in here."

— — —

Joe followed Braedon down the metal ramp from the *Verity*'s cargo hold into the warm sun. As he stepped onto the red dirt, his handheld signaled a message from his TSS commander, Ian Mandren. Joe ignored it, making a mental note to report in later once he had something useful to pass on. Trouble at the border and missing scientists weren't exactly breaking news for the TSS. Maybe he could investigate a little more after Braedon revealed his latest scheme.

He took a deep breath of the fresh air before he spoke. "So where are we *really* going?"

Braedon gave him a sly smile and then rubbed his hand over the back of his neck. "I can't keep anything hidden from you. Are you always reading my mind?"

"No, reading you doesn't require that much work. I know you well enough. If you have an agenda different from what you've told Iza, it's best I'm made aware of it ahead of time."

Braedon pouted in annoyance before he shrugged and kept walking. "You're right. Guess, I better work on hiding my feelings. Maybe that's my trouble with Cierra. Though I think she actually *is* reading my mind."

He easily kept up with Braedon's brisk pace. "Braedon, where are we going?" he asked, grabbing Braedon by the front of his shirt.

The teenager sighed. "All right. I've been monitoring my father's activities, and he's been attempting to hire several high-ranking scientists."

"Do you think your father is involved in these disappearances?" Joe released his grasp.

"I dunno, it's possible. When it comes to that artifact, he's obsessed. Let me put it this way: if this is related to that thing, he wouldn't lose any sleep over abducting a few people." Braedon waved him forward. "I have an idea. I'll tell you more on the way."

Joe thought hard about that as they trudged along the road leading into the city. Braedon's father, Victor Arvonen, had proven himself a real threat to Iza and the *Verity* in the past. He was prepared to fire on the ship and his own son in pursuit of the artifact. If the artifact gave the man more power within the Taran Empire, there'd be plenty of reason to report it to the TSS.

They passed from the pasture lands and onto the more spacious and populated transportation roads. Perhaps he'd have a chance to make a call in private.

After four kilometers in the heat, Jovani's shirt was sticking to his back and he cursed the planet's large sun. Braedon, his hair dripping with sweat, hired the first available transport. He didn't even protest the price, which Jovani thought was exorbitant. The small shuttlecraft sat four comfortably and blew cool air on their seats while the driver sped past residential buildings. The neighborhood transitioned into a commercial district, and the buildings grew taller and more ostentatious the closer they got to the city center.

"There were several well-known scientist types that I grew up with. They know my father and will have seen his requests in the Sensationals. If they can help us figure it out, I can ruin his plans," Braedon explained.

Joe gave him a sidelong look. He'd been wanting to investigate on his own. Once again, his connection to Braedon turned out to be much better. After they had gathered proof against Arvonen, the TSS would have the justification they needed to move against him. "When did you first realize you were the son of a megalomaniac?"

Braedon squinted his eyes and laughed. "When he pulled me into his office and told me that power was the only thing that mattered. He said, 'It's our birthright, Son. It's our duty as a family to acquire it at all costs.'"

Joe raised his eyebrows.

"Yeah, I was five years old and he'd missed my latest accomplishment. Later, I found it was almost an exact quote from a VR game I was into at the time."

"Wow, you handled it well, considering."

"If by 'well' you mean setting fire to my home. Then gambling away my inheritance, before disappearing in a stolen ship of my father's, then yeah. I've adjusted pretty well to being raised by a selfish and power-hungry man."

"Okay, maybe the fire was a little over the top, but otherwise," Joe said with a smile that made Braedon laugh.

The city bustled around them as the shuttle zipped in and out of traffic. Joe spotted a grouping of six large buildings designed to look like they were twisting into the sky at nauseating heights.

Braedon pointed up at one of the tall, twisted buildings. "That's where we're going."

The shuttle let them out near the building entrance, and they entered the airy lobby, passing through the building's security checkpoint.

"The labs here are where the top scientists work on innovative new technologies," Braedon explained. "I have a friend in the astrometric lab who might know what's going on." He ambled to the elevator and ran a hand through his hair.

"What's her name?" Joe asked.

"What makes you think it's a girl?"

"You've touched your hair no less than three times since you caught sight of your reflection coming into the building. Once just before you pressed the call button."

Braedon laughed as he looked down at his shoes. "It's not like that, she's not interested in a gamer like me. Besides, I've got my eyes on someone else at the moment."

"Yes, yourself," Joe said punching him in the arm.

"When did you realize you were in love with Iz?"

Joe felt the punch in his chest whenever he thought about her. His TSS training kept his features neutral. "I'm not sure I'm in love with her yet, but my feelings for her aren't shallow."

Braedon nodded as if he understood. Considering his current situation with Cierra, it was possible.

They reached the eleventh floor of the building and Joe immediately noticed a change in the ambient energy intensity. A palpable shift in the air.

"Something's wrong," Joe said as he kept his back pressed to the wall, scanning the halls for activity.

"What? What's going on?"

"They're already here," Joe said.

"Who's here?"

"Your father and his people, at the end of the hall. We need to move quickly." Joe sprinted ahead.

He held up a hand for Braedon to wait as he drew his pulse handgun and peeked around the corner. He didn't spot anyone, but he could sense them coming.

"Stay back. They're coming," Joe said.

A moment later, a man and woman dressed in white lab coats came running in their direction. Their pursuers, presumably the men Arvonen sent, appeared from around the corner, closing the distance fast. Both were a head taller than Joe and wore fitted navy suits with masks over their faces.

Against Joe's instruction, Braedon peeked around to get a look at the corridor. "We have to help them!" he pleaded.

Without hesitation, Joe used his telekinetic ability to push the masked men away. They flew backward, as if caught in an invisible wind, and then collapsed on top of each other in a heap on the floor.

Braedon reached out, grabbing the female scientist as she reached out to him, her blue eyes wide with panic.

"We need to get out of here fast," Joe said. "Any ideas?"

"I'm resourceful, remember? Follow me." Braedon held tight to the woman's hand as he ran to the closest stairwell.

"Thank you," the male scientist said as he followed.

Joe groaned. "Where are we going? Those guys are going to be right behind us." Joe dashed down the stairs behind them. While he could easily disable the pursuers, he was already close to violating the TSS code of ethics by using his telekinetic abilities to slow them down. Considering the thin ice he was treading with the TSS, he didn't want to push his luck.

Braedon continued forward, undeterred. "We'll get to someplace they'll stand out and we'll blend in."

IZA WAS ABOUT to leave the flight deck when Trix held up her hand. "Captain, we're receiving an incoming transmission for Cierra."

Iza huffed, checking the local time. "Did you ping her?"

"She is not responding."

"Fine, put it on hold," Iza said with a sigh. "I'll let her know. Head down to the cargo hold and I'll meet you there."

Cierra was a gifted Healer, but the woman was almost intolerable; she was never where she should be, and she treated their everyday technology as if it contained some kind of transmittable disease. Iza jogged from the flight deck to Cierra's cabin just beyond the infirmary doors. It only took a minute to reach it before Iza pulled back a fist and pounded on the door.

Bomaxed incense. The stuff seeped beyond the edges of the cabin door.

"Hey, open up!"

The door eased open and the musky heat that blew into her face made Iza take a step back and cough. Iza glanced inside, and through the haze she noted the abundance of plant-life and a fountain of running water that dominated the cabin. *When did she accumulate so much junk?* The stone fountain had an invisible water source, using engineering Iza had never seen in person before. There had to be more than a dozen plants of different varieties in shades of pink, purple, and blue accenting the green.

Iza scowled. "Really? Are you trying to turn my ship into some kind of botanical lab?"

Cierra rested a hand on her right hip, her curves accentuated by her pink bodysuit with a sheer overlay. As usual, she was barefoot—an enduring safety hazard on the ship—which showed off her painted pastel pink toenails. "I believe I can decorate my cabin as I see fit. If you'd like, I'd be happy to add some botanicals to the flight deck or your cabin as it does wonders for the brain energy."

Is she insulting my brain? Iza wondered. Cierra had a tendency to be just cryptic enough to make it impossible to tell.

"No, thanks. Keep your nature inside your own cabin. Don't think I didn't notice what you did in the kitchen," Iza said, pointing an accusatory finger at her.

Cierra lifted one shoulder in an apathetic shrug.

"You realize if they're not bolted down, those pots you put everywhere could go flying," Iza said. *Not that the sheep would be safe, either, but that's not the point.*

"I've used a special adhesive to keep the pots from shifting, don't worry, Captain. I will tend to them as I do all of my plants. Is there a reason for your appearance at my door, or did you only come to berate me about my choice in decor?"

Iza had to bite down on another retort. Cierra Quetzali had a tendency to get under her skin. No wonder she and Braedon fought so much; she was a haughty little thing. She doubted he'd tolerate her at all if she didn't have the big curls, tight figure, and prominent gray eyes. Iza let out a huff and held back her remarks, allowing the annoyance to show on her face.

"You're getting an incoming call on the flight deck. If you prefer, you can take it audio-only right here."

"No, if I'm to use the technology I would prefer a face-to-face conference."

"Fine." Iza turned away from her. *Is she purposely trying my patience?* Iza glanced down at her handheld again. If she didn't hurry, the client would be upset and the haul might scatter to the winds. She needed to get moving. "The call is on hold, so all you have to do when you get to the flight deck—"

"I would like for you to come with me, Captain," Cierra said.

No, I've got better things to do. Like pull my hair out from the roots. Iza tried to keep the dismissiveness from her tone, "I have business to attend to."

"This won't take long. My parents will want to meet you, to see where I am living and with whom. Besides, if I'm not mistaken, the ship's computer systems haven't been behaving properly and I'm the last person to be able to fix something on the spot." Cierra strode out of her cabin toward the flight deck.

"Appeasing your parents isn't my responsibility."

Cierra waved a hand. "If I break your ship, it won't be my fault."

Iza glared at the other woman's back while she sauntered down the corridor. *No wonder Braedon can't break free from her. She's a master manipulator.*

The last thing Iza wanted to do was listen in on a call between Cierra and her parents, especially since it took daily meditation to keep from kicking her off the ship mid-flight, but she wasn't about to leave the flight deck unattended after

Cierra made that kind of remark. Cierra's feelings about the technology were obvious by how she lived, but if it hadn't been clear enough, she also refused to engage with Trix. Iza didn't expect them to be friends, but she demanded respect for Trix not only as crew but as her oldest friend. She might be an android, but Trix was a sophisticated, sentient being. Her loyalty had been tested and proven, whereas Cierra was about as helpful as a pebble underfoot.

Iza slumped into the captain's seat while Cierra accepted the video call, touching the console like it was infected.

A man and woman matching Cierra's dark complexion, but with graying hair and lined faces, appeared on the front display.

"Daughter, how are you? Until we received your message, we thought you were lost to the cosmos." Her mother's concern was evident in her cat-like eyes.

"Mama, Baba, things haven't been as I expected. However, I am well."

Iza listened to Cierra recount her tales and watched her father and mother sitting side-by-side engaged in the story. Behind them, a framed picture of a small cottage in a large wooded area reminded Iza of where they'd found Cierra on Leveckis. Perhaps the image served as inspiration for her living choices.

Cierra had her father's eyes, though his were kinder and more rounded at the edges. Her mother had the curls, but she kept them tamed under a bright floral scarf wrap. Several of the curls refusing to lie down, escaping at her neck and above her ears.

"You have abandoned your home to travel the stars. That doesn't seem like you," her father said. His playful smile and wink charmed a smirk out of Iza. They knew her well, it seemed.

"True, but circumstances required it. I am serving here as a Healer for the *Verity*. This is her captain, Iza Sundari," she said with a sweep of her hand.

Caught off-guard, Iza scrambled out of her seat and stood beside Cierra. "It's a pleasure," she said with a slight bow and raised one hand in the traditional formal Taran greeting.

"The pleasure is ours. We're happy to hear you are taking such good care of our daughter. She's not one for space travel, so I'm sure she is eager to get her feet on solid ground," her mother said.

"I am, you know me too well." Then, as if Iza was no longer standing there, Cierra continued, "Any news?"

Her parents shook their heads, uncomfortably looking to each other and then back at the display. "Not a word. Do you think she lives?"

"I know she does," Cierra said with a sigh. "Abby is too stubborn to be snuffed out. Perhaps she's been incarcerated for illegal activity. Give her time. I'm sure we'll all see her again before long."

Iza was debating whether to continue standing or to take her seat again when Cierra abruptly signed off.

"My love to both of you and stay strong." She held a fist to her chest.

"We will, Biscuit, and we love you," her father said as he and his wife each lifted a fist to their chest.

The exchange gripped at Iza's heart, and she had to work to clamp down the envy that sprang up. Instead, she bit back the tears that stung her eyes when she thought of her own parents.

Cierra turned to Iza. "Thank you, Captain. Now, I would like to spend some time outside the ship."

"Sure, your time is your own. You have at least a few hours while I conduct my business and wait for Braedon and Jovani to return. You'll find plenty of solid ground, but this area isn't as lush as you're accustomed to."

"It will be more than sufficient to rejuvenate me." She paused. "You seem distraught. Are you well?"

Once again, Iza was grateful that telepaths like Cierra couldn't read her. She left the flight deck without another word.

On her way to the cargo hold, Iza's thoughts drifted from her parents to the jarring dream she'd had the night before. In it, she had been standing hand-in-hand with Jovani beneath a giant ship, which frequented her nighttime visions. Her happiness of being in Jovani's presence was overshadowed by the feeling of being watched, like a cold brush of fingers over one shoulder. Someone seemed to follow her every step. But, when she glanced over her shoulder to see who was there, she was a second too late to catch them.

Iza shook off the flood of anxiety that gripped her chest as she reflected on the unsettling dream. She needed to focus on what was real and right in front of her. She had a job to do.

Trix studied Iza when she entered the cargo hold. "You have an accelerated heart rate and your pupils are dilated. Your temperature is a degree higher than normal. Is there something wrong?" the android asked, concern audible in her monotone voice.

They'd been together too long for Iza to hide anything from her. Trix could decipher even the most complex emotions from Iza, whether it was thanks to being an adaptive AI or just because she'd been through so much with Iza that she'd witnessed a wide range of emotions. Regardless, the android's nasty habit of frequently reciting everyone's biometrics, especially hers, made Iza testy.

"I'll be fine. Let's just get this haul and get out of here."

The two disembarked the ship and headed toward the nearby rendezvous spot. According to their contact, the sheep would be walked to the pickup point.

"Your parents were good people," Trix said suddenly. "They cared for each other and for you."

Since when did Trix decide it was okay to talk about my parents? She knows how much it bothers me. To speak on their behalf about their feelings was even worse.

"You didn't know them, so don't defend them. If they'd cared for me at all, they wouldn't have Left," Iza said without turning to face Trix, the tightness in her chest threatening to wring tears out of her.

"It was your mother who Left, choosing to die rather than care for you as a young child. Your father didn't have a choice. He cannot be blamed for what happened."

Iza shrugged. It didn't matter because she blamed him, anyway. Regardless of how stupid and childish, her father's death ruined everything. It had set her on the path from living in a happy home to being a street kid.

"Maybe not, but it didn't help," Iza grumbled.

"You need them," Trix said, surprising Iza again.

Iza stopped to face her. Despite the sun in her eyes, she looked over the android with concern. Perhaps she was malfunctioning. "What are you talking about?"

"Braedon, Jovani, and Cierra. You need them."

"There must be something wrong with your systems. You're going to need to run a self-diagnostic." Iza huffed. "I don't need anyone."

Iza did a mental checklist of her current crew. Cierra was a Healer and helpful in a crisis, but not required. Braedon was as resourceful as he'd claimed, but again, Trix had and could do most of the work he did with less yammering. Thinking of Jovani, she paused. A former TSS Agent was certainly an asset, but she'd been taking care of herself for the last twelve years. She wanted him, that was undeniable. *That's not the same thing, though, is it?*

"Your serotonin levels have continued to rise since their arrival. Your general mood is elevated and the tension in your shoulders and posture is gone. I believe their absence would be detrimental to you, like the loss of your parents."

"Doubtful. More likely, it's the temperature on the ship. I thought I told you to adjust it." Iza raised a hand to shield her eyes from the sun's rays while she glared at Trix. "I'm done talking about them, are you?"

Trix was probably reading her biometrics, and Iza's rising blood pressure should be enough to convince her to leave it alone.

Trix nodded. "Yes, I am done speaking of them."

Iza turned and faced the horizon. "Good. Let's go get some sheep."

—

After thirty minutes of waiting in the hot, blazing sun for her contact to arrive with the two dozen promised sheep, Iza's mood had soured.

At last, the herd ambled toward her, letting out soft bleats. They roamed the area, feeding on blades of thin grass that stuck up from the red dirt.

"Aww, they're cute," she commented to Trix. "Too bad they're so tasty."

Trix shook her head. "You organics are very strange."

While being sniffed and nibbled on by sheep, Iza conducted the official exchange with the bearded man tending the flock, using her handheld to confirm the pickup. She received the second half of her credits, and that concluded the transfer.

The man's beard was almost the length of his hooked staff; perhaps he'd been a shepherd his entire life. He was accompanied by a small boy, who stood at his side wiping his nose on the back of his dirty hands while he followed their every move with large, wide eyes.

"Keep them together and don't let any of them stray too far," the bearded shepherd advised. "They'll die without the herd. You're all they have for protection and they'll follow you if you give them a reason to trust you."

Iza nodded. "There won't be far for them to wander in space." She gestured to Trix. "Let's get them on board."

The android nodded and then began a perfect imitation of the sound the shepherd had made to herd the sheep, urging them toward the *Verity* with ease. She carried a small rod that she used to guide them gently up the ramp of the ship. They followed her as they would have followed the man.

The man and his son stared open-mouthed as Trix led them on board.

"Daddy, is that a robot?" the little boy asked.

"Yes, son, don't go near it or it'll bite you faster than you can shout for help," he said without a change of expression.

The hackles on the back of Iza's neck rose. It wasn't uncommon for people in the outer colonies to speak that way about an android. They hardly had occasion to see a Lynaedan, let alone interact with one as sophisticated as Trix. They didn't understand the AI made her even more intelligent than a mere robot.

"That's not true at all." Iza kept her voice soft and patient. "She's kind and helpful. Trix has been with me since I was a kid. She took care of me when I didn't have any folks. Want to get a closer look?" Iza offered.

The boy's eyes grew as round as plates and he nodded eager to get closer.

"No, thank you." The man snatched his son's hand. "We'll be on our way. We've got other livestock to tend." He turned and moseyed off, dragging his son behind him. The sound of the man scolding the boy for being curious about the android carried on the wind to Iza's ears. It was a shame that there were still those who didn't understand what a marvel Trix and her people were.

"All the sheep are secured. Shall I close the ramp?" Trix asked when Iza boarded behind the last of the sheep.

"Yes, keep them inside our makeshift pen, but leave the hatch open for Braedon and Jovani. They said they'd be joining us soon enough."

Iza was surprised Cierra had also come down to care for the sheep. She sat with her bare feet hanging off the ladder, speaking softly to them.

"We'll have the livestock off soon enough, so you won't have to monitor them," Iza said, wishing the woman would stay out of her way.

"It's no trouble. I like being around them, they're so fresh."

"True, but we won't be eating these, they're for delivery only," Iza said unable to hide her mischievous smile.

"You're joking but it's not funny," Cierra said, keeping her voice light in front of the sheep. "I would never eat one of these precious creatures. They're so trusting, and their eyes are like a mirror of their souls. How can you even think it?" She reached out scratching one under its chin.

Iza thought about it a moment, then answered honestly. "All I know is if I was hungry, I would eat one without any hesitation."

Cierra scoffed.

Iza ignored the other woman's indignation as she made her way up the stairs to the flight deck. The humming coming from her cabin stopped her for a moment, and she remembered the dream again. The sensations had been so real, but so far she'd seen no sign that they were precognitive. Iza wondered, not for the first time, if there was something to the dreams and their connection to the metal sphere she kept in her nightstand.

Perhaps the dreams only amplified her desires. Even now with Jovani off the ship, she could sense the pull of him. It was unnerving, the effect he had on her emotions. But, there was also the giant alien ship and the anxiety of someone watching her. Those weren't things she'd experienced It had taken time for the fear to fade even after she'd gotten out of bed. Even now, she glanced over her shoulder more than usual.

Trix joined Iza on the flight deck in short order, and they settled in to wait for Braedon and Jovani to return.

A klaxon alarm broke the silence, and Iza turned to Trix to

see what was going on.

The android stood in the center of the flight deck listening for a moment. "Braedon, he is in trouble."

"Braedon? What's he up to?"

"He is signaling us to meet him at specified coordinates. There are people that need our help immediately. That is all."

Iza was already moving toward the doorway. "We'll take the shuttle." She swore under her breath. *Braedon, what have you gotten in the middle of now?*

THE COORDINATES BRAEDON had provided in his emergency signal directed Iza and Trix to a quiet neighborhood east of where the *Verity* was docked. They'd settled in between several other small craft parked around a communal landing pad, offering a small measure of anonymity while they waited.

Unlike the dusty outer reaches of the city, this area had been transformed into a manicured landscape fitting of the central worlds, complete with tree-lined streets and grassy yards. However, with seven single-family dwellings to a square block, the living quarters were too tight for Iza's comfort. *How can people live so close to each other by choice?* In city centers or on a spacecraft, she could understand how people didn't have another option, but out in the suburbs, it seemed strange to build homes almost on top of each other.

Though the streets were wide enough to accommodate a high volume of traffic, the surroundings seemed eerily empty for mid-afternoon. Only a few people strolled by on foot while Iza and Trix waited in the parked shuttle for Braedon to arrive. There seemed to be nothing more going on than people trying to avoid the boiling heat of a summer day. The climate controls in the dilapidated shuttle hadn't been working properly for weeks, and she felt the heat of the day seeping in and slowly cooking her.

Iza peeled off her jacket and shirt, exposing her white tank top, and dropped the rest on the floor beside her. "Check it again. Are you sure we're in the right place?"

"Yes, these are the coordinates." She paused. "A dampening field has just been activated in this area. Our outbound communications and sensors are now blocked."

"Naturally." Iza's eyes scoured the street, looking for any signs of the trouble. *I should be used to this with Braedon by now.*

Just when her visual search turned up empty, an incoming audio-only communication lit up on the front console.

Trix assessed it. "The origin is masked. It appears to be a hack through the dampening field."

"Sounds like Braedon's handiwork." Iza opened the channel. "Hello?"

"He's already here," Braedon said through panting breaths. "We can't get to you."

"Okay, calm down. What in the bomaxed stars is going on?" Iza demanded. "We're where you told us to be. Where are you?"

"My dad is—" The audio abruptly ended.

"Braedon?"

"We have lost the signal," Trix stated.

Then, Iza spotted a small shuttle zipping through the trees. The aerodynamic design of the craft was sharp, with two rear wings that jutted out on either side. It moved methodically down each street before dodging between the homes, as if searching for something.

"Keep our ident masked," Iza said as she tracked the other shuttle's movements. "Based on what Braedon was about to say, what are the chances that's an Arvonen shuttle?"

"Ninety-five percent."

Iza groaned. "We need to stop him before he gets a hold of Braedon."

"Devyn," Trix said correcting her.

"No, he'll always be Braedon to us. I don't care what his father calls him."

"With the localized dampening field, we do not have the ability to track the signal. We will have to wait for him to come to us."

"Where is the *Arvonen One*?"

"I estimate they are in orbit above us to maintain the field blocking communications in this area."

"Can we knock it out?"

"Not from here. The *Verity* could do it, but I cannot remotely interface with the *Verity* from within the dampening field."

Iza let out a slew of curses as she watched the other shuttle continue its search. There was no way to get another message to Braedon. Besides, any further communication between them would only risk exposing his location.

"I recommend we search on foot. They are ignoring anyone who is not male."

"We? No way. They'd spot you in a heartbeat, and I can't afford to lose you, my friend. Better I go alone. Between the two of us, I blend in much better around here." Iza slipped out of her pants, leaving her blue shorts underneath exposed.

"How are you going to avoid being seen? They will recognize your face from before, and no doubt they will be looking for you, too."

Iza knotted the bottom of her white tank and took her hair out of the braid, allowing it to fall forward on her face. "I've got a plan," she said, grabbing some rope from the back hatch. She gripped it in one hand. "Open the hatch and stay put."

"Keep your head angled down so they cannot scan your face."

"Got it. Stay powered down here until I signal," Iza said, opening the hatch in preparation to jump out.

"There is no way that you will be able to get a signal through," Trix reminded her.

Iza called out over her shoulder. "You'll see this one, I promise." Then, she leaped out of the shuttle and down to the street.

Her movements were casual but all business. She ignored the way her stomach growled at the smell of grilling meat coming from one of the houses; Cierra had no idea what she was missing. Iza didn't want anyone to take more than a casual glance at her as she walked the streets, so she moved like someone looking for something. She put two hands on either side of her mouth and started calling out in a high-pitched, frantic voice.

"Blacksheep! Blacksheep! Where are you?"

She passed by a few people who shook their heads sympathetically. As far as they could tell, she'd lost her pet. Iza continued searching down the second street. The large trees formed a canopy overhead, where birds and small creatures made their homes in the branches. They chirped loudly to each other as Iza passed. She noted the proximity of the Arvonen shuttle as they made another sweep of the street. As instructed, she turned her face to the ground.

"Blacksheep!"

A rhythmic knocking caught her attention. It was probably

some kind of code, but instead of staring in the sound's direction, she dropped to one knee to pretend she was tying her shoe.

No sooner was she on the ground than a white fluffy dog with brown and black markings, standing as tall as her knees, came bounding out of a nearby house. It stood on its hind legs and began licking her face as soon as it reached her.

"What the...?" Iza was about to shove the dog away when she noticed a passerby on the street watching her.

"Oh, there you are, Blacksheep!" She scooped up the dog and tried to pretend that his lapping tongue on her face wasn't gross.

She then casually strolled toward the house where the knocking sound was emanating from. The moment she reached the front door, it flew open.

Jovani stood framed in the doorway. "Nicely done," he said.

Iza put the dog down, and he ran inside. "What's going on here?" she asked, waiting for her eyes to adjust as she stepped into the darkened residence. "You were supposed to go back to the *Verity*."

"There were complications," Braedon said from the adjacent living room.

"Yes, we noticed. What's your father doing here and how did he find you?"

"Him showing up here might be a coincidence," Braedon said. "My dad, he found me, but I don't think he was looking for me, specifically. I think he's looking for them." He pointed to a red-haired man and lean woman with a crop of short brown hair, who were huddled on the floor away from the windows.

"Oh." Iza looked them over. "Why?"

"They're scientists." He gave her a significant look.

"Wait, you think your father is the one snatching them?"

Braedon nodded.

"What does he want with you?" Iza asked the man and woman.

"We're not sure," the man replied. "All I know is that someone offered us an obscene amount of credits to join a secret project, and when we declined, they came to take us by force."

Iza placed her hands on her hips. "Who are you and what exactly is it you do?"

"Elyse, metaphysicist," said the woman, raising her hand to speak.

"Natanael, astrophysicist." The man placed his hand on his chest.

Iza stared blankly at the both of them. "I'm sorry, you're going to have to be more specific than that."

Natanael rolled his eyes impatiently and pointed to the woman. "Space and the universe." Then to himself. "The effects of space and time on us."

Iza nodded, but she still wasn't sure it made any sense to her. "Am I missing something? What's the connection between them and your father?" she asked Braedon.

"My father was looking for a map. It was supposedly inside a wooden-like box impossible to open. Remember when we first met, I was trying to get away from one of my father's thugs? They were after me because I'd stolen the *Verity*. Back then, my father had been using it to transport some things he didn't want found. I didn't realize the box was inside when I took it. Later, when I found it, I realized it was important and stashed it back inside one of the cargo hold containers. I ran into a little financial trouble and Karter Hyttinen agreed to impound the ship, hold it for me until I could pay to get it out. I never in a million years thought he would sell it out from under me. Then, I ran into you and when you mentioned getting a H3X, and your vicinity to the one I'd lost, I knew it couldn't be a coincidence. When I went back for the box, though, it was gone. I'm pretty sure Karter has it now, which explains why my father didn't shoot him out of the sky when he showed up threatening to take it from you."

Iza nodded in understanding. Karter had leased her the ship, but he didn't have the box or the sphere inside it. In fact, she could hear it humming even now. Iza knew Victor Arvonen wanted it, but she still didn't know why.

"Where does he think this map leads?" she asked.

"I'm not sure, but he's obsessed with finding whatever it is," Braedon said, scratching his head.

The sphere had quite a few etchings on it, but Iza wasn't sure how it could work as a map. However, it was a new clue that she didn't have before.

"If he's snatching scientists like us, then I suspect he believes the map isn't of Taran origin," Elyse speculated with more enthusiasm.

"Aliens?" Iza snickered.

"Yes, it shouldn't surprise us that species other than ourselves have populated the universe," Natanael continued. "Consider the history of our own worlds. We've barely scratched the surface and we're finding more planets each day. Especially now that the Taran government is encouraging new technology research and colonization, I suspect the Taran Empire could double its reach by the time our grandchildren are old."

Iza waved a hand to dismiss his philosophy. "Later. Right now, we need to get out of here without that Arvonen shuttle spotting us. Whose house is this?"

At the question, the white fluffy dog nudged her with his nose. Iza and the others looked down and laughed.

"Yours, huh?" Iza turned to the others. "How did you know to send him out to grab me?" She scratched him behind the ears.

Jovani shrugged. "We didn't. He ran out the back door on his own. It wasn't until you brought him back that we realized what he'd done."

"What, really?" Iza stared at the animal as it stared up at her. "Well, aren't you special?"

He barked in response and wagged his curled tail happily.

"To answer your question, though," Jovani said, "the place was empty and we let ourselves in."

"These biometric locks are so easy to hack. People think they're safe, but—" Braedon cut off at the sound of the Arvonen shuttle making another sweep along the street.

"And we're not safe here, either." Iza began putting together a plan to get the attention of Trix in their own shuttle.

"Yeah, we need to move soon." Braedon peeked out the window. "They're searching the houses on foot now."

"They'll find us and take us, like they did the others." Elyse clutched Natanael's arm. His features were neutral, but there was a sheen of sweat on his face and his cheeks had two bright-red circles on them. He was probably just as frightened as she was.

"Do you know where he took the others?" Iza asked.

"No, only that several of our colleagues, leaders in their fields, have been missing for over a week. No one has heard from them since," Natanael replied.

Iza would ponder that information later. For now, she needed to make sure they all got out without getting themselves caught. "Do you still have your pulse gun?" she asked Jovani.

"Yes, but we won't be able to shoot our way out of here. I can hold off a couple, but I'm not sure how many more are on that shuttle. They could have someone actively shielding their heat signatures the way I'm doing for all of you."

It was then that Iza noticed the fine sheet of sweat on his brow and realized it wasn't from the heat outside, as the house was cool. He was using his abilities to keep them hidden.

"I'll need you to push yourself and do your mind thing. That, combined with my distraction, will help Trix find us, and we can get these scientists someplace safe." She sighed. "However, that doesn't solve the *Arvonen One* problem. Right now, there's no one on board to protect the *Verity*. Cierra is there alone, with no idea what's going on over here."

She had no idea how to deal with that particular wrinkle. If the *Arvonen One* struck out at the *Verity*, not only would it strand them on Galminus, but they'd lose Cierra, their cargo of sheep, and their home.

"We've got Jovani," Braedon said. "If we can't get through the dampening field in time, he can reach out to her and so she can get to safety before they can fire on the ship." He looked at Jovani to confirm.

Jovani nodded. "She'll be my number one priority if they spot us."

Braedon bit his bottom lip in worry. "I might be able to keep them from firing on us, but I'll need access to your shuttle's controls, and we'll have to be outside the dampening field."

Iza looked at both the harried scientists. "You'll need to keep up."

Before they could answer, the front door flew open, and everything went sideways.

THE ROOM WAS upside down from Iza's vantage point on the floor, where she had been pulled underneath Jovani to cover her from pulse fire.

Jovani telekinetically threw both of the large men back, closing the door quickly behind them. He was moving so fast, Iza had hardly caught her breath when he pulled her to her feet and prodded her toward the back door.

"Those look like the same guys from Kinterin," Braedon said, rushing the scientists out the back door ahead of Iza.

"Yep, get the scientists to the shuttle. Trix is waiting for you at the coordinates you sent us."

"What about you?"

The small dog was alerting the entire neighborhood to their location and his displeasure at having his front door knocked in.

"Oh, no!" Jovani stopped short. The panic in his eyes told her she wouldn't like what came next.

Iza's body lifted into the air as a large explosion leveled the house behind them. She fell hard and fast. It was exactly like a nightmare she'd had once. She braced herself for the impact of the ground, screaming the whole way down. Only when she felt the soft touch of the grass under her back, indicating she was on solid ground again, did she risk opening her eyes.

How did that happen?

Jovani must have used his abilities to lower her softly to the ground, and the dog was happily licking her face. For a minute, the only thing she heard was the ringing aftermath of the explosion.

Iza stared at Jovani's mouth. He was saying something, but she couldn't make it out over the buzzing in her head. Jovani grabbed her by the hand again and raced forward, but he was going in the wrong direction.

"Wait, the shuttle is back that way." Iza pointed with her free hand.

Jovani shook his head, and this time she heard him. "No, we need to let Braedon and the scientists reach the shuttle. Trix can come and get us after we lose the Arvonen shuttle."

"But the dampening field," Iza countered.

"It can't dampen this," Jovani said, tapping his head twice with one finger.

The dog's curled tail wagged happily at this game of chase, excited about whatever would come next.

"Settle down, you," she said. "Can't you do something about him? Use your telepathy to tell him to beat it or something?" Iza waved a hand in the general direction of the dog prancing at her feet.

Jovani smiled and shook his head. "It doesn't work like that."

"This must be the most exciting thing to happen to you in your whole life," Iza said to the dog. He was quiet now, at least, so he wouldn't give away their position. However, he wouldn't stop following her no matter how many times she pointed him away.

While they ran down the street, dodging knee-high bushes and racing between houses and trees, a loud boom sounded behind them. They stumbled in the yard of the next cottage house, falling to the ground for long enough to look back. Though Iza couldn't see the source of the sound, it reminded her that it wasn't safe for any of them yet.

"They're bringing reinforcements. We need to keep moving," Jovani said as he jumped to his feet. He grabbed her hand and tugged her along after him.

The dog had taken their momentary rest as permission to get comfortable, and he was now laying down in the grass with his legs spread in all directions, panting. Their escape must have exhausted the poor thing. Iza looked around for a fenced area where she could secure him in, since it was clear he wouldn't leave her side.

A low engine roar sounded above. Iza was about to take cover when she realized it was her shuttle. She breathed a sigh of relief as Trix lowered the craft over open pavement in the middle of the street between the trees.

Jovani ran to it and held out his hand to help Iza on board. In spite of herself, Iza looked back at the white dog with the brown markings as he ran anxiously back and forth, then hopped on his hind legs, begging to follow them. He howled in pain as Iza climbed aboard.

"Bomaxed dog," Iza said, shaking her head at her irrational feeling of guilt for leaving him behind. He already had a family somewhere down there, even though his house had been leveled. "He's better off down there. Space is no life for a dog."

Jovani put a hand on her back. "We could drop him off somewhere where it's safer."

"What if his people come looking for him?"

"He seems determined to be with you." Braedon shrugged. "Maybe *you're* his chosen person."

Iza glared at him, and he lifted his hands in surrender.

"Uh oh, we've got company," Braedon called out just before a volley of pulse fire hit the hull.

Iza couldn't take her eyes off of the dog.

Jovani groaned. "This is ridiculous." He used his abilities to telekinetically lift the small dog onto the ship.

As soon as his legs touched the deck, the dog leaped into Iza's arms, licking her face in gratitude.

"What are we going to do with you?" she asked him.

"We can decide later. Strap in," Jovani said.

Iza put the dog down and wiped the wet from her face while she raced to a seat next to the two bewildered scientists. As she secured the flight harness, the dog, in a move of pure genius, tucked himself in underneath her seat behind her legs.

"Trix get us back to the *Verity* double-time. We need to get going before they discover where we are," Iza instructed.

"That will be impossible, since the *Arvonen One* is now between us and the *Verity*," Trix replied from the pilot's seat up front.

"What?" Iza swiveled to look out the viewport.

To her horror, the *Arvonen One* flagship hovered in the sky half a kilometer from their position. Worse, their weapons were hot.

Iza swore as *Arvonen One* fired. The blast rattled the shuttle, prompting the dog whimper beneath her.

"Keep us low, Trix," Iza ordered, hoping that would make them a difficult enough target to buy a little time. "We need another rendezvous option with the *Verity*. Can you contact

Cierra?"

"What for?" Braedon asked from the seat next to Trix.

"You can fly the shuttle and Trix can interface with the
Verity. But we would need to switch the ship from manual to
remote, and Cierra is the only one on board."

"Maybe..." Braedon didn't seem convinced.

Iza didn't have the time or patience to argue. "Trix, get
Cierra on the comms."

"The dampening field is still in place," Trix reminded her.

"I can get past it, hold on," Braedon got to work.

The shuttle rocked from another blast. Trix dove the
shuttle below the top canopy of the trees lining the street to get
as much cover as possible.

"Hurry, Braedon!" Iza urged.

"I'm working on it!"

"*Arvonen One* requests that we surrender," Trix said, then
banked hard left to avoid another hit.

Iza scoffed. "Screw that."

A minute later, Cierra's voice came through. "Yes,
Captain?"

"Cierra, we've run into some trouble in the form of the
Arvonen One. I need you to switch the *Verity*'s control matrix
over to auto so Trix can remotely bring you to us."

"I don't know how," Cierra said. Her voice quivered with
nervousness.

"We're dead out here if you don't."

"Hey, you can do this, Q," Braedon cut in before Iza could
yell at her any more for slowing them down. "Listen, go to my
station at the front of the flight deck. Put in the sequence
exactly as I say."

"Okay," she said. There was a pause while she got into
position. When she spoke again, her voice seemed far away and

afraid. "There are so many lights. I don't know what I'm looking at."

"Don't worry about it at all. Just listen to me," Braedon said calmly. "There's a blue button on the bottom right. It should be flashing. Do you see it?"

"Yes."

"Good. Press that one twice."

"Okay, I did it."

Braedon smiled. "Now, there should be a row of yellow buttons on the left. Press the third and the fourth ones together, and then press the green one that comes up."

"I don't see the green one." Panic pitched Cierra's voice.

"The Arvonen shuttle is now closing in from behind." Trix sounded a little panicked herself.

"We need to make a run for the *Verity*," Iza decided. The approach with Cierra was wasting time they didn't have. "Try to stay ahead of the shuttle and avoid *Arvonen One*."

"*Arvonen One* is preparing missiles. We will not sustain a hit of that magnitude."

"I've got it, hold on," Jovani said as the shuttle spun out of the way of the larger ship and raced toward the *Verity*. Iza had witnessed him do some incredible things with his telekinetic abilities, but she wasn't convinced that blocking a missile blast was within his capabilities.

"I need the cargo door open, Braedon!" Iza called out.

"Cierra, do the sequence again in the same order, make sure that you hit the two yellows at the same time."

"Oh! I see the green one now."

"Good girl, now sit back and let us do the rest," Braedon said beaming with pride. "Trix, I've got the shuttle." He turned to the console and input the commands.

Braedon and Trix coordinated their movements to

intercept above a park. The *Verity*'s cargo door opened to receive the shuttle—a tiny target, but a necessary risk. Braedon deftly lined up the approach, and the shuttle slotted into its berth, coming to rest with a jolt a safe distance from the pen housing the sheep.

Braedon grinned. "Am I good or what?"

"Get us out of here!" Iza unstrapped her harness.

"Yes, Captain." Trix closed the cargo hatch, then a moment later sent the *Verity* on a steep upward trajectory.

Iza hopped out from the shuttle and ran up the stairs to the flight deck, with Trix, Jovani, and Braedon close behind. Cierra was standing in the back corner of the room when they arrived, her arms crossed.

"Good work," Iza told her and she dropped into the captain's seat.

"I'll be in my cabin." Still trembling, Cierra rushed from the flight deck.

Maybe this will convince her to go live on a planet again, Iza thought to herself, but she knew that was wishful thinking.

"Sensors indicate that the *Arvonen One* is moving into an intercept course," Trix warned.

Naturally. Iza studied the location of enemy craft on the holodisplay. "Braedon, do your best to stay ahead of them while we get to the jump point. Trix, plot a course for Beurias."

Braedon took the flight controls. "I'm on it."

The *Verity* broke free from the planet's atmosphere, and the view on the front display changed to a dark starscape.

"Two minutes until we can jump," Trix reported. "*Arvonen One* and the shuttle are still in pursuit."

"Evasive maneuvers. Get us out of here as soon as you can," Iza said.

The graphic indication of the *Arvonen One*'s plasma beam

range was getting dangerously close to the *Verity*. Braedon accelerated with the sub-light engines, using the maneuvering thrusters to change trajectory just enough to throw off the pursuit ship's weapons targeting. If they'd been hauling anything heavier than sheep, they might not have been able to outpace the other vessel.

Tense minutes passed while Trix completed the necessary computations for the subspace route. "Preparing to jump," she stated at last.

A blue-green swirl of light encapsulated the ship, and it slipped into subspace. Iza couldn't be sure, but it seemed like there was a slight hesitation at the moment of transition that she hadn't noticed before.

"That was close," Jovani said, collapsing into the chair at the tactical console.

"Too close," Iza said. The dog, whom Iza hadn't even realized had followed her from the shuttle, leaped into her lap, trying to lick her face. "Not now, mutt, I've got work to do." She dropped him to his feet and turned to Trix. "What was that?"

"What was what?"

"Is there something going on with our jump drive or nav console? That transition seemed a little sluggish."

"No all systems appear to be functioning normally," Trix answered.

"Things have been anything but normal lately." Iza sighed. "Braedon, go check on Cierra and make sure she didn't touch anything else."

"I'm certain she wouldn't. She probably needs a cleansing just to get over the amount of tech she handled today."

Iza rolled her eyes. "Whatever you say. Jovani can you set the scientists up in an empty cabin where they can shower or get some rest? Then show them where they can get something to eat if they get hungry. Everywhere else on the ship is off-limits."

"Sure, but, there's something you should know," he said.

Iza only half-heard him, distracted by the dog. He ran from the flight deck, heading toward the cargo hold.

She chased after him. "Stop... you!" She faltered, realizing that she didn't know his actual name.

At the base of the stairs descending to the cargo deck, the dog had become fixated on the sheep. His curly tail wagged with excitement while his tongue hung out of his mouth. His brown eyes were locked on the sheep, making them shift uncomfortably in the pen, unable to move away from him in the tight quarters. Seeming to think it a new game, the dog moved toward them and then sat down before taking another couple steps forward again.

Iza didn't want him getting any ideas.

"Iza," Jovani called from behind her.

She lifted a hand to stop him from saying anything more. "I'm sorry, it'll have to wait. I need to find a place for the latest interloper far away from the sheep."

5

WITH IZA DISTRACTED by her new canine companion, Joe set about getting the two scientists settled instead.

After giving them a brief introduction to the ship, he went to his cabin and pulled out his TSS-issued handheld from the bedside table. The latest incident with the scientists might not be enough to free him from his exile, but it was certainly something his superiors would want to know about. Such situations were precisely what he'd been sent to the outer colonies to monitor. He hoped Agent Mandren, his former trainer and direct superior, would be pleased with his detailing of events.

In the last few months, Joe had been meticulous about sending regular reports, but lately he had found his attention was divided between his duty to his mission and his assignments on board the *Verity*. Iza needed his focus, as did the crew. Even though most of what they did was legal, a lot of it was squarely in the gray area for most civilians and well out of bounds for an undercover TSS Agent.

He wanted to talk openly with Iza about what was really

going on, but he was hesitant to cause her any more stress. Even though he couldn't telepathically glean impressions from her in the way he could with most people, her body language said it all. She was barely holding it together. It was clear it had something to do with Karter, since Iza's demeanor had started to change the moment Karter had gotten them out of the trouble with the Tararian Guard and Arvonen. There was something else, too, but he couldn't figure out what it might be.

For the time being, Joe would be quietly supportive. Even when Iza tried to distance herself from him, Joe sensed her desire to be close. She was putting on an act. He couldn't think of a reason why, but he'd play along. She was too important to him to give up without a fight.

When he finished writing his summary of pertinent events for the TSS, Joe found himself wondering how many other Agents besides himself left gaps in their official reports. Perhaps his feelings for Iza were influencing him even more than he'd realized. *Worries for another time.* He sent the report and returned his official Agent handheld to the drawer of his bedside table.

Joe wandered up to the galley, where he found Cierra and Braedon seated at the table. Braedon was hunched over, absorbed in his handheld, while Cierra looked like she was trying to incinerate the device with the power of her mind.

Wanting to steer clear from their drama, Joe walked to the refrigerator without making eye contact.

The basic furnishings in the *Verity*'s galley came standard with most hauling ships, though the previous owner had made some nice improvements. One wall lined with touch-sensitive cabinets served as storage for their dry or packaged foodstuffs and utensils. Upgraded refrigeration units next to the cabinetry helped preserve fresh produce longer. The opposite wall held the cooking appliances and the sink.

Joe selected a piece of fruit from the refrigerator, but when he bit into it, the taste and texture were off. He spat out the bite and threw the whole thing into the trash, realizing it was spoiled.

The rancid taste had ruined his appetite, so he turned to leave.

"Not like that!" Cierra exploded.

"It's my project. I didn't ask for your input in the first place," Braedon said, snatching back his handheld.

Don't get involved. Joe continued toward the door.

"Jovani, be the tie-breaker," Cierra called out.

"Um-no." Braedon shook his head.

"What is it?" Joe asked tentatively.

"His opinion is as good as anyone else's," Cierra insisted. "Tell Braedon he's making a mistake with the costuming." She snatched Braedon's handheld from him and pointed at the screen.

Joe looked down at the device and saw it was a comic, like the ones he grew up reading as a boy back on Earth. Braedon had chosen a clean style with a minimalist but sleek feel.

"You're writing a comic? How many pages have you done?" Joe asked as he began scrolling through it.

"Only a few. I just wanted to get some ideas down," Braedon said his voice quieter than usual.

Joe noted that Braedon had included some of their crew's experiences on Phiris. He couldn't tear his eyes away from the raw grief he'd drawn on Iza's face. Braedon had drawn himself as the hero in the story, and Joe was lying unconscious in Iza's lap. Though he looked sickly rather than just passed out, it wasn't a bad drawing.

"It's good. Don't show Iza, though. I don't think she'd like what you've done with her." Joe waved a hand in front of his chest and cleared his throat.

"I told you," Cierra said. She gave Braedon a light slap. "He doesn't listen."

"I'm a great listener. Right, Trix?" Braedon called out when Trix came into the galley.

She reached for her cooking apron before answering. "I believe I am the better listener. When Jovani told me about the TSS, I listened."

Joe's mouth fell open. *What is she doing?*

"What, Jovani telling you his old Agent stories?" Braedon elbowed Cierra, and she squirmed away from him.

"No, he still has TSS friends. He spoke to one the other day," Trix said.

"That's enough about the old days. Come with me, Trix," Joe said, grabbing her by the hand and leading her into the corridor. He spoke low enough for only her to hear. "What were you saying?"

"I do not understand. What do you mean?" Her facial expression more blank than usual.

"You were basically telling Braedon everything. What's wrong with you? I thought you were going to keep it a secret."

Trix tilted her head to one side and looked at him in confusion. Then, her eyes filled with tears that spilled down her cheeks.

"What's wrong, Trix?" Joe asked as he put a hand to the side of her tear-streaked face.

"Nothing," she said, her voice devoid of emotion.

"You're crying."

"It is the secrets… they are spilling out of me."

Joe ran a hand through his hair. At a loss for what to do,

he led Trix to the relative privacy of the cargo hold.

"This couldn't have happened at a worse time. I can't deal with this right now," he murmured under his breath as he looked her over. "Why is this happening?"

"I do not know."

"What's going on with you two?"

Joe spun around to see Cierra descending the stairs.

"Can't two friends talk in private?" Joe retorted.

"Ah, you're getting advice about Iza." Cierra smirked. "Carry on."

"What are *you* doing down here?" Joe asked, not that he cared. Mostly, he wanted to know if he'd be able to resume his conversation with Trix in privacy or if he should find another location where they could talk.

"I'm looking for the crate of seasonings I brought on board. Have you seen it?"

"No, I haven't."

"Are you sure you two are okay?" She looked him over.

Joe waved her away. "We're fine. Trix is just helping me out, like you said."

Cierra looked at her and then back at him. He could feel her pressing against his thoughts.

"Don't," he said in a warning tone.

"You're hiding something," she stated confidently.

"So are you." He telepathically pushed back at her hard enough to let her know he could do more if she persisted.

Cierra let out a sigh and shrugged before picking up the edge of her robes. "I'll look for that crate later." She sauntered toward the upper deck.

Only when Cierra was out of sight and her mind was no longer near did Joe risk speaking again.

"Trix, there's something going on with you."

"I am sorry. I cannot keep these secrets of yours anymore. She has a right to know who her father is," Trix said. Her voice didn't tremble, but her eyes filled again.

What is she talking about? Joe's brow knitted. "I don't know what you mean. What about her father?"

"I cannot tell, but it will not be long before all the secrets come pouring out. I cannot stop them."

"Is there something corrupting your operating matrix?"

Trix shook her head. "I do not know. He is dangerous, but she must know the truth. I cannot keep it from her."

Jovani let a curse. "You need a self-diagnostic and a recharge. Go to it now and we'll see if we can get you working again, okay?"

"Yes, Joe, you are right."

"My name is Jovani, remember? I'll be back to check on you." He directed her toward her charging station at the back of the cargo hold.

The last thing he wanted to do was expose his secret to anyone else on the ship. It was bad enough that Trix knew. Karter would use it to his advantage. Joe was prepared to avoid him at all costs, but now he had to worry about Trix telling anyone who happened by.

"Jovani?" Trix's voice reminded Joe of a scared child.

"What is it?"

"I am afraid of what's coming. You will have to protect her. She may not be able to handle what is out there."

"Out where?"

Trix abruptly shut down.

Joe rushed to her. "Trix! Can you hear me?"

"If she's charging, you'll have to wait," Iza said, entering the cargo area.

Joe gathered himself. "Ah, okay. That was strange."

Iza came to attention. "Strange how?"

"It might be nothing, but she was acting kind of… erratic," Joe said.

"Okay, so it's not just me thinking that." Iza groaned. "If it's not one thing with this ship, it's something else."

"What do you mean? What else has been going on?"

Having found the part she was after, Iza jogged back up the stairs. "You mean besides the temperature in here rising by the hour and the communications being spotty?" She didn't slow as she spoke.

Joe followed her to the upper deck. "Could an issue with Trix cause the ship to act up, or do you think it's the other way around?"

"I have no idea. Sucks when the engineer might be part of the problem, doesn't it?"

"How do we—"

"The refrigerator isn't keeping my food fresh," Cierra yelled from the galley down the corridor. She ducked back inside the room.

Joe frowned. "I noticed it, too."

Iza rolled her eyes. "I'll deal with it later." She continued forward without breaking stride.

When they passed by the doorway to the galley, Cierra was standing just inside with her arms crossed, tapping one foot impatiently. "This is why I don't like living on ships. I need to touch soil again with my bare feet."

Iza waved a hand. "I've got bigger problems than what you do with your bare feet. We're on our way to Beurias. Feel free to roam around in the dirt when we get there." She jogged the rest of the way to the flight deck.

Joe flashed Cierra a sympathetic smile before racing to catch up to Iza. She was mumbling to herself about taking on passengers instead of crew as she dove inside an access panel on the wall behind the tactical console.

"Here, let me help you with that." Joe reached over and held the new temperature regulator valve while she removed the old one.

Iza traded parts with him as she tightened the new valve into place, testing the gauge. Joe examined the old part. It looked pristine, as for as he could tell.

"It doesn't look burned out to me. It might be something else," he said.

"I've replaced everything else. I don't know what else to do." Iza wiped her wet brow with the back of her hand, leaving a smudge behind.

Joe put the old valve aside, confident they might be able to use it again once they discovered the real problem. Iza stood up and adjusted the temperature, waiting for the cool air to fill the room. She smiled when the vents started blowing cool air onto the deck.

"Nice work, Captain." He moved closer to her with the hopes of pulling her in for a kiss.

To his surprise, she didn't resist as he planted his lips onto hers. He pushed aside the doubts from earlier and let the kiss deepen as he gripped her hip with his left hand while reaching under her curls to cradle her neck. When they parted, both he and Iza were breathless.

For a moment, she looked at him the way she had when they first realized the connection between them. Then, a shadow passed over her eyes and she pulled away from him.

She picked up her tools. "Let's get back to work."

— — —

Iza cleared her throat and stepped away from Jovani. *Stars! He's a good kisser.* His proximity made her forget about her contract with Karter and wish she'd never made it. *Why does he always have to smell so amazing?*

"Iza—" Jovani started to protest, but he cut off when Trix chose that inopportune moment to return to the flight deck, far sooner than she should have for just having started a charging cycle.

Trix sat in her place at the front control station, and Iza took in her movements and manner. There *was* something off about her. Plus, thinking back on it, Iza recalled Trix recharging the night before, which meant she should have a sufficient charge for days.

"Hey, Trix, how are you feeling?" Jovani asked after exchanging a concerned look with Iza.

"I am fine, thank you for asking, Jovani. Your heart rate is elevated, and you are perspiring below your hairline and along your upper lip. Are you well?"

Iza tried to conceal her amused smirk. *She seems to be her old self.*

Jovani rubbed the back of his neck. "Yes, I'm fine. It's just a little warm in here."

"The ship is regulating the temperature on board at a chill factor of twenty. Would you like to lower the number?"

"No, tried that," Iza said. "We just finished replacing the temperature regulator, and at least cold air is blowing for the time being. Something is still off, though." She frowned at the exposed innards of the console, wishing she knew more about environmental systems.

"I will run another diagnostic," Trix stated.

Iza nodded absently.

"Jovani was supposed to tell you about the new jump drive

we had installed," Trix blurted out.

Jovani's eyes widened.

"The *what*?" Iza stared at Jovani, then Trix, and back again.

"I've been wanting to talk to you about it, but there's always something..." Jovani trailed off.

That was all the confirmation Iza needed, but she wanted to see for herself. "Show me."

Trix brought up the technical specifications of the new jump drive installed behind her back, intentionally buried beneath the conventional interface. Iza's heart thudded against her chest and she kept looking for something to hit. There was nothing except Jovani's sad eyes and Trix, whose mouth was turned down in a confused frown.

"How? Why?" Iza demanded. It was the betrayal of her friends lying to her for more than a month rather than the upgrades themselves. Her ship had quadrupled in value with that upgrade, but she couldn't think of a reason for why they would keep it from her. "I trusted you," she whispered.

Jovani's gaze flew to Trix, and she turned matter-of-factly toward Iza.

"Jovani authorized the upgrades," Trix said.

"And you went along with this?" Iza was dumbfounded. In all the time she'd known Trix, she couldn't ever remember a time when the android had kept anything from her.

"It was an improvement that would not harm you or the ship while giving us a tactical advantage against Victor Arvonen and Desirae Hyttinen, who were actively pursuing us at the time," Trix replied.

Though the reasoning was sound, there was one glaring issue in Iza's mind. "But why didn't you tell me?"

"That's complicated," Jovani started to explain.

Iza rounded on him. "I take it you're the one who arranged

it? How did you even get your hands on one of these jump drives?"

"There's a guy who owed me a favor."

"A guy?" Iza tried to wrap her mind around the idea. "This is unbelievable."

"Are you unhappy with the upgrades?" Trix asked.

"I'm furious that you decided to modify my ship without my consent! Neither of you signed a contract to own this ship. I did. You don't appreciate what I had to sacrifice for this ship. I have nothing else to give." Iza slapped both of her hands against her thighs in frustration.

"Don't yell at her, she was only helping me," Jovani said stepping between them.

"Oh, helping *you*? And what's your ulterior motive for modifying *my ship*?"

"Keeping you out of jail, for one!" Jovani shot back. "Why don't you just admit we made a valuable improvement and move on? Or is it too hard for you to admit that you're not the only one who can get things done around here?"

Where did that come from? Iza's mouth fell open. "Wait, what?"

Jovani's hands dropped to his sides and his shoulders fell forward as if he were trying to retreat into himself. "I'm tired of bending over backward to help out around here and getting absolutely nothing but suspicion and coldness from you. Next time, it's all on you."

Iza regretted her outburst, but it was too late. Jovani stormed off the flight deck.

"I apologize, I should not have helped him without talking to you," Trix said.

There was nothing to be done about the upgrades now. Trix had never gone behind her back to do something before and the change in her behavior had to be due to Jovani. Iza didn't like it, and she wondered what else she'd have to contend with if Jovani stayed.

Iza lowered her voice a bit now that she'd gained control over her temper. "Look, I'm the captain here and I decide what's best for my ship. Don't go around me again. Is that understood?"

"Yes," she said.

Iza noticed the glistening in the android's eyes and moved in closer. "Trix? Are you crying?"

Trix reached up and wiped the tears from her cheeks. "No. We will arrive at our destination in four hours. Would you like me to prepare the shuttle?" Trix asked, suddenly back to her normal robotic self.

Iza reached out and put a hand on her shoulder, checking to see if her eyes were still leaking. "Run a self-diagnostic. I need to know that you're okay."

"Yes, Captain." Trix turned away from her and stared out the viewport.

Once they were back on Beurias, Iza would arrange a trip to Lynaeda. It had been several years since they'd been there. Trix wasn't a machine that needed tuning up, but she was special. Iza couldn't imagine what she'd do if there was something seriously wrong with her friend.

"How long have we known each other?" Iza asked.

"Since you were ten years old," Trix said without shifting her gaze from the viewport.

"Do you remember the day we met?"

"Yes. I was pursued by a group of children who did not like androids. You came to assist me."

Iza nodded. "Why?"

"Why did the children not like androids?"

"No, why did I help you?"

Trix fell silent for a moment. If she was an organic person, Iza would assume she were evading the question. In this case, she thought Trix might be trying to determine if she could answer.

"I believe it is because you viewed me as worthy of saving."

Iza smiled. "Yeah, and don't ever forget it. You've never given me a reason to mistrust you."

Trix finally turned back to look Iza in her eyes. "Do you mistrust me now?"

"I don't know."

"Do you trust Jovani?"

That was the real question, wasn't it? Iza didn't know if she trusted anyone other than Trix—and now even that was uncertain. Despite being on the ship together and the crazy connection between them, what did she really know about Jovani, other than what he'd shared with her the one night they fell asleep in each other's arms? Because of her contract of engagement with Karter, she couldn't risk being alone with him. Not only did she want to tell him everything, she wanted to reassure him he would still be a part of her life if it was still something he wanted.

Instead, she answered Trix as honestly as she could. "I want to."

IZA WAS WITH Braedon on the flight deck as they neared the end of their subspace jump to Beurias. He kept turning back in his seat to face her, and she'd had enough of it.

"What?" she snapped.

"You know what you did, and it's wrong," he said. "I'm trying to keep my mouth shut, but I feel like I need to say something, despite my better judgment."

"You should follow that feeling."

"I like you and Jovani together. I think you're pushing him away, though I don't know why. I'm the first to admit I don't understand what you women are thinking, but in this case, I might be able to help you. Since you're not telepathic and neither am I, we need a little more help than most."

"Really?" Iza asked the question with as much sarcasm as she could muster, but he still managed to ignore it.

"Jovani has strong feelings for you. You should have seen him when I first met him. He was as cold as ice and closed off from everyone. He actually sat in that dive of a restaurant trying to fit in with his obnoxiously bright shirt." Braedon gestured at his chest to emphasize his point. "Every local in the sector knows the place isn't worthy of the credits they charge to eat there."

"Yet, you were eating there," Iza said, crossing her arms over her chest.

He shrugged then kept going as if she hadn't interrupted him. "He was hopeless. Then, he met you, and I swear I've never seen anyone do such a quick one-eighty. The guy is all about you. Give him a chance."

Iza nodded but said nothing more. Braedon wasn't wrong, but she wasn't about to tell him so.

"Are the scientists ready to get dropped off?" she asked to change the subject.

"Yeah, I think they've had enough excitement. It was nice of you to let them come with us this far."

Iza loosened her arms and waved away the compliment. The dog had hitched a ride on her ship, too. Although between the three, the dog seemed to be the least trouble.

"It was a good thing you did for those scientists," Iza told Braedon. "Though, you never told me how you happened upon them in the first place."

His feet seemed to shuffle back and forth while he tapped out a silent rhythm with the fingers of his right hand on the console. "I thought I was keeping my business to myself?"

"We're beyond that now. Do you want to tell me, or do I need to go to the scientists and get their side of your story?"

Braedon sighed. "Okay, I've been reading the Sensationals lately, just for fun, and I saw that a call had gone out from my father looking for scientists. When we found out about the missing scientists at the border, I got suspicious that there might be a connection. So, I looked into it. What I didn't anticipate is that we'd walk into a lab in the middle of an attempted abduction."

"Why didn't you say anything before about your father's activities?"

"I didn't have any solid facts. I know my father can be obsessive, but honest, I never thought him capable of kidnapping people. It wasn't until I saw his henchman going after those scientists that I believed it." Braedon shook his head. "He must be desperate. We need to track down that box and find out what's on that map."

Iza nodded vaguely, not sure it was a good idea to reveal her secret at the moment. She couldn't keep the box and sphere inside hidden for long.

Victor Arvonen had the resources to chase her indefinitely; it was a wonder they hadn't run into his people since they escaped him last time. Since her business dealings were legitimate, there were records of her movements. She took what precautions she could, but this new information about Mr. Arvonen's scientist 'recruitment' cast his dealings in a new light. Without a doubt, kidnapping was the least of his offenses. Iza wasn't sure the sphere was worth losing her life over.

"Braedon, I know it seemed like the right thing to do to help those scientists when you saw they were in trouble, but getting involved is a huge risk for us. We already had a target on our backs because of your father's obsession with this ship and what he thinks is on it, and this brought them right back on our tail."

"It was a calculated risk, but I couldn't just leave them there."

Iza sighed. "You're a good guy, but it's your soft heart that keeps getting you into trouble. Every time you stick your neck out for people, you get hurt or you get someone else hurt."

"Doesn't mean I shouldn't help people. Look at you." He smirked.

"What about me?"

"If I hadn't come along, you'd still be riding around in that shuttle with Trix. Jovani and I brought a little muscle and a lot of heart to your world. Admit it, you love having us on board."

"I'll admit no such thing," she said, rolling her eyes. "The two of you are hardly worth the trouble you've caused me. Thanks to you and Jovani, I've been doing more rescuing than hauling."

"You just made my point. You care about people, even if you don't want to." He looked quite satisfied with himself.

Little twerp. But he was right; she was already too attached.

It probably was time to tell them the truth about the box she'd found in the cargo hold. They deserved to know what was driving Braedon's father to kidnap research scientists. If they could learn more about the sphere and what it could do, they might be able to predict his next move. It was clear the old man was a danger to the Taran people. The Enforcers might even intervene. Iza imagined herself speaking to Desirae Hyttinen and getting her to arrest the head of the Arvonen Dynasty.

Ha! That would be the day. It would never happen, but she might find someone else who'd be interested in learning about the man's proclivities and have enough clout to do something about it.

Braedon frowned at his console. "Hey, Iz, did you input new coordinates?"

"No, why?"

"We're no longer heading toward Beurias."

She quickly brought up the subspace route on the front holodisplay. The original beacon sequence had been replaced by a new route leading away from their intended destination planet.

"Stars! I didn't even know you could change a route once the jump was initiated."

Braedon shrugged. "I didn't, either. Maybe it has something to do with that new independent jump drive?"

"Maybe."

Neither of them had had time to look through the new settings, now that the dummy interface mimicking a traditional drive had been stripped away. It did make sense that the additional computational capacity and finer-tuned equipment would be able to do more than she'd ever dreamed possible. However, that didn't alter the fact that neither she nor Braedon had changed their route.

"There's something wrong with the navigation," Braedon stated the obvious. "This new course is locked in, and I can't change it."

"Bail out from the jump, then. There's an emergency protocol to drop us back into normal space, right?"

"There is, but everything has been locked out."

Iza checked for herself, not that she doubted Braedon's assessment. Sure enough, a number of commands were grayed out, and many others were non-responsive.

She swore under her breath. "Where in the stars is the ship taking us?"

"Nowhere, really. An imaginary dot in the outer colonies that doesn't belong to any landmass. I can't even get a fix on a star in the general vicinity."

"Trix, I need you on the flight deck, now!" Iza yelled into the comms system.

It didn't take more than thirty seconds for her to arrive. She was wearing her cooking apron.

"Are you connected to the ship?" Iza asked the android.

"My systems are currently integrated, yes," Trix said.

"I want you to initiate an emergency termination of this subspace jump and return us to normal space."

"Yes, Captain."

There was a pregnant pause as they waited for a starscape to appear out the viewport. However, ribbons of blue-green light continued to swirl around the ship.

"What's happening?" Iza demanded.

"Nothing. The ship's navigation control is not responding," Trix replied.

"Are you saying we don't have control of my ship?"

Braedon shrugged. "I don't know what to tell you."

"You've got to be kidding me!" She glared at Trix. "So much for our fancy jump drive. Now the bomaxed thing is taking us wherever it pleases!"

"Whoa, what's going on?" Jovani asked as he cautiously stepped entered the flight deck.

"You broke my ship, that's what," she snapped back.

"Actually," Braedon said from his console, "I don't think this is the independent jump drive's fault. Rather, the navigation system is enabling the ship to behave this way, but the instructions aren't originating from within the system itself."

"What *is* controlling it, then?" Iza asked.

"I don't know."

Iza looked at her engineer. "Trix?"

"Yes, Captain, I can see evidence of command code directing the navigation system, but it will take time to identify its source."

"What are our options?" Iza looked around the faces of her crew.

"We could force a shutdown of the jump drive if we pull

out the PEM," Jovani suggested.

"Jovani is correct," Trix stated. "Though such an action would also disable a number of other systems throughout the ship, and it is possible that some components could sustain damage."

"Do we have sufficient antimatter reserves to reach Beurias using the sub-light pion drive?"

Trix nodded.

"Well, I'm not about to let my possessed ship take me to the middle of nowhere, so I guess we don't have any choice other than to risk a manual shutdown. Trix, get down to Engineering and prepare to pull the PEM on my order."

"Yes, Captain." The android ran off the flight deck toward the aft of the ship.

She didn't like the idea of pulling out the power core from the ship, but the jump drive was incapable of operating without the Perpetual Energy Module. Disconnecting the power source was the only way to force an exit from subspace while the nav system was non-responsive. Even so, they needed to be smart about managing the risks.

"Shut down all non-essential systems," Iza instructed Braedon. "Hopefully, we can minimize damage to components by shutting down things properly."

"I'm on it."

A couple of minutes later, Trix came over the comm. "I am ready to manually disconnect the PEM on your order."

"Ready on my end," Braedon said.

Iza braced. "Do it, Trix."

The lights flickered as the ship switched to its backup power reserves. A moment later, the ethereal light outside the ship snapped back to a starscape, and the blue-green ribbons dissolved into mist.

"Okay…" Braedon said slowly, "I think we're stable. Backup systems seem to be working. It'll be a bit of a trek to Beurias from here, but we can make it on sub-light engines." He swiveled around to look at her. "We got really lucky, Iz. We could have been stranded in the middle of nowhere."

"Good job noticing the course had changed," she told him, giving him a nod of praise. "Set in a sub-light course for Beurias, as quickly as you can safely get us there."

"Already done." He grinned at her.

"Great, then you can use the transit time to figure out what's going on with my ship. Can you hack into the system?"

"I can try."

It amazed Iza the speed at which he tapped on the console. The coding he was doing was so far above her knowledge that she had no idea how he could read any of it.

Trix returned from Engineering and took her usual seat on the flight deck. Braedon asked for her input a few times while he worked, and Iza left them to it.

Jovani sat stoically at the tactical station, stealing occasional glances in Iza's direction. She made a point of ignoring him, since she hadn't decided if she was going to remain angry with him for going behind her back or be flattered that he'd call in a favor as big as getting her a coveted independent jump drive. If Karter had been smarter, he would have known to woo her with tech rather than fancy clothes.

After ten minutes of feverish work, Braedon threw his hands in the air victoriously. "I did it."

"Define 'it'," Iza clarified. "Do you know what's wrong with the ship?"

"Yes and no," he said. "There's some kind of command protocol running in the background. It'll take a lot longer to figure out how to contain it—or eradicate it—but for now I've been able to wall off the navigation system."

"Meaning?"

"Meaning if you reconnect the PEM, we can jump to Beurias in two minutes rather than spending four-plus days in the black taking the slow boat."

"Sounds a lot better." Iza ventured a smile. "What do you think, Trix?"

The android sat in her seat, completely unresponsive.

"Trix?" Iza stood up and took a step toward her friend.

Jovani also came over to examine her. "She's been acting off the last few days, flipping between emotional and distant at a moment's notice."

Iza looked into Trix's eyes, but her expression was blank, vacant. "Trix, what's wrong?" She shook her head when there was no reply. "We need to bring her to Lynaeda. She needs her own people."

"We can't go anywhere with the ship in this condition," Braedon said. "I feel confident that my patch will get us to Beurias, but any farther than that would be pushing our luck."

"All right. I'll re-initialize the PEM and we can jump to Beurias. We'll drop off the sheep and then get the maintenance crew at Apex to look over the ship and see if they can figure out what's wrong. As soon as it's safe to travel, we're going straight to Lynaeda to find out what's wrong with Trix." Iza rushed toward Engineering.

Jovani followed her. "Iza, it'll be okay," he called, running to walk abreast with her.

"Yeah, well, that remains to be seen."

"Hey." He gently caught her arm, stopping her in the corridor. "I'm here for you. I hope you know that."

"By going behind my back."

"I didn't mean for it to be like that. All I've wanted is to keep you safe."

She could hear the sincerity in his voice. As much as she wanted to be upset with him, she felt the anger giving way to the desire she'd felt for him since the moment they met. He touched her face lightly between his finger and thumb, tilting her head up so he could look into her eyes. Iza willed her legs to keep her upright.

"I'm worried about you," he murmured. "You're not getting enough sleep. It's starting to show."

"I'll be fine."

"I can't help it," he said, resting one hand on her shoulder "Agents are trained to make predictions and act instead of waiting for things to fall apart. You're in charge, and if you'd prefer I remain off the flight deck, I'll accept that."

"No, I appreciate your help." Iza needed to touch him, and she lifted a hand to his arm. "I shouldn't have lost it with you before. I was just caught off-guard. It means a lot to me you want to look out for me. Aside from Trix, no one else has ever cared enough to do that."

"Get used to it. I hope you understand I would never try to overstep your authority. I may not have said it directly before, but I respect you." His hand traced the edge of her face pulling her closer.

"It's nice to hear you say it."

He gave her a reassuring smile. "I know you've been through a lot, and things are still a mess, but I want to support you in any way I can."

"Well, you can start by helping me with the PEM."

"All right. Let's get the ship to Beurias."

7

BRAEDON'S COMPUTER PATCH didn't provide full navigational control once the PEM was reinitialized, but he was able to successfully plot a course to Beurias and complete the subspace jump. When the ship had malfunctioned, Iza had resigned herself to thinking the sheep delivery would be late. Thanks to Braedon's hacking, however, they were able to successfully complete the drop-off on-time and collect full payment.

That turned out to be a good thing as soon as she found out how many credits Apex Enterprises wanted just to take a look at the ship to see what was wrong, let alone what the repair bill might be. Iza decided to defer that worry for another time.

While the Apex mechanics began their evaluation, Iza and her crew waited on the *Verity*'s flight deck so they could keep an eye on what was being done to the ship. Several hours passed in tedium, but then the communications console lit up with a flurry of incoming messages.

"They're addressed to you, Iz," Braedon said over his shoulder.

"From whom?" Iza asked.

"From everyone," Braedon shrugged. "I'll pull them up on the holodisplay."

The list of messages was endless. "Some of them are vid messages, some are text. It looks like they're still coming— about two or three every minute. How's you get so popular all of a sudden?"

Iza caught the word 'congratulations' in one of the message's subject line and almost choked. *It can't be.*

"What are the messages about?" Jovani asked.

"It doesn't matter, delete them all," Iza said, hoping the blue-hued lights in the flight deck would hide her blush.

"But there's so many," Braedon said. "Are you sure? There might be real messages mixed in with the junk."

"Delete them all. Set the inbox to reject all first-time senders and just find out what's wrong with my ship."

"Iz, there's a brand-new message from Karter coming in on the vid," Braedon said.

She groaned inwardly. "Put it through to my cabin, I'll take it there. Trix doesn't have a place of her own. Can one of you walk her to the gym for now? She can sit in there until we can get her some help. The scientists should be getting off, see that they do."

Iza left the flight deck, shaking her head. *What else could possibly go wrong today?*

She reached her cabin and noted the message light flashing. Before she could answer it, the white dog she'd picked up on Galminus began weaving through her legs and pawing at her. It occurred to her that he'd been locked up for several hours and it was probably time for him to do his business down in the cargo area again. She resolved to tend to him right after the message.

She sat down on the foot of her bed and began playback of

the pre-recorded video message. Karter's face came on the screen, and the dog began growling low in his throat.

"Yeah, I feel the same way." She scratched him behind the ears in reward.

"Iza, this is an urgent matter. I see you just landed on Beurias. Your timing couldn't be better. I need you in my office immediately. What we must discuss can't be handled over comms. Come meet me at your earliest convenience."

In that case, is 'never' okay? The cryptic message from Karter annoyed her, and she rolled her eyes at having come all the way to her cabin for this. She didn't have time to talk to him or anyone else. Trix was in serious danger. If they didn't figure out what was wrong with her, she might be permanently damaged. Iza imagined all the worst scenarios.

"Come on, Pooch," she said, inviting the dog out of the cabin to follow her. She would at least take care of him before she met Karter.

As soon as she set foot outside her cabin, Braedon came running. "Iz! Look at this!" He beckoned her to follow him back to the flight deck.

Oh no. Iza froze in horror as soon as she saw the front viewscreen.

"It's all over the Sensationals. Karter is getting married," Braedon continued.

"What?" Jovani asked, coming back onto the flight deck. He must have secured Trix.

"I don't care about any of that frivolity." Iza stepped back away from them both before Braedon could anything more. "I'm on my way to meet with Karter now about some other business. I'm sure if he's engaged, he'll tell me himself."

Braedon chuckled. "Yeah, he will, since they're saying he's engaged to *you*!"

"What?" Iza and Jovani asked at the same time.

"It's everywhere! They're saying that you and Karter are engaged. Can you believe it?"

"That's ridiculous," Jovani said shaking his head.

"Absurd, right? Well, they don't have anything more than a bunch of pictures of you coming in and out of Apex. They're linking the two of you together because some anonymous source claims you are secretly engaged. You and Karter Hyttinen, a Lower Dynasty heir." He slapped a hand against his thigh as he laughed hysterically.

Iza was feeling less angry about the leak and more bothered by the hysterical laughter. She hoped Braedon's reaction was a commentary on their incompatible personalities rather than a judgment of her being unworthy of marrying into highborn life. Granted, most people who were elevated to dynastic standing didn't have juvenile detention records, but she'd always considered herself to have the looks and brains to be desirable.

"It's an easy mistake for desperate reporters to make, considering your recent visits here. It might have happened to anyone," Jovani said, trying to reassure her by rubbing her arm.

Braedon shook his head. "No, way. First of all, Karter is from a powerful dynastic bloodline and owns more than most. This is probably some sort of slander campaign perpetrated by a corporate rival or something. I mean, stars, it's more likely that he'd marry his cousin than someone from the streets like you. No offense."

"Offense taken," Iza said, trying not to let the hurt show through. So it wasn't just that she and Karter were a bad fit; Braedon really did see her as being unfit for highborn life. Well, she was good enough, regardless of what he thought. "Enough with the Sensationals. I've got a meeting with Karter. I need the two of you to hold things down while I'm gone. Oh, and take the dog out, too."

"Haven't you named him yet?"

"No, because he's not staying."

"He's the only one you haven't kicked off the ship yet." Braedon lifted his eyebrows two times fast.

"That's because he doesn't get on my nerves. Just take him out and stay off the Sensationals. That stuff will rot your brainpan. I'll be back."

"Give our regards to your fiancé!" Braedon's laugher followed her off the ship.

—

The outside of Apex Enterprises was littered with Sensationals cameras. Iza had to swat at the buzzing machines as she ran for the door of the showroom building. No doubt, her presence at Apex would be seen as confirmation of their engagement. They should have held a holoconference instead of meeting in person. *What was he thinking?*

Karter's assistant, Becca, showed Iza in without any undue ceremony or formality, expertly fielding two calls while escorting Iza.

When Iza entered Karter's office overlooking the Apex showroom floor, he was sitting at his large, crescent workstation. He'd dressed in an impeccable dark-blue suit that seemed to be made for his lean and muscled form. He wore a metallic bracelet that caught the light against the dark skin of his left wrist when he gestured.

Things in his office were exactly as they had been during her last visit. The hydroponic trees he kept at the doors still rustled lightly as she entered. He gave her a nod and held up one finger to her while he continued his virtual meeting. The facial images of the group were in a three-dimensional semi-circle around him as he spoke.

"Ladies and gentlemen, I appreciate your feedback. Keep in mind, however, that this company has been and will continue to be run by my family. We have everything under control. Despite what you may believe or have heard, nothing has changed."

A chorus of voices erupted in murmurs and discontented conversations.

Karter held up two hands, as if in surrender, and spoke again, "As I've stated before, everything will be resolved immediately. Continue to trust in me and this company, and I will usher in a bright new future for all of us. My next appointment has arrived, so I must tend to other business now. Thank you for your time. I look forward to seeing you at our regularly scheduled sessions next week."

He disconnected the call with a huff and rubbed his eyes. He rose slightly from his chair and held out one open-palmed hand. "Iza, welcome. Have a seat. I believe we have much to discuss."

"The Sensationals?" Iza asked. She crossed her arms over her chest and leaned back in a chair across from him.

Karter sat back down and dimmed the lights using the controls on his touch-surface desktop. He folded his hands neatly in front of him. "Yes, I saw them. They've been camped outside the building for the last twenty-eight hours. Becca has been fielding calls all day. I wondered when you were going to come clean."

"Me? Don't even try it, you snake. I know it was you."

"No, I had nothing to do with it."

"Sure. So it's just a coincidence that I didn't hear anything about it until I got to Beurias? It *had* to be leaked from here. Your office, in fact."

"I told no one of our arrangement." Karter looked off into the distance, as if trying to read the wall behind her.

If he didn't, then how is the news public? Iza scowled. "Are you sure you didn't put the contract someplace where it could be discovered? Your assistant might have—"

"No, she knew nothing of it. In fact, she thought it was a prank until I confirmed it with her, and only her."

"Well, that's funny, because *I* didn't tell anyone. So someone, who either has access to your paperwork or who knows how to get access, has leaked the information," Iza said with raised eyebrows.

Karter sighed. He rubbed his chin thoughtfully. "Yes, you're right, but it's not too late to use this to our advantage."

"How, exactly, is exposing a very secret engagement to our advantage?" Iza asked. "I didn't want to do this in the first place."

"Take a moment and imagine the possibilities. This could be an opportunity for both of us. If we officially announce our engagement at a public event, we could find out exactly who leaked the news."

"How would that reveal anything?"

"By exposing anyone who's not happy about the news."

Iza scoffed. "Well, that includes me. And from the sounds of it, the people you were just speaking with, so I'm not sure that will work."

"It's all I can do at the moment. Don't you have a coder on board your ship?"

"Yes, but—" Iza nodded. "Oh, you want them to trace the information and find the origin stamp?"

"Exactly. The information is out now. We should do the

opposite of what they'd hoped to achieve. We'll announce it officially with a laugh at whoever leaked the news prematurely and we'll pretend that it's only slightly off-schedule."

"How come I get the idea that you've already made up your mind?" Iza asked.

Karter only laughed. "I've always found you fascinating. It must be your intelligence."

"Spare me the flattery. What's your plan?"

"You'll meet me at the Blue Hills Estate this evening. You'll come late at night when no one is watching our movements too closely. Then, you'll stay within the estate until tomorrow evening when we throw a lavish party where the announcement will be made."

Iza didn't know which she hated more: being on display or being on Karter's arm. She let out a long-suffering sigh. "I can't." She shook her head. "Now's not a good time. Trix is in trouble and I need to get her to Lynaeda right away."

"That's something your crew can see to; I'm sure Trix is beloved by them all. You, however, are the only one who can do this particular job."

"What choice do I have?"

"None, really. The contract still stands, until someone else can take your place. If you want to keep your ship, I'll need you to stand at my side as my bride-to-be in that dress I sent you."

"Oh, you meant for me to wear that thing? I misunderstood, sorry. I needed something to clean the floors— I've been a little short on help lately—so I'm afraid it's ruined." She shrugged her shoulders.

He smiled. "If it wasn't to your taste, a new dress can be found. While we're on the subject, I would be so pleased if you'd smile during the announcement."

"Don't push it. You may be a bomaxed good liar, but

anyone who knows me will see through it immediately. Best to tell those closest to me the truth of things."

"No, I don't think that's wise. Whoever leaked the information might still be after more information. We should keep it between us."

"Unless you can block your thoughts, it's not going to be possible. They can't read me, but unless you've gained some telepathic abilities I don't know about, Cierra and Jovani will be able to read you and know the truth."

"Don't worry about me. Just don't tell them about the contract and I'll keep the rest carefully hidden to the best of my abilities," Karter said with a smile as he narrowed his almond eyes. He leaned forward to take her hand but Iza snatched it back from him.

"Fine, I'll do this announcement thing, but that's it. Your mechanics better figure out how to repair my ship. After tomorrow night, I'm heading to Lynaeda no matter how this 'engagement' shakes out. Are we clear?"

"The H3X was in excellent condition when I gave it to you. What did you do to my ship?"

"*My* ship, and I haven't done anything to it. In fact, I'm warning you. If you've sold me a defective spaceship or embedded some kind of bug that's messing with its systems, you're going to have to deal with more than a few Sensational scandals before I'm through with you."

Karter gave her his brightest smile as he raised two hands. "I'll make sure my best mechanics are on the job. In the meantime, pack a bag and I'll send a driver around to pick you up after midnight. I'll be busy until then, so don't reach out. I'm not sure that our calls are safe."

Iza rolled her eyes. "I'm not the one with a mole."

She strolled out of his office with a hard look at his assistant on the way out.

Becca, dressed in her usual black business attire, bobbed her head up and down as she spoke to someone calling about the engagement. She glanced up as Iza walked out.

"No, there is no truth to the rumor. I'm not sure where you learned of it, but nothing of the sort has come from this office. Good day," she said then looked away from Iza as another call was answered. "Apex Manufacturing Enterprises, this is Becca, how can I help you?"

Her voice faded as Iza descended the steps. The woman seemed frazzled, but was it possible there was more to it? Maybe Jovani could find out if any of Karter's people leaked the information.

Iza stopped short. *How willing will Jovani be to help me once he learns the truth about my engagement to Karter?*

JOE WATCHED ON the flight deck as Braedon slowly lost his patience with the Apex mechanical crew. The unsuspecting workers, not knowing Braedon, had no idea that his silence wasn't a good thing.

The distraction was just what Joe needed after the news about Iza and Karter's engagement. He wanted to believe it was a ruse—to what end, he didn't know. But given Iza's odd behavior over the past several weeks, he had to give more credit to the stories in the Sensationals than he might otherwise. The question was, though, did she have any intention of following through with a marriage?

"No, I've tried that already!" Braedon yelled at the Apex engineers, interrupting Joe's thoughts. The young pilot launched into another explanation about what had happened.

Joe had to admit, the ship's malfunctions were a genuine mystery. The moment Braedon's patch was disabled, the navigation system defaulted to plotting a course to the same coordinates in the middle of nowhere. The thermostat continued to act up no matter how many times they tried to calibrate it. The refrigerator in the galley refused to regulate temperature and humidity correctly. And those were just the problems they'd been able to identify so far.

For a short while, Joe had been concerned that his covert jump drive upgrades to the *Verity* had adversely impacted the ship in some way, or that the TSS had unknowingly slipped in spyware during the upgrades. After listening to the Apex mechanics, however, he was convinced that the issues were unrelated to his interventions. Iza had made enough enemies that it could be a deliberate attack, or maybe the problems were just a terrible coincidence.

Regardless, they needed to find the real cause for the malfunctions or Iza might find herself without a ship, which would leave Joe without transportation and put his undercover TSS mission in jeopardy. Worse, Joe didn't want to have to explain to TSS High Commander Wil Sietinen why the independent jump drive Joe had begged him to approve was on an impounded ship sitting in a scrapyard because no one could fix it.

By late-afternoon, after hours of running into dead ends with the mechanics, Joe could almost feel the anger radiating off of Braedon when he sat down next to him. Instead of speaking first, Joe waited for his friend to broach the subject.

It took all of five seconds. "They've been at it for hours, and they're no closer to finding the cause of the malfunctions than before," Braedon grumbled. "Some systems came back online on their own, though to hear them talk, they're to be credited for that." He let out a short, incredulous snort. "It's like the ship's running a bomaxed fever. It's blazing in here!"

Joe tugged at the collar of his shirt. "Maybe Cierra is secretly a technological wizard and this is her sinister plan to turn the entire ship into a massive greenhouse."

Braedon cracked a smile. "You joke, but you may be onto something."

Joe turned serious again when he looked at Trix's empty seat. "Any word back from Lynaeda?"

Braedon shook his head. "No, though we received a message marked '*Verity* Crew'. I didn't peek because I figured we'd all want to look at it together, since it's probably from Iz. Then the dumb thing got locked inside the system. The whole ship is breaking down! It's like living on a freaking death trap."

Something about the message being marked to the '*Verity* Crew' made Joe doubt it came from Iza. She'd never directly called them her crew. Though they'd become more than just visitors, Joe knew she hadn't fully accepted him or Braedon into her life yet.

I can't force her to trust me. And he couldn't fault her for being cautious. After all, he hadn't even told her his real name. *I need to come clean.*

—

While Braedon went down to Engineering to berate the Apex mechanics about their general incompetence, Joe decided to use the down time to reach out to his best friend, Emery Valackas. It'd been more than a month since they last spoke, and Emery had been demanding an update.

"I was just telling my fiancée you were a bomaxed idiot." Emery was notorious for starting conversations mid-flow. His bright, topaz eyes lit up the screen in delight underneath the dark curls falling down into his eyes.

Joe sat in the captain's chair on the flight deck, smiling at the holodisplay. Their stop on Beurias was the longest they'd been anywhere in a while, and Joe was glad for the opportunity to catch up with his friend. "I'm calling you now, aren't I? Things in my new assignment have been more exciting than I originally anticipated."

"Who are you trying to fool? You're in the outer colonies, how eventful can it be? Though, it looks like you found yourself a ship." Emery chuckled.

"Things haven't been too bad." Joe glanced around him. "Though I lost an arm."

Silence. That got Emery's attention. He leaned forward.

"Got it back though," Joe continued, "but that's why I couldn't contact you. Not even the High Commander knows I was rejuvenating an arm in a private hospital." He flexed the arm muscle like they used to back at Headquarters when they were both younger and training to become TSS Agents.

"Are you serious? Whoa, it's a good thing you're well, because with news like that, your sister is liable to kill you for not making it to the wedding."

Joe smiled. His best friend bonding with his older sister had thrown him at first. Now, though, after his brief time with Iza, he understood the power of that pull firsthand. It wasn't something easily severed, even for the love of a brother or a friend.

"Do I even want to know how it happened?" Emery asked.

"It's a long story, I'll save it for later." Joe wanted to shift the focus off of himself. "How are the wedding plans?"

Emery laughed and rubbed a hand through his thick, dark curls. "Wow, where did that come from?"

"What do you mean?"

"I don't think you've ever brought up the subject before. What's really going on with you? Do you have some kind of terminal, incurable disease?" Emery asked.

Joe thought back to his first days in the outer colonies and remembered how rough it had been. He'd had no friends, no place to stay. Then, it all changed when he met Braedon. He didn't realize it then, but the kid would bring so much more than a ship into his life. They'd gotten into some trouble along the way, too, but that wasn't all together unexpected when dealing with a Lower Dynasty rebel who had a Robin Hood complex.

"To be honest, I really like it here," Joe said.

"So, who is she?" Emery smirked.

The question caught Joe off guard. He hadn't even hinted at Iza. "What?"

"I've never heard you so animated. I'm pretty sure if you're not dying, then you're already in love. So, what's her name?"

Joe struggled to find the right words to define his relationship with Iza. "Well, there *is* someone," he began.

"I knew it!" Emery slap his hand against his thigh out of the camera's view. "It's obvious there's something different about you. Where did you meet her, what does she look like, and when's the wedding?"

Joe laughed. Emery had bonded and fallen fast and hard, it was no wonder he'd leap straight to the happily ever-after. How could Joe begin explaining Iza? Things with her were so different. Her mind was closed off from him, and lately he couldn't even be sure she still felt the same way.

"Don't get ahead of yourself," Joe said. "Not everyone falls in love in a week and gets married the next day."

"It wasn't like that. Skyler and I didn't talk about getting married at all in the first four days." Emery winked.

"Save me the details. You and my sister getting together is still weird to me. I am happy for you both, though. I hope you can believe that," Joe said, hoping his voice sounded as sincere as he felt.

"You sound like you actually mean it this time." Emery's eyes darted to the left, and Joe realized his sister was listening in.

Joe shifted in his seat, not sure how much to say in front of her. It was easier to focus on Emery and pretend they were alone.

"I do. Before, I might not have completely understood what you two have, but lately," Joe rubbed the prickling at the back of his neck, "it's starting to make more sense."

"You didn't mention how you met this mystery woman," Emery said. His powers of persuasion were weak, but he saw through Joe faster than most.

"Actually, she captains the ship I'm on. That's sort of how we met," Joe said. With his sister listening in off-screen, he didn't mention the prison ship.

"The captain? This just gets better and better. Does she know who you are, I mean about the TSS stuff?"

"No." Joe shook his head and bit his lip. Though he wanted to tell her, his position and post depended on no one knowing his true identity. As it happened, he'd already blown his cover with both Trix and Karter.

"So I guess you won't be bringing her to the wedding."

Joe shook his head. The fantasy of dancing with Iza with many of his classmates and former teachers looking on was something that he'd dreamed about. However, attending his sister's wedding with Iza wasn't meant to be.

"Fair enough. Come on, what's her name?"

"Iza." It came out more like a whisper, as if just saying her name would bring her to him.

"Iza—sounds exotic. Can't wait to meet her," Emery said. "But *you're* coming, right?" It was hard to ignore the hope in his voice.

"I'll do my best," Joe promised and meant it.

"Don't show up without a gift. We're expecting something expensive." Emery teased. Joe saw Skyler's fist come from the left side of the screen and hit Emery in the shoulder.

"Okay, sounds good," Joe said, laughing.

"Your sister says hi." Emery braced himself for another hit.

Joe hadn't spoken to Skyler in over two years, when Skyler and Emery had told him about their impending nuptials. It had been a rough time for all of them when Joe didn't take the news well. Emery hadn't understood why Joe was so upset then, and he probably never would. Joe's relationship with Skyler was too complex to properly articulate, so he normally just shut down rather than trying to justify his behavior.

Joe cleared his throat. "I'm glad you two are doing well. Take care." He waved at the camera. He was taking the coward's way out; the shame of it crept up his neck and into his cheeks like a heat rash.

Emery glanced to his left and then nodded, dropping his shoulders in resignation. "Yeah, Joe. you too." He'd finally learned—some things he couldn't fix. Despite Emery's eager optimism, Joe appreciated the effort. He would make a great addition to their family.

Joe ended the call and slumped in the captain's seat. He hated that every talk with Emery inevitably circled back to his sister. That's what hurt so much. Emery had been *his* friend. *His* person to talk to and help him forget about how his life had been turned upside down.

But then Skyler had stolen his best friend. Perfect Skyler, the older sister who'd decided his fate without even realizing that's what she was doing.

Joe forced himself from the seat with a frustrated groan.

He wiped the communication logs so no one could trace the call back to the TSS, and then he headed to his cabin.

"Wow, what's with you?" Cierra asked when she passed him in the corridor.

Joe normally kept his thoughts guarded from her, but he knew he was wearing enough emotion on his face to give an accurate impression of his mood. As he passed by her, he decided to share a telepathic hint of the storm brewing just beneath the surface.

Cierra nodded as she took in the mental impressions. "Family is complicated."

"You really have no idea," he muttered and continued on his way.

He'd had what he would consider a typical childhood in America, if Hollywood movies were a proper indication. Skyler was the golden child, excelling at everything she tried. Joe had given up trying to compete with her by the time he was a teenager, happy to have fun rather than stress about being Number One at anything.

Then, their parents had been killed in the line of duty during a mission gone wrong. Until then, Joe and his sister had no idea that their parents were Tarans stationed on TSS special assignment on Earth. When an Agent came to recruit Joe and Skyler to follow in their parents' career footsteps, Skylar had jumped at the chance to go off to become a TSS Agent herself; she'd always dreamed of being some kind of superhero.

Joe, on the other hand, had gone off the deep end. His temper got the best of him most days, and he never seemed to be able to keep it under control. The doctors tried to tell him it was an issue with abandonment, or some such nonsense, but he didn't buy it. He didn't blame his parents for dying, but he didn't like being a part of the lie once he learned the truth about

Earth's place in the galaxy. The Taran Empire was right there, just beyond Earth's technological reach. They hadn't rescued his parents in time, and then they'd convinced his sister to join their ranks and leave everyone they cared about on Earth behind, in the dark.

Joe had no choice: either lose his sister, too, or join the TSS to maintain a connection to the only family he had left.

Despite having entered the TSS in the same cohort, the experience ultimately drove Joe further from his older sister. He resented her, as unfair as it was, for choosing a path that led away from their home. He didn't need to follow her, but at sixteen, he'd been too alone and scared to see another option. Sure, the TSS was great in a lot of ways, but he grew bitter about struggling with things that always came so naturally to her.

In the end, the TSS managed to turn Joe into a mediocre Agent with an average skillset. Whenever he saw his sister, though, the anger and resentment was impossible to conceal. Instead of fighting with him, Skyler had avoided him. After many years of practice, they'd found that keeping their distance was for the best.

I followed her so we'd have each other, and then I did everything I could to force her away. He shook his head.

At least Emery had found a way to maintain a relationship with both of them, against the odds. Maybe, one day, Joe would find common ground with Skyler, but that still felt like a long way off. For now, though, he had found a surrogate family aboard the *Verity*. And maybe, just maybe, Iza could become even more than that.

IZA'S CONVERSATION WITH Jovani, Braedon, and Cierra went much like she expected when she told them that she wouldn't be around for a couple of days.

"Of course, we'll continue to oversee the repairs and pick up any supplies you may need," Braedon said. "There's this sweet little shop near the city where we can get fresh fruit for almost nothing. Cierra wants to go so I'll get extra for the rest of us who want their fruit whole."

"There's nothing wrong with blended fruit." Cierra crossed her arms defensively.

"Maybe not once in a while, but I'd like to use my teeth while I still have them," Braedon complained.

Iza ignored their bickering. "Jovani, reach out to Lynaeda tell them what's going on with Trix. Find out if there's anything we can do for her until we are able to bring her to them."

"I'll take care of her." He reached out and rubbed his hands up and down both of her arms.

Does he know I feel chilled to the bone, or is it just something he does for someone he cares about? Either way, she welcomed the contact. She'd need every bit of energizing she could get before spending two days being paraded around as Karter's newest acquisition.

"If they say it's necessary, leave my shuttle here and take the *Verity* to Lynaeda," Iza told him. "Trix is the priority. She's been down for almost a full day, and I'm worried about what's going on with her internal systems if she remains inactive for any longer. If I could get out of this job, I would."

"You didn't say exactly what your plans were," Braedon said.

"No, I didn't," Iza said, ignoring his implied question. "If you run into trouble or you're not sure what to do, contact me. I'll get back to you as soon as I can. Oh, and check on the dog for me too. He needs to go out at least twice a day. Let him run around the ship a few times, it will tire him out a bit."

"Cierra and I know how to care for a dog, we've got this. Everything will be fine," Braedon assured her. He seemed almost too eager for her to go.

Cierra nodded once, as if she were also eager for Iza to be away.

"Why do you always look like you're about to get into trouble?" Iza asked them.

"Because they usually are," Jovani answered with a smirk that made Braedon frown. "Don't worry, I'll make sure Braedon stays out of trouble this time."

Iza nodded, still not sure about leaving Trix but knowing she didn't have a choice. "Thanks, you're a huge help. I'll make it up to you."

Jovani waved a hand at her. "Don't worry about it, that's what friends do for each other. Just be safe."

Iza smiled. *He's amazing.* She stared at his smile a moment longer than normal to commit it to memory. It would disappear once he learned the truth.

—

Karter was sending his driver to pick up Iza at 01:00 in the dead of night. The others had long since gone to bed when Iza opened up her cabin door to creep out. It was better this way—fewer questions, she reasoned. However, the questions would come later. Then she'd be forced to answer them.

Iza was only bringing a small bag of clothes, which she'd slipped the ancient box inside. She didn't want it to wind up in someone else's hands while there were so many unknown people on board her ship. It was safer with her, though she'd probably sleep better without it.

There was a light creak of metal when she tried to close the door behind her. While she was struggling to make it close softly, the dog slipped out into the corridor.

"No, not you. Stay," she said in a loud whisper, which he happily ignored. His curled tail wagged with joy at the prospect of going out. "I should have known it was a mistake not to drop you off some place at the first opportunity."

She crept along the corridor near the gymnasium with the dog trailing quietly behind her. Iza opened the door to look in on Trix. The android was still standing in the room with her eyes staring off into space and her head slightly tilted. It was as if she would say something any minute.

"I'll be back, I promise. Jovani will take care of you and we'll get you home soon. Don't give up." There was no blink or response from Trix as Iza reached out and touched her shoulder.

Seeing her friend that way broke her heart, but Trix was an AI in an android body. She wasn't lost. They'd get her to

Lynaeda, and they would know what to do.

Having said her temporary goodbyes, Iza snuck off the ship to wait for her ride outside with her dog in tow. She had forgotten how cold it got on Beurias in winter, which was made to feel even more extreme after living in the sauna-like environment on board the *Verity*, thanks to the broken thermostat. Iza checked the weather report on her handheld and saw that snow was in the forecast for the following evening. She couldn't help but take it as an amusing sign about how her engagement announcement would be received.

Karter's driver pulled up, and Iza's jaw dropped. The sleek shuttle was built for speed, complete with a mirror-finish hull that made it almost impossible to see in the dim light until it was nearly on top of her.

The dog let out one loud bark in her defense, and she realized she should have made some kind of leash for the little beast. "We have to be on our best behavior," she told him.

The shuttle's side hatch swung open vertically, Iza slid into the back bench seat. The dog hopped in and sat down next to her.

Up front, the driver, a pale-skinned man with sandy-brown hair tucked under his black cap, cast a skeptical gaze at the dog.

"Don't even think about saying anything," Iza warned him.

The driver turned forward and initiated the takeoff procedure.

Iza composed a short message to Jovani, with a delayed send scheduled for the morning, to let him know that she'd taken the dog with her instead of leaving him behind as planned. With one hand resting on the dog's back, she watched the blurred view as the shuttle sped to the Blue Hills Estate.

The lights of the city blended together in streaks reflected off the glass. Like in many places at times when most people were in bed, there was a small contingent still awake—scattered lights in distant windows of the city's towers. Iza remembered that life, conserving her energy during the day so she could run the streets at night. She had seen little back then, having avoided the central planets in favor of spending most of her time in the freer outer colonies. There were plenty of cities out there that didn't take notice of a street kid living in alleys and looking for a quick score. She'd grown so much since then, seen magnificent cities and glimpsed from afar opulence that was out of reach for all but a select few.

Despite her experiences, nothing had prepared her for the sight of Blue Hills Estates. Ten minutes outside the city, the outline of the massive mansion took her breath away. Lights illuminated almost every window of the four-story building, no doubt because staff were busy getting the mansion prepared for the upcoming festivities.

"This is it?" she asked, trying to sound wholly unimpressed just to see if she could get a rise out of the driver.

He didn't respond. It seemed he had about the same level of conversation ability as one of Cierra's vegetables.

Iza glanced down at the dog, and he looked up at her expectantly. At least someone was listening to her.

After landing the vehicle, the driver opened the shuttle's side hatch without a word.

"Well, thanks for all of your help," she said sarcastically.

She slung her pack over one shoulder as she slid out from the shuttle, and the dog followed her. The two scaled the twenty-two steps to the door. Before she could knock, the door swung open.

"Good evening, Miss Sundari," said the formidable older gentleman who answered the door. "My name is Brooks.

Welcome to the Blue Hills Estate. May I take your bags?" He scowled down at the dog, who sat with his tail still wagging and his tongue dripping saliva on the marble floors.

"I've got it, thank you," Iza said.

Brooks ushered her inside to a foyer boasting ostentatious sparkle and decadent details. An enormous crystal chandelier hung from the center of the ceiling, casting tiny rainbows on the elaborate carpet woven in shades of blue, which led to a curved staircase with a carved marble banister. Painted ceramics and chiseled metals accented the adjacent halls. As old as it all seemed, none of it held a speck of dust.

"This way, Miss," Brooks said when she stood staring too long.

"Iza will do," she corrected.

Brooks led her into a small study to the right of the foyer. Floor-to-ceiling shelving housed physically bound books. She stared at them in awe. Iza couldn't remember when she'd last seen an actual book made with paper. A fireplace in the corner cast the room in a warm glow and heat that made it welcomingly cozy, especially on such a chilly night. Two chairs sat on opposite sides of a small table in front of the fireplace, where two glasses of some unknown citrus-colored drink were waiting.

"Please, have a seat. Mr. Hyttinen will be here in just a moment," Brooks said before he left the room, closing the door behind him.

Iza took her time taking in the rest of the ornate furnishings and the view out the large window overlooking the front grounds. At one time, the estate had been someone's actual home, though it was hard for Iza to believe it. Now, the Hyttinen Dynasty used the estate for various political and social functions.

With Karter nowhere in sight, Iza picked up her drink and made a cheers to herself. *If I have to be fake-engaged, at least I can do it in style.*

—

A knock on the door and the dog's growl startled Iza to attention.

She didn't realize she'd been sleeping until she felt the drool on her chin. She hastily wiped it away and stood up when she saw Karter enter the room, settling into her annoyed expression. "Took you long enough."

The dog pranced toward Karter and almost glued his nose to the cuff of Karter's pant leg to see if he was friend or foe.

If only it were that easy to tell, Iza thought to herself.

"I had imagined you'd be coming alone." Karter peered down at the dog with no little distaste. It only made her happier that she'd allowed the mutt to come along.

"He insisted." Iza shrugged.

"Fine."

Iza made a noise at the back of her throat to warn the dog to stop his attack. He wisely trotted behind her and sat down.

"I see you made yourself comfortable," Karter said, eyeing the two empty glasses on the table. He smoothed the jacket of his tan suit, which complimented his dark-brown skin. "I apologize for the inconvenience. I very much appreciate your patience. It took some work to clear a path to where you'll be staying the next couple of days." "Well, I'll show you to your rooms."

Rooms... plural? She brushed past him, careful not to stumble in her sleepy haze. She wondered again what he hoped to gain from this false engagement.

"Was this your family's house?" Iza asked.

"Hardly. We use it to host parties and other functions to impress each other." The last part he said with a little bitterness.

"So, you're not all about the parties and dynastic shoulder-brushing?"

"I have no problem socializing with people of my class as long as it doesn't require me to lie. I hate putting on false pretenses just to keep what I have," he said, his jaw tight.

It seemed to be a sore subject, but she was already exhausted. It wasn't worth the fight that would come from asking him for more details. Instead, she followed him in silence while he led her through the mansion. As they passed through the kitchen, she debated about grabbing something to quiet her grumbling stomach, but promise of sleep won out.

The dog however, had other ideas. He whined and scratched at one of the food drawers as they passed.

"When was the last time you fed your dog?"

Iza thought over her day and realized she hadn't asked if Braedon had done it. "I think he ate this morning, but I'm not sure, to be honest. I've been a little busy."

Karter surprised her by stopping to dig into the back of one of the large cold storage fridges to grab a large bone with some meat on it. The dog went crazy at the sight of it, but Karter, to his credit, held fast to the bone. The dog to followed him, eyes glued on the bone.

"Please forgive the unconventional route to your suite. I placed you on the far end of the manor to reduce accidental foot traffic passing by," he said, ignoring the dog's impatient whining. "But in the morning, you'll have a lovely view of the gardens, despite the snow."

"At this rate, I hope you don't expect me up before noon."

"Well, there's quite a lot to do tomorrow. I also hope you can find the time to practice our dance."

"Pardon?" Iza raised her eyebrows.

"It is the custom for a newly engaged couple to lead off the first dance, with friends and family looking on."

"You mean *your* friends and family," she said.

"In all fairness, your family and friends are invited, as well. Since the event will be public, it's about time they knew."

Iza had no intention of inviting anyone from the *Verity* and she had no real family. She lifted one shoulder and let it drop. "I don't know anyone who would want to come to this farce."

"Your mother, perhaps? Once we track her down, we could—"

"Don't bother. I have no intention of contacting her, let alone invite her to this."

"Iza, she's your mother. I would think you'd want to know what happened to her."

"That woman, who I thought Left after my father died, walked out on me and never looked back. End of story, no twist, no happy ending." Iza let the bitterness fill her mouth.

"I do wish you'd consider it. She may have some explanation. But, of course, the choice is yours."

He fell silent again, and they continued without another word. Even the dog was patiently following the meaty bone in his hand without complaint.

After four flights of stairs, they reached the top floor and proceeded to the end of the hallway on the left. Iza stopped counting the doors after seven when it was clear that they were going as far to the end as possible. Iza couldn't make out anything but stars through the window at the end of the hall.

"Here you are." Karter motioned, at last, to a set of double doors. "Press your palm to the reader." He pointed to a biometric scanner on the right side of the door.

Iza pressed her hand against the plate.

"Would you like to initialize?" asked a synthesized voice.

"Yes, authorization by voice, Karter Hyttinen."

"Voice authorization recognized. Room initialized and assigned."

The lock released, and Karter opened the door for her. As she passed through the threshold, the lights turned on automatically, revealing a large suite with two connecting doors leading to the other rooms. The bed in any other space would be garish, but in this room it was merely the focal point with its canopy draped in a soft white fabric and gold accents. Large picture windows on either side of the bed faced into the room. Another large bay window with an off-white seat occupied the space opposite the door, which the dog promptly claimed as his own.

Karter opened the two closed doors on the left, revealing a clothing closet and a shoe closet already filled with luxurious garments.

"Who's are those?"

"They're yours, if you want them." Karter waved a hand at the items as if it were nothing.

The clothing inside had to be worth more credits than everything she owned put together. Despite the pretty designs and fine materials, she couldn't imagine wearing them on a haul.

"You are free to explore the rest of your rooms on your own time. You must, however, stay here until tomorrow night, as I don't want to ruin the big reveal. Try to get some rest. Tomorrow will be a big day for you." He finally tossed the meat bone to the dog, who leaped to catch it. Karter held his hand away from himself to keep from soiling his suit or touching anything.

"Thanks," Iza said, but it came out more like a question.

Karter saw himself out and closed the door behind him. Iza heard the lock bolt into place as soon as he was through the door. Iza took a glance around the room and decided that she would explore in the morning. Tonight she just wanted to go to sleep.

She slipped out of her boots and noticed that she'd tracked caked dirt onto the carpet. More careful with her jacket, she placed it inside out on top of the window seat. Only then, when she opened her bag to unpack, did she realized that she'd neglected to bring something to sleep in, just another set of day clothes.

Iza dropped the bag to the floor in a huff. The distinct *thunk* called her attention to the ancient box she'd hastily thrown in. She fished it out and opened the box. The sphere hummed in her palm as she stared at it, wondering what kind of map it was and where it led.

For the first time, the dog whined on the floor and backed away from her.

"Can you hear that, boy?" She placed the sphere back into the box and snapped the lid shut. He seemed to settle, returning to his gnawing on the bone.

Iza slipped the box inside of the nightstand to the right of the bed for safekeeping. She stripped out of her clothes and dropped them on the floor before she climbed between the silky sheets. As she drifted off to sleep, her thoughts circled around Jovani, wishing he was there next to her. They'd laugh about the waste of credits to stay in such a fancy place and enjoy the perks of such a comfortable bed.

10

THE NEXT MORNING, it seemed the temperature controls on the *Verity* were finally working again. Overnight, it had become unbearably cold due to the overly compensated thermostat, but Joe couldn't help thinking that part of the chill was Iza's absence. Their bond intensified whenever they were together, and he'd become accustomed to her presence. Even Emery had noticed the change in him immediately. Was it obvious to the others, as well?

Shortly after he awoke, Joe got a message from Braedon summoning him to the flight deck, saying something about there being a message addressed to the crew.

Joe took his seat at the tactical station, his usual spot, and looked expectantly at Braedon to share whatever had him so worked up. Cierra was standing next to Braedon's work-station with her arms crossed, tapping one of her bare feet.

"So, let's have it," Joe prompted when Braedon kept fidgeting rather than starting to talk.

"All right, remember yesterday when we got that message addressed to the '*Verity* Crew'?" Braedon began, and Joe nodded. "Well, I forgot about it because I spent all afternoon dealing with those knuckleheads from Apex. Apparently, since we didn't open it within twelve hours, it got resent with a higher priority tag. Well, *this* version of the message has a dynastic seal on it."

"Whose?" Cierra asked.

"Hyttinen. I guess that means it's from Karter." Braedon turned in his seat at the console and pulled up the message. "Should we open it?"

Joe wanted to punch him. "Obviously!"

A virtual invitation unfolded to the sound of fanfare and an explosion of color as a calligraphy script wrote out the message in real time:

> *Greetings!*
>
> *Crew of the* Verity, *we cordially invite you to the engagement announcement of the Karter Hyttinen, heir to the Hyttinen Dynasty, and his bride-to-be, Iza Sundari, this evening at 19:00.*
>
> *Our family is pleased to offer you food and drinks during your visit to Blue Hills Estate. However, weapons and recording devices are strictly prohibited. Please also note, this is a formal affair, and we cannot admit those dressed inappropriately.*
>
> *We look forward to sharing our happy day with you,*
>
> > *Warm Regards,*
> > *The Hyttinens*

Braedon and Cierra turned as one to stare at Joe while he continued to gawk at the screen, which still flashed with short bursts of color like fireworks over the invitation. *So it is true.*

Movement caught the corner of his eye, snapping him back to the present. He turned to see Trix wander onto the flight deck.

"Trix?" Braedon said, leaping up from his console and running to examine her.

The shock was wearing off as Joe joined the others circling Trix, who seemed to be back to normal.

"How are you?" Joe asked.

"I am functioning within acceptable ranges." Trix turned to Joe and her eyebrows furrowed. "However, my internal chronometer is not functioning properly, as it cannot account for the missing time. When did Iza become engaged?"

— — —

For the first time, some elements of Iza's recurring dreams had changed. Usually the locations and people were vague except for herself or someone like Jovani standing next to her. The location was unfamiliar, as usual—what looked like a market or small town with lots of food stands and people buying local.

Iza brushed at the dust on her arms and in her eyes as she struggled to take in the people around her. The smell of cooking meat drew her attention, and she turned where a man was serving sandwiches of smoked meat. She was hungry, but a cold shadow on her back made her turn her head, searching the crowd for the cause of the chill.

One young man stood out from the others—familiar but not. He looked directly at her and the anger on his features was unmistakable. The charge of electricity between them traveled over her skin in a flash as she stared back at him, wondering what she'd done to offend him. His mouth moved as if he were speaking but no words reached her ears.

The dog let out an eager yip, startling her awake. The sun was already streaming through the windows. *When did the sun come up?*

The dog had bounded to the door to attack whoever was knocking. Iza pulled the covers up over her chest and stared at the door in horror. Karter had assured her she wouldn't be leaving the room. *Why would anyone be at the door?*

"Miss Sundari, I have your lunch tray. You must open the door if you'd like to eat today."

At the promise of a meal, Iza's stomach responded before her feet touched the floor; she must have slept through breakfast. She disregarded her pile of clothes on the floor and rushed to answer the door. Whoever was bringing her lunch was going to see her in her undergarments.

There were two white-uniformed women at the door, wearing black aprons. The elder, who appeared to be in charge, had her gray hair pulled away from her large forehead and up into an organized mess on top of her head. She looked Iza up and down with her sharp gray eyes, lips pursed. Then, she gave Iza an almost imperceptible nod before waving a young red-haired woman with a long braid into the room.

The younger woman blushed at the sight of Iza in her underwear, but she quickly turned her attention back to pushing a food cart with drinks and a water bowl into the room. She couldn't resist scratching the dog behind his ears as she set the water dish on the floor. "He's so cute, what's his name?"

"Never mind that!" the older woman scolded, and the younger snapped to attention. "Excuse my companion, Miss Sundari. My name is Barbara, and this is my assistant, Georgie.

We'll be seeing to your needs today. Mr. Hyttinen allowed you to sleep in, but he has a full schedule for you this afternoon."

"Does he?" Iza said, stepping forward with her hands on her hips in challenge.

"Yes, Miss, he insists that you be ready for this evening's festivities."

"What, exactly, does he have planned?" Iza was being sarcastic but Barbara answered as if the question had been sincere.

"A light lunch, a bath with oils followed by a full body massage, followed by a briefing about this evening's guest list. After tea and crackers, Georgie and I will dress you for the ball this evening."

"Dress? Like a child?" Iza asked.

Georgie let out a nervous squeak, which Barbara answered with a cluck of her tongue and a glare.

"No, of course not, Miss Sundari. We're only here to facilitate your transition into high society. It is our understanding that you are not accustomed to associating with Mr. Hyttinen's business partners or family. He doesn't want there to be any embarrassment, thus the need for discretion and your confinement to these rooms."

The nerve of him making her out to be ignorant and backward gutter trash. Iza pulled herself up, squaring her shoulders and looking down at the woman with as much disdain as she could muster. "Despite Mr. Hyttinen's instructions, I've had plenty of contact with his associates and his family, as a matter of fact. Don't confuse me with someone who's going to fit into his mold. Are we clear?"

"Perfectly. We meant no disrespect, Miss Sundari."

Barbara's quick apology cooled Iza's anger against the woman. It wasn't her fault; she was just following orders. She had no idea her employer was a bomaxed self-absorbed idiot.

"Let's start with that. Stop calling me 'Miss Sundari'. Since I'm to be treated like a child and confined to my room, you can at least do me the courtesy of calling me by my first name. I don't require, nor welcome, the pretension."

"Mr. Hyttinen would never allow it," Georgie blurted out before covering her mouth with both hands for her impertinent outburst.

"He's not here, so we'll keep it between us." Iza smiled, lifting the metal top off of the breakfast plate. "This looks amazing. I'm starving."

— — —

Karter traversed the halls of the Blue Hills mansion with purpose, trailed by Becca and the estate housekeeper, a stout woman named Mildred. Things were going almost as well as if he'd planned them himself. Now that he was in the swing of things, planning the engagement party had become as much fun as acquiring new transport storage facility. As he checked off one item and then another in his planner, he immersed himself in the details.

"I want the kitchen prepped and ready in an hour so we can go over the menu one last time. How are we coming with the rest of the house preparations?"

"Everything else is going well," said Mildred. "The guest rooms are ready and some of the overnight guests have already begun arriving."

"Already?" Karter stopped in his tracks.

"Several of your friends are by the pool. One young lady has requested access to the gardens this afternoon. Despite our warnings about the cold and falling snow, she insists."

"Raquel," Karter said shaking his head. "She can do what she wants. It's fine." Karter made a mark within his handheld and moved on to the next item. "That's all for now, Mildred. I think everything is in order. If you don't hear from the catering company about the delivery time, get the company manager on the line and I'll speak with him myself. He won't survive if he thinks he can get away with being late tonight."

"Yes, sir, Mr. Hyttinen. Miss Drejas," Mildred bobbed and dipped to the right, heading down the corridor toward Iza's room.

Karter watched her walk away and then turned back to Becca, lowering his voice.

"The Sensationals. What have you discovered?"

"Only that whoever leaked the information is well-connected and bankrolled the entire process from beginning to end. No one is talking. The only way to find out who sent the original message is to trace it through the Net. We don't have access to the tech and Investigator Hyttinen has been less than inclined to help us."

"Really? I guess I shouldn't be surprised by her being so petty. I'd hoped she'd come around." Karter sighed.

Becca referenced the checklist on her tablet. "You have the kitchen inspection at 13:30. You left some time for tennis and a shower before your massage at 16:30. Would you like me to have some food brought to your suite? You haven't eaten anything since breakfast."

"No, I'll have the chef make me a sandwich or something while I'm in the kitchens. I won't risk running into my mother's cousin and her obnoxious daughter after my relaxation hour. In fact, I think I'll get it out of the way early."

Karter turned with purpose toward the large staircase leading to the foyer, where maintenance workers were hanging the large red curtain they would use for their reveal. With the news out, it wouldn't be the surprise he was going for, but it would be better than nothing.

"Check in with Barbara and make sure that Iza isn't giving her any trouble. She gets antsy when she's caged up." Karter grinned.

"I will make sure she has everything she needs. The hair and makeup artists are on their way, and they have a few designs for you to approve."

"Send them to my handheld. What about you? Did you receive the dress I ordered?"

"Yes, sir, it's…" Becca paused a moment, her eyes darting from left to right. "It's lovely. I'm surprised you thought of me on such an important day."

"You're the most important person in my life next to Iza. I can't imagine what I'd do without you." His hand reached up and touched her cheek. It was gentle and out of character, and the moment he realized it, his hand dropped to his side. "Did you bring it?"

Becca's smile faded only a little when she answered, "Yes." She pulled a small velvet bag from her pocket and handed it to Karter. "It's beautiful."

"It was my grandmother's. I hope she likes it."

"I'm sure she'll love it," Becca said, reassuring him with a touch on his arm.

He stiffened, pulling back from her. "Where is my mother?"

"She, Maeve, and Desirae are in the community room where the spa has been set up." Becca looked down at her tablet then back at him. "They're getting facials at the moment."

"Fine, I'll seek them out while they least expect it. I don't want a repeat of the Baellas anniversary ball last year."

"Sir, Investigator Hyttinen may be with them," Becca warned.

Karter waved away the warning. He'd need to face her eventually, and it was better to do it now instead of in a room of his guests at the engagement party. His family members had been made aware of the engagement ahead of time. For the rest of the guests, Iza would be a surprise, depending on how much they believed the Sensationals.

As expected, the women were all having their treatments done early before the other guests arrived. His mother was on her back while someone rubbed something brown over her skin. His mother's cousin had her eyes covered while a technician rubbed at her face. Desirae was face-down while her legs were massaged. She had great legs he noted, along with everything else. It was everything above the neck that was crazy—a trait she clearly got from her mother.

Desirae's mother, Maeve, had married into the Hyttinen family, becoming a cousin to Karter's mother by marriage. She'd been trying to maneuver her daughter as a partner for Karter since they were young. The intensity and frequency of the hints had been off-putting enough, but the fact that Maeve had had both her and Desirae's names changed to Hyttinen, despite having no blood relation, made the situation even more uncomfortable. Though Karter did his best to steer clear of both of them, they had a way of inserting themselves into his business at the most inopportune times.

"Mr. Hyttinen," the three workers said in unison, looking up from their clients as he entered. They bowed their heads with respect.

"As you were. I'm just here to chat with the ladies of my life."

"Clear the room," his mother said between her teeth,

already guessing at his intentions. She was like a hawk these days, always looking for a reason to peck at him.

The three workers hurried away.

"I must say, I'm surprised that this was the big secret you were keeping from us. Your earlier behavior makes sense now," Desirae said as she rolled over to face him on the nearby massage bed, pulling the white towel forward to cover herself.

"As your mother's favorite cousin, this has come as a surprise. I'd always hoped you and Desirae would get together, but I guess it's not meant to be," Maeve clucked her tongue. She wore a green jewel-toned necklace that she never took off. The rings she habitually wore on each finger were resting in a small glass dish on the table at her side. "I'm disappointed in you, Karter. Why would you align yourself with someone so far beneath you? Couldn't you find anyone more suitable?"

"Iza's perfectly suitable," he said, keeping the disdain in his voice at bay.

His mother let out a humph. "She's a nobody from the streets of nowhere, doing nothing and no one has even heard of her."

"She's suitable for me, and that's really what should matter most, Mother."

"It's almost as bad as picking an employee. I warned you if you took on an employee you'd lose it all. And I'm not alone; the investors are behind me."

"Only because you've poisoned them against me with your talk of dividing the company. Enough. I will run Apex Manufacturing Enterprises as I see fit, without your meddling."

His mother waved a hand in the air.

"It's shocking how he speaks to you these days, Phaedra," Maeve said with another tsk of her tongue. "His father would never stand for it." She nodded her head once as if to confirm it.

"You didn't even know my father," Karter bit down on the words harder than intended, and the three women's heads snapped up to stare at him. "I apologize. I'm just tired. This is an important day. If you'll excuse me, I better get some rest." Then he added as an afterthought, "If you don't see me until this evening, don't take it personally. There's important business to attend to, as some guests have already arrived."

Karter strolled out of the spa room with the women chattering about his ill-advised marriage to a commoner. But they didn't know Iza, and they didn't know his plan. Everything was exactly the way he wanted it.

11

THE DAY PASSED in a blur of pampering, fittings, and walk-throughs. As evening fell, butterflies erupted in Iza's gut. The mere idea of dancing in front of over two-hundred guests with Karter gave her anxiety.

An engagement party should be an exciting affair, but Iza was dreading it more than anything else she'd done in her life. She'd dreamed of being with someone, perhaps even getting married, but not like this. Not to Karter. And the false pretense made it that much worse.

Now that the reality of her contract was setting in, facing jail time and losing her ship was nothing compared to the prospect of losing Jovani. When Jovani dove in front of her and lost his arm, she thought he'd never be the same. Her deal with Karter saved his arm and his life. However, the price was weighing on her. Tonight, she'd have to reveal to Jovani that she was engaged to Karter with no further explanation—unable to tell Jovani that her heart belonged to him and everything with Karter was just an act. He would hate her and she wouldn't blame him.

Barbara and Georgie arrived at 16:00 to prep her for the evening. Though they'd brought a tray of snacks for her to consume, she couldn't bear to swallow anything. The pressure of the evening was crushing her like a giant wave of water against a rocky cliff.

Iza leaped out of her skin when Karter knocked on the doors promptly at 17:30. Georgie let him in, and he sidestepped the dog to inspect Iza's appearance. He'd dressed in an immaculate steel-gray formal suit, a perfect complement to the liquid-silver gown they had poured her into. The soft texture of her dress seemed to match the design in the gray-on-gray pattern.

"You look resplendent," he said as he sauntered in an appreciative circle around her.

"You clean up well, too," she said and meaning it.

"It's even better on you than I imagined."

"I haven't embarrassed you?"

"Not yet," Karter said, taking her arm. "But it's still early."

He probably hadn't meant to be funny, but the casual way he'd said it made her relax a little.

Then, he pulled out the ring. A giant white stone set in a silver band that matched the dress.

She gawked at it as he slipped it on her finger. The weight of it sobered her mood.

"Ready?" he asked.

"Let's get this over with."

Karter led her back down the corridor, but this time they turned toward the front foyer and down to the landing where the East and West wings met. They headed toward the bright-red curtain designed to block the view from the rest of the wide staircase below. Iza could hear the chatter of the guests and the tinkling of glasses on the other side.

He had a flair for the dramatic, she mused.

"Ladies and gentlemen, your attention, please." It was Brooks who introduced them in a loud voice that bellowed over the crowd of people below. Their voices fell to a hush, and he continued, "The Hyttinen Dynasty is pleased to welcome you to the Blue Hills Estate in celebration of the engagement of Karter Hyttinen and Iza Sundari."

There was a rumble of murmurs as the crowd waited for the curtain to part and reveal the couple.

Karter put on his most charming smile as the curtain parted, and Iza did her best to not look like she was about to throw up. The crowd below them erupted in applause and cheers.

Karter took slow measured steps, giving her time to keep up with him and not lose one of the fancy silver shoes she wore. When they reached the bottom step, he stopped.

"Thank you all, for welcoming Iza into our family. We hope to have all of you back here for the main event early next year."

Iza's head snapped up and she stared hard at him. Karter refused to turn a centimeter in her direction. *When did we agreed on a date? Not going to happen.* Iza tensed when he grasped her hand tight in his own. She was merely a stand-in serving his interests for the moment. She was about to hiss the important fact into his ear when someone called out to her from behind.

"Well, Scrap Rat, looks like you're coming up in the world," said Captain Douketis. He'd dressed in a formal suit the color of dirt. Without his large sandy hat hiding his dog-like features, he looked even more canine.

"Why would you steal an invitation to this?" Iza asked, keeping her tone level as he approached with Reis on his arm;

a head taller than him, she was hard to miss. She was stunning, draped in a soft black velvet dress with a V-neckline that plunged toward her navel. Her bright pink hair had been recently treated and added to her eye-catching ensemble. It was too bad about her crooked nose, but Iza thought her makeup design did decent job of hiding the defect.

"Karter invited all the haulers who work with Apex Manufacturing. We wouldn't miss it for the world." Sarcasm dripped off every word.

It was then Iza realized what Douketis was saying. *All the haulers.* She repeated the words in her mind slowly. Karter had invited everyone. That meant her people on the *Verity* would also be in attendance.

Stars, no. She searched the crowd for Jovani but didn't see him among the guests. *He wouldn't. He couldn't.*

She spotted Karter talking to a group of businesspeople nearby and stormed over to him.

"You told them?" she hissed in his ear.

"Who?"

"Everyone on my ship. You invited them here to this?"

"I wouldn't intentionally leave out your friends. What kind of man do you think I am?"

"The dirty-rotten bomaxed soon-to-be-dead kind," she fumed, trying to keep her voice to a whisper as to not make a scene. "I never asked you to do that. In fact, I specifically recall telling you *not* to do it."

Karter reached out for a glass of rosé sparkling wine with fruit garnish and put it in her hand, but she wasn't thirsty. Rather, she was close to throwing the pink bubbly drink in his face.

Karter's mother, Phaedra, approached a moment later as if she'd been waiting for it. She plucked the glass from Iza's hand, deftly placing it on a servant's tray.

"She'll look like she's overindulging in all the Sensationals," she said, wagging her index finger. Her manicured nails were exceptionally long and pointed, Iza noted, making them look more like talons. The conniving older woman kept a smile plastered on her face as she spoke unnaturally between her teeth. "Water only."

"Mother, don't be fastidious. No one will believe she's not drinking at her own party unless she's pregnant. Let's not give the Sensationals anything more to discuss."

Iza ignored their exchange, still scanning for any sign of Braedon or the others. *Maybe they didn't come.*

Then, her world came crashing down when she spotted Cierra, inexplicably barefoot. *Does the woman ever wear shoes?* It was a formal ball in winter. Aside from her feet, she dressed more like the future wife of a dynastic heir than Iza did.

Seeing Cierra confirmed it. Jovani knew the truth, and she hadn't even been the one to tell him. *Where is he?* She'd have to ask Cierra. It didn't sit well with her, but it was the only way without seeing him to know for sure he was somewhere in the massive well-dressed crowd.

"Tell me I'm not the only one bored already?" asked a woman with long blonde hair. Her playful blue eyes seemed to dance over the room before landing on Iza. "You appear to be a woman who needs a drink," she slipped an arm into hers and grabbed the nearest pink drink from a servant tray and handed it to Iza. "Drink up, your smile's fading."

Iza did so and noticed the effects on her empty stomach immediately. She tried to smile but her concentration was on searching the crowd for any glimpse of Jovani.

"My name is Raquel, I'm an old friend of Karter's. He's been very secretive about you. This engagement seems so spontaneous. I can't imagine he has the capacity for it, with that large stick up his rear end, so it must be you."

Iza choked on her drink and laughed. She wasn't wrong. Karter did meticulously plan everything.

"I'm sorry we haven't met before. Do you live here on Beurias?" Iza asked.

"Most of the time I avoid it, to be honest. Parties like this where highborn exhaustingly try to impress each other are rarely exciting. However, meeting you, I think this one might be different."

Iza liked her easy manner and her honesty.

"Ah, I see you've met Raquel. She's an old friend," Karter said, taking Iza's arm again and guiding her away from Raquel.

"So she was telling me." Iza pulled away from him and stood on her own power. The shoes hurt, but she didn't want to hold on to Karter any longer than necessary.

"I'll catch up with you later, Karter," she said with a formal curtsy.

"Careful around Raquel," he said, nodding in her direction.

"She seems nice. How come you haven't tried to marry her?" Iza asked louder than was appropriate.

Karter glared at her. "What makes you think I didn't?"

Iza hadn't considered that he'd had time to ask anyone else. *I guess I'm not the only woman who's hesitant about being tied to him.*

Iza tried again and failed to reach Cierra before the chimes indicated their first dance. Karter reached for Iza's arm and she followed him to the center of the foyer floor, where the music was already playing. They hadn't actually practiced, and suddenly Iza worried she'd make a fool of herself. The song was a slow one, though, and Karter moved in a predictable rhythm allowing her to follow with little work.

"You're doing fine, try to relax," he said.

"You're not the one wearing heels and a dress made of liquid metal. I'm doing my best not to sweat in this thing, but I'm sure I'm failing."

Karter laughed a little. It was the first time she realized he'd been nervous, too, as some of the usual mask of calm he wore slipped away.

"I think we're putting on a convincing show, don't you?" she asked.

"Yes, quite the show. However, my interests are still at risk. Worse, my cousin will insist I dance with her, so prepare yourself."

Iza wasn't sure what that meant, only that she wouldn't have to spend the entire night dancing with Karter, which was a good thing. She was already counting the minutes before she could retire to her room and contact Jovani. Perhaps he hadn't come because they were busy on Lynaeda. Possibly Trix had taken a turn for the worse. Again, she scanned the crowd for any sign of him or Braedon. She'd have to get to Cierra and find out what she'd be walking into.

The music ended and again the surrounding crowd broke out in applause. As predicted, Karter's cousin Desirae took his hand and forced him to dance with her, leaving Iza on her own. She was lifting the hem of her dress and preparing to leave the center of the room when she looked up and saw Jovani.

The room fell away and his blue eyes held hers, trapped. The music had already begun playing several bars as he made his slow approach, but it didn't matter. Iza couldn't move. All the excuses she wanted to give him remained lodged in her throat. His eyes wavered over her first in appreciation and then in disappointment. She thought he might turn away and leave her standing alone in the middle of the dance floor without a partner. But he didn't. He took a step forward and held out his hand to dance with her.

Without a moment's hesitation, she met him the rest of the way, clasping one hand in his and putting the other on his shoulder.

His left hand on her back and his right hand in hers, he took her on a slow turn of the room. Neither speaking, just staring at each other. It wasn't the only time she wished she could speak to him with her thoughts. Instead, there were only the silent gazes and the disappointed frown of his mouth as he led her around the dance floor.

When the music ended, they stopped moving, but his hands didn't release her until Karter joined them.

"Well, don't you two make a lovely couple? I better break this up before people get the wrong idea about you two," Karter said.

It was in that moment that Iza realized what Karter had done, what he'd planned to do all along. He wanted to ensure that Jovani didn't have a chance and felt discarded.

She glared at him with unbridled hatred. He'd played her again, but this time he'd be sorry. Their engagement was public, but that didn't mean she'd marry him, and she was just about to say so when Raquel returned.

"You look ready to spit fire. I better make you laugh and quick," she said dragging Iza away from the dance floor.

The guests were murmuring. Raquel was right, she was causing a scene. The whole point was to keep up the false pretense. It wouldn't do any good to lose everything now.

"Karter can be such a fool. Whatever he's done to make you mad, I'm on your side," Raquel said.

Iza smiled as she was handed a glass of water. When she

took a sip, though, she realized it wasn't water.

"Nothing but the best for you, don't worry. I knew you'd need it after that hot and heavy dance with Mr. Gorgeous Blue Eyes. Tell me he has a name."

"Yes, it's Jovani Saletas."

"Jovani, I like it," Raquel said, licking her lips in a way that made Iza want to laugh.

"He is handsome, isn't he?"

"Yes, and clearly his brooding eyes are only for you. Some day you must tell me the story but not tonight. That a girl, smile a bit," she said with encouragement. "Keep these stuffy shirts guessing. Let's go find a place to sit down. I'm sure those two-hour heels have to be killing you by now."

This time, Iza did smile. Raquel seemed to understand her in a way that no one else ever had.

Iza followed Raquel to a nearby floral-print bench seat near the kitchen door. A rush of air entered each time the servants came in and out. The window behind the bench seat revealed the snow outside was coming down harder than ever.

"Are you a doctor or something?" Iza asked.

"Nothing so glamorous. I play in the dirt digging up old junk that long-dead people barely noticed when they had it."

"An archaeologist," Iza nodded.

"Yes, and it's as tedious as it sounds. How are you holding up?"

"Were Jovani and I that obvious?" Iza asked, worried now she hadn't held up her end of her bargain with Karter.

"Only a little, but I think we caught it in time. He must be special to you, for him to throw you so off-balance."

Iza's mouth went dry. To admit her feelings for Jovani was to admit her engagement was a fake. It was in that hesitation she heard a commotion coming from the kitchen.

"What's going on?" Iza felt the change in the energy. She glanced around at the unconcerned guests and wondered why no one else seemed to notice it. *Something's wrong.*

There was another crash in the kitchen and they both stood up.

"I don't know, maybe we should—"

Raquel's next words were cut off as the kitchen door flew open and several masked men armed with pulse rifles barreled into the party.

IZA REACHED FOR her handgun, forgetting it was upstairs in her suite along with the sphere and dog. She wouldn't be able to get there without bounding up the staircase or exiting through the kitchen, which was now blocked by a man and a short woman, both wearing masks.

The woman's head swiveled in Iza direction before her attention snapped back to pointing her rifle at the party guests.

The man directed Iza and Raquel to sit back down on the bench.

Someone must have neutralized the security, since there was no alarm. Iza couldn't see any staff members nearby, which likely meant that they'd been locked up somewhere. No doubt the criminals had heard there would be a formal event this evening that would be attended by an impressive guest list of the Taran elite. There was a lot to potentially be gained from such a gathering.

Iza wondered, then, where Jovani had gone. *Stars, I hope he snuck in a weapon.*

"Ladies and gentlemen, thank you for coming this

evening." The man speaking kept his face covered but his arms were spread wide in welcome. "I wish we could introduce ourselves, but for now we'd like to remain anonymous. It's wonderful to see such fine people as yourselves dressed up for an evening out and dinner provided by Mr. Hyttinen himself. However, every event like this one comes with a price. This evening, the price is your prized possessions. Please place all your valuables in the little black bags provided by my associates."

Iza watched them making the rounds holding out the bags. The way one of the intruders moved reminded her of someone, though she couldn't place it.

The two people at the kitchen door moved forward, each holding out a bag. Raquel was already grumbling about buying new jewelry for the event.

"Not everyone is insured," Raquel complained as she tossed her necklace in the man's outstretched black bag.

The young woman turned to Iza, holding out her bag but not speaking. She was close but Iza couldn't make out her features under the mask. However, a small green lock of hair peeking out of the mask caught her attention, very similar to a girl who had blue hair the last time they'd met.

"I don't have anything valuable," Iza said.

"The ring."

That's when Iza recognized the young woman's voice; they'd shared a prison cell not that long ago on Sarduvis when Investigator Hyttinen had accused Iza of hauling illegal goods. Iza dropped the engagement ring that Karter had given her only two hours before into the bag. Then she remembered the earrings and the necklace and put them inside, too.

"Don't forget the bracelet," said the man, who'd finished collecting Raquel's items. He held out his bag for Iza's metallic bracelet. She dropped it in.

When the man moved toward the other party guests to assist with the collection, Iza lowered her voice and spoke to the young woman guarding her. "Viper?"

The intruder's head jerked up before she realized her mistake.

"Hurry, don't dally now," said the man serving as the spokesperson for the group. "We've overstayed our welcome as it is."

Viper took the cue and darted back through the kitchen.

"It's been a pleasure, everyone—no doubt more so for us than for you. But it's time to bid you goodnight. Please don't get up and don't follow us. We wouldn't want anyone to get hurt on such a fine evening." He bowed slightly and darted out of the room after his companions.

Iza kicked off her heels and was about to pursue them when she caught sight of Karter. He was being led at rifle-point toward the corridor. As much as she wanted to follow the thieves to try to stop them, it would be poor form to not come to the aid of her fake fiancé.

Iza counted to ten before leaping up and trailing the intruders escorting Karter. She'd learned a few tricks traveling among criminals, and one of them was that taking hostages wasn't the kind of thing that brought in the credits. Karter made a horrible hostage since he was far from weak and there were few with the money to pay his ransom.

Iza kept herself hidden behind the nearest marble pillar, watching Karter's captors. They began attaching their harnesses to dangling black ropes.

Iza was plotting her move when she felt a tingle on her arm. She looked to her left and spotted Jovani, who'd done the telekinetic equivalent of tapping her on the shoulder. They made eye contact.

He held up a handgun for her to see. It wasn't his, but she imagined he'd got it from one of the thieves. He gave her a grin that made her heart quicken and then nodded once, giving her the signal to go ahead when ready. He'd cover her whatever she did.

For the moment, Iza waited and observed, looking for the right target.

The thief who had their pulse handgun pointed at Karter bent over to adjust their harness, which pulled up the back of their hood. Iza glimpsed a flash of unmistakable bright pink hair. *Reis! Of course, that rat Douketis would pull this kind of stunt.* Suddenly, the brazen break-in made a lot more sense; there had been help from the inside.

Knowing from experience that she could take her, Iza ran up behind Reis without a sound. She grabbed the woman's wrist and twisted it behind her back, wrenching the pulse handgun free. Using her other hand, she gripped Reis by the throat and pulled her ear toward her face.

"Hey, Pink, you'll be leaving without this prize," Iza said, expecting Karter to make a run for it. When he just stood there with his mouth hanging open, she yelled, "Run!"

Karter bolted. Pulse fire rang out as Jovani covered Karter's escape.

Reis glared at Iza for a moment before her rope pulled taut. She zipped up to the ceiling with the rest of her gang.

Iza ran over to where Karter had joined Jovani in the corridor.

"Are you okay?" Jovani asked.

She nodded. "I think that was Reis."

Jovani's eyes widened with surprise. "From the *Iron Dog*?"

Karter frowned. "But they were on the guest list."

"Yeah, makes me question your choice in acquaintances," Iza said. "And here everyone was questioning *my* suitability for mingling with highborn."

Jovani didn't look happy to be reminded about the engagement, but it was worth it to see the displeased look on Karter's face.

"I don't know why they would try to capture me," Karter said. "Holding me wouldn't help any of the people I can think of."

"Well, we can't stay here," Iza told him. "Pack a bag and be ready to leave."

Jovani looked even less enthusiastic about that.

"Why?" Karter objected. "The thieves got what they wanted they don't have any reason to come back."

"You're assuming they weren't trying to get at you for ransom or something else."

"I can't leave," Karter complained.

Iza shrugged. "Fine, stay here, but you'll be on your own. I'm going back to my ship and going after them." She turned to face Jovani. "Gather the rest of the crew and let's get back to the ship. They might have left a trail that we can follow." She thought for a moment. "Did Braedon come? I only saw Cierra."

"He's back on the ship with Trix. She's better."

"Better how?" Iza asked.

"Moving around and talking again. You'll see soon. We need to go." Jovani's voice was tight but he'd gone into Agent mode again. Like her, he was used to burying his emotions. It wasn't something that went away because you quit working for the TSS.

Iza picked up the hem of her dress and led the way back toward the foyer. "Tell Braedon to prep the *Verity* for departure and track the *Iron Dog*. Is my shuttle here?"

"Yes."

"Get Cierra and meet me there. I need to get out of this dress."

"Among other things," Jovani grumbled. He marched ahead with purpose.

"I heard that," she called to his back.

Saying anything more would draw unwanted attention. Groups of guests standing around were lamenting loudly over their lost gems and jewelry.

Their complaints prompted Karter to look down at her hand, and he noticed for the first time the missing engagement ring.

"They took it?"

"They took everything," she replied dismissively.

Iza wasn't the least bit sad about it, but Karter's eyes darkened and he tightened his right hand into a tight fist as if preparing to hit something. "Those people are going to pay for this. I need a minute to get my things together."

She took a step away from him. "Pack a bag and then meet me back here. Don't take too long. We don't want their trail to go cold."

"Are you leaving?" Raquel asked, coming up behind her. Iza snapped her mouth closed, hoping that the woman hadn't overheard their exchange.

"Yes, it's not safe here. You should go, too."

Raquel nodded but still seemed distracted by all the commotion. She took a step to leave but then stopped and stared at the people rushing around her. She seemed lost. It dawned on Iza that she'd probably never been robbed or had anything like this happen to her before. Iza couldn't count the times she'd been in similar situations.

"Go home." Iza gave her new friend a light push toward

the door. It seemed to work, as she turned and slowly made her way out while guests rushed past her toward their own transports.

Iza headed up the stairs. She hoped rather than believed the thieves hadn't bothered with the guest rooms.

—

By the time she reached her room, Iza had a sinking feeling. All of the doors leading to her suite were flung open and the contents of the rooms were spilling out into the hall. It appeared anything small and valuable had been taken, no doubt to be sold for credits within a day.

When Iza reached her suite, the door was open like the others. She cautiously stepped inside and surveyed the damage. Most of the furniture had been turned over, and a handful of small items were missing.

A light whimper from behind the bathroom door made Iza's heart leap into her chest. She cracked open the door and the dog almost leaped into her arms. He continued to whimper and lick at her face.

"Sorry about that, boy. You did your best. You probably have a strong bite but they had pulse rifles."

Whoever had gone through her room had been thorough. Even the decorative pillows from the bed were on the floor along with the bedding

The sphere had been in its box inside the nightstand. When she reached for the drawer and found it missing, she wasn't surprised. It was an organized, timed effort and the crew had been efficient.

Her backpack underneath the bed had been opened but her clothes were of no value and remained inside.

She was dressed and ready to leave in under five minutes. The bag felt lighter and empty without the sphere, but this wasn't the time to worry about it. She'd go after Douketis and get what was hers.

She raced for the front doors with the dog bounding after her.

When she reached the foyer, her path was barred by Investigator Desirae Hyttinen. She was trying to round up the guests again and keep them all from leaving. Iza swore as she bolted to the side.

Desirae didn't seem to notice her in all the chaos, but more Enforcers were arriving. They were directing the guests into the other rooms and away from the crime scene. Iza had to get out of there or she'd be kept with the rest of the guests and questioned for hours while the *Iron Dog* got away.

Iza debated for a second about telling the Enforcers about the *Iron Dog*, but she didn't have evidence to prove that it was Douketis behind the job. He'd been at the party and Reis had been with him, but other than the *Iron Dog* being in orbit, she couldn't be sure. Viper was with them, as well, which could mean it was more than one crew making out on the robbery. It made sense considering how many moving parts were involved and the number of rooms that had been searched in such a short time.

No, with all the bureaucracy involved when dealing with the Enforcers, she'd be much better off on her own.

Now, if she could only get past Desirae without being spotted. Fortunately, Karter's arrival provided just the opportunity she needed to make her exit with the dog. He saw the problem immediately, it seemed, because not only did he lead the distraction, he made sure that Desirae's back was to the door. Iza heard him speaking as she slipped past them.

"I want them to pay for this. Bring the criminals to me."

"Of course, I'm sorry that your party was ruined." Desirae didn't sound sorry. Iza wondered if Karter had heard the false note in her response.

"I'll be away while all of this gets sorted out. If you have any questions for me, I'll be happy to answer them."

"You may need to come in, but for now, I won't hold you. I know how to contact you."

Iza was outside by the time Karter spoke his next words. She didn't look back as she ran for her shuttle.

Karter wasn't far behind her, and he caught up to her midway down the path to the line of transports waiting to transport guests home.

His handheld signaled, and he answered it without hesitation. The voice of the speaker carried in cold night air. "Karter, where are you? The Enforcers are trying to get a statement from everyone, but you and your bride are nowhere to be found."

"Don't worry Mother, I'll be safe. You should leave the estate but don't go home. It might be safer for you if you stayed at our cottage instead."

"The cottage? A woman of my station can hardly be seen socializing with country folk at that cottage," she said with disdain.

Karter shook his head. "Have it your way, Mother. I'll be out of touch for a bit while I get my affairs in order. Take care of yourself."

"I always do," she said then ended the call.

Iza snatched the handheld from him and threw it onto the pavement. A credit to its design, it didn't shatter into a million pieces as she'd thought it would.

Karter blinked at her. "What did you do that for?"

She spoke to him as she would a confused child. "Someone is trying to kill you or abduct you. We can't take the risk that your devices aren't being tracked."

"Can't I just disable—"

"Not good enough." She picked up the device and smashed it against the rocks ringing a bush next to the path.

"You enjoyed that," Karter commented.

Iza couldn't argue with that.

When they reached her shuttle, the hatch opened. Iza climbed inside and the dog hopped in after her. Jovani was in the pilot's chair and Cierra was seated beside him.

Iza saw the tension in Jovani's shoulders when Karter climbed aboard. He stared from her to Karter, his expression cold. He lifted the shuttle off the ground.

"Some party you threw there," Cierra said. It seemed she was doing her best to diffuse the tension, and Iza was grateful.

"I assure you, the robbery was not intended to be the entertainment," Karter said. "About the robbery— Wait, what did you do to my shuttle?" He glanced around the interior of the craft.

"It was never *yours*. You were a salesman and you sold it to me years ago." At the time, the small craft had been filled with useless finishes that interfered with her ability to fit more cargo. Though its exposed components, wiring, and mismatched furnishings might now look rough around the edges to someone stuffy like Karter, her modifications had made the vessel far more functional for her needs.

Karter folded his arms with a huff as he leaned back on the bench seat.

There were more Enforcer patrol craft circling the area around Blue Hills Estate. Iza wasn't in the mood to talk to anyone else that evening.

"Slow and steady," Iza said to Jovani's back, "we don't want to draw too much attention to ourselves or they'll never let us leave."

"If you'd bothered to take care of this shuttle, it wouldn't look like an outer colony criminal was trying to get away with something," Karter muttered.

Iza rounded on him. "You don't get to have an opinion about my things. I've owned this shuttle outright for years, like the *Verity* is mine now, too. If you want to complain about the scorch marks on the hull, well you can thank yourself, because some of your shadier dealings have had a tendency to get me shot at." She pointed to one of the patches on the interior bulkhead. "When that happened, I believe your response to the situation was something along the lines of, 'You're on your own'."

"I see." Karter crossed his arms. "Well, you assured me I'd be safer with you, but from the damage to this shuttle, I'm not so sure that's true. As I was about to say before, do you really think the robbery was about the items or about me?"

"I'm not sure, but I plan to get back the items those thieves stole, and I expect to be paid for my work. If anything happens to you, I won't get what I want, so I'll be keeping you very safe," Iza said with a wink.

Karter cleared his throat and turned to Cierra. "I don't believe we've had the pleasure." He turned over his palm in formal greeting and she returned it.

"Cierra Quetzali, Healer."

"Ah, of course. You were the one who cared for Jovani before he was turned over to my team."

Iza saw Jovani's back straighten. Something more must have happened between them while he'd been seeing the doctors on Beurias, though she couldn't imagine what Karter would want with him.

Jovani managed to pilot the shuttle to the *Verity* without a word or glance behind him.

There was no way for her to explain to Jovani her reasons for being engaged to Karter. Karter had virtually tied her hands in that department. *Bomaxed contract. What does Karter hope to gain by driving me away from Jovani?*

13

ONCE THE SHUTTLE was docked on the *Verity*, it was time to get down to business. "Jovani, secure the shuttle and meet me on the flight deck," Iza instructed as she opened the shuttle's exit hatch.

"Yes, Captain."

Ouch, and there it is. She'd expected him to be angry and this was the result. She already missed hearing him say her name.

Iza reasoned with herself a moment. She couldn't tell him everything, but some of the truth would be better than nothing.

I could say something like: 'So, I want to introduce you all to my fiancé. Yes, I hate him but we're getting married.' No, that doesn't sound right.

Iza led the way off to the shuttle with Karter falling behind at his casual speed. Karter never seemed to move with any hurry, and running didn't seem to be in his skill set. The dog lagged behind, sniffing the cargo hold for unfamiliar scents.

"Cierra, it's best you join us on the flight deck," Iza said.

"What I have to say concerns you, too. Karter, try to keep up."

As soon as the group entered the flight deck, Braedon turned around in his usual seat. "Wait, what's he doing here?" He eyed Karter.

"He's with me," she said simply. "Trix, I can't believe it's you." Iza moved to her friend, looking into her eyes to make sure she was back.

"I am functioning normally, though there are gaps in my internal clock."

"Don't worry, we'll get it all sorted out. I'm just glad you're back to you."

"I'm incapable of being anyone else."

Iza smiled. "That's true."

"May I ask about your engagement to Karter?" Trix tilted her head.

"I'll get to that soon enough. It's not a long story."

"What? Just tell us it's fake." Braedon stared at her wide-eyed. "You hate him. I'm pretty sure you hate him. Maybe hate is a strong word, but, no, I'm pretty sure you hated him," Braedon rambled. He was talking so much there was no way to get a word in. She waited for him to finish.

"It's complicated," she said.

"In the past, you have remarked, 'He's such a conniving weasel. Remind me not to underestimate that parasite.'" Trix imitated Iza's voice perfectly.

"That's an insult to the parasite community," Jovani commented under his breath.

"Who happens to be my fiancé," Iza reminded everyone, keeping her tone gentle.

"Still here." Karter gave a slight wave of his hand.

"Would you like me to find him an empty cabin or will he be lodging with you?" Cierra asked.

Iza raised an eyebrow. "Look who's suddenly full of jokes. I'll worry about Karter's accommodations. We have some things to discuss beforehand. It's best that we're all together for this, including you."

"Is he going to be with us for a while?" Braedon asked with a disdainful glance at Karter's satchel.

"It's undecided, and like I said—complicated. Moving on. Were you able to track the *Iron Dog* before they jumped?"

"Unfortunately, no."

Iza's hands dropped to her sides. They were too late.

"I did, however, find another way to track where they're headed," Braedon said, sitting back with his legs outstretched and his hands behind his head.

"Well, out with it!" Iza groaned.

"People dealing with stolen goods need to off-load it, and fast. While you were heading back here, I did some digging. I found a suspicious auction going down in several days, and up for grabs are some pieces that may interest us. For example, dynastic heirlooms, jewels, rings, necklaces, earrings of all kinds. In the mix are some pulse rifles. There aren't pictures of anything, but it certainly sounds like the kind of stuff taken tonight, and likely the weapons used in the heist.'"

"That does sound like our stuff," Iza assessed. "Do you have a location?"

"Yes. If we start now, we can use the conventional jump drive to keep up appearances and still make it to Hubyria a day early."

"What do you mean by 'conventional jump drive'?" Karter asked. "As opposed to...?"

Iza ignored him. "Hubyria? Why in the world would they host an auction on that barren rock?"

"I'll admit I've had occasion to pass by during one of

Hubyria's auctions," said Braedon. "The items are genuine, unique, the guest list is limited, and their sales discreet."

"I see. I take it you know all of this from personal experience?" she asked.

Braedon gave her a significant look. "I have a past. We all do."

Iza had been wondering why Braedon had been to the mining colony before. It also went a long way to explain how Yeaga had been able to fund the miner's rebellion. Iza had always suspected that those sorts of underground dealings were more common in the Outer Colonies than anyone realized. People had been living on the edge, just trying to get by, for a long time. Any side income steams—especially those that didn't get reported to the central authorities—could make life a lot more comfortable.

"Plot a course to Hubyria," Iza instructed.

"Wait, didn't you hear me?" Braedon scoffed. "Sometimes I feel like you're just ignoring half of everything I say. This proves it. Is it because I'm younger than you?"

Iza put her hands on her hips and waited for him to get to the point, knowing that an interruption would only lengthen the delay.

He got the hint. "This event is *invite only*, and we're not on the list."

"But you can get us on the list," Jovani said. He seemed to have perked up at the revelation about Hubyria having an underground auction house.

"Of course, I can." Braedon threw up his hands in the air as if insulted. "The thing is, we don't have enough credits to get a buy-in, and that's the only way in after they've sent the invitations out. So unless you've got ten thousand credits lying around, we're going to have to find another way in."

"You'll have your credits to get in, and enough for a plus one," Karter offered.

Braedon raised his eyebrows and looked at Iza for confirmation. Good, she didn't want Karter getting any ideas about telling her people what to do.

"Do it."

"You've got it," Braedon said. "I'll request two buy-ins. We should have our answer by the time we arrive." He paused. "Wait a minute, pictures of the party are just hitting the Sensationals. Wow, Iz, your body is amazing in that dress! Please tell me you kept it."

—

As soon as they were in route, Iza made the choice to begin disseminating pertinent information. She took a deep breath and looked around at everyone in the room.

"As you know, Karter is the owner and sole proprietor of Apex Manufacturing Enterprises. Apex is a subsidiary of DGE and has afforded many captains with the opportunity to earn their ships. Karter gave me such an opportunity with the *Verity*." True. "During that time, not only did I learn he was an excellent businessman, but he would make an excellent match for me." Lie. "We were engaged shortly after and now our engagement is public."

Iza kept her voice monotone and businesslike. Even with the lies, she felt like getting everything out in the open had lifted a weight off her chest. Then she saw the look on Jovani's face and she wanted to curl into a ball and hide. The betrayal and disappointment were clear.

"That being said, we decided on our private engagement before I knew any of you." Lie. "I apologize for the deception, but it was in our best interest that the news not be public until we wanted it to be." Truth. "Now that you all know, you will understand my reasons for wanting to keep Karter safe."

She'd done her best to keep the truths and the lies straight and hoped she'd sounded at least half-convincing. Though she knew it would be a hard story for anyone to accept.

Iza waited for Trix to ask her inevitable question.

"You once said Karter was a snake that could never be trusted. Have you since changed your opinion of him?" She never disappointed her.

"Ouch." Karter rubbed his chest as if stabbed in the heart.

"Heat of the moment," she said.

"I'm offended."

Iza looked up to see Jovani staring back at her. She told the truth. "Nobody's perfect."

She took another deep breath, resting her fists on her hips, then changed her mind and crossed her arms over her chest.

"Before we reach the *Iron Dog*, there's something you should know. When I originally purchased the *Verity*, I found something in the hold in a compartment behind the stairs." Iza glanced up and caught Braedon's eye. His mouth fell open in understanding.

"Yeah, I didn't mention it before because, well, it was none of your business. All sales being final and all that. I figured whatever it was might fetch a good price at some point. It was a small box made of an organic material like wood. I couldn't get it open for the longest time, but then one day it opened. A little sphere made of metal, like nothing I've ever seen before, popped out. I kept it hidden at first because I didn't know it had any significance. That was before Mr. Arvonen caught up to us."

"Stars! You've had the map this whole time?" Braedon shook his head. "You've known about it from the beginning?"

Iza nodded. "But I didn't know what it was, so I wasn't as careful with it as I should have been."

"What's it look like?" Karter asked.

"It's the strangest little thing, a perfect sphere with etchings all over it. If it's a map like you say, it's not like any map I've ever seen." Iza swallowed back the part about the humming and the dreams. If anyone else had been having the experience, they'd have spoken up by now. Telling them she had a strange connection to the thing would only make her sound more crazy and less credible.

"Can we see it?" Braedon asked, rubbing his hands together in anticipation like a kid waiting for a piece of candy.

"Would you like me to run an independent analysis on the device?" Trix asked not waiting for her answer.

Iza hadn't thought of that. An independent analysis from Trix might have been able to tell them more about the map's origin and history than she was able to glean from the onboard computer's assessment.

"I took it with me to Blue Hills Estate," she said, dropping her gaze.

"So the thieves have it," Karter said, disappointed.

"We should get it back," Braedon said, stroking his chin. "We've already got our buy in; we'll use it to get close to the artifact and take it back. Then we can find out where it leads."

"No." Jovani didn't raise his voice, maybe that's what made it feel so intense.

"What do you mean?" Iza asked.

"Mr. Arvonen wants the artifact. If they have it, all we have to do is let him take it from them."

"I think we're forgetting about the scientists he's

kidnapped," Cierra said. "We have to consider the innocent."

"I'm not forgetting about them. I'm thinking of our safety. Mr. Arvonen almost blew our ship out of the sky for that thing," Jovani said.

"That's nothing compared to what he'll do if he gets it," Karter said in his unhurried way, pacing back and forth as he spoke. Iza realized in that moment, Karter was actually nervous.

"What do you know about him that we don't?" Iza asked.

"Victor Arvonen has an obsession with gaining more power. It has influenced every relationship in his life, including his son." Karter looked over at Braedon and Braedon stared back.

Braedon clamped his mouth closed his lips pursed in anger.

"Tell us something we don't know," she said.

"After I got possession of the H3X and sold it to you, Arvonen reached out to me. He demanded I get it back by any means necessary."

"That's why you sent Douketis to Hubyria. You were trying to make sure I couldn't come up with the money."

"I made a deal and I meant to keep it. However, Arvonen can be persuasive. He threatened my dynasty and my family. He's too close to getting what he wants to let anything get in his way."

"What does he want?" Jovani asked. It seemed his Agent instincts were activated, as he was leaning forward, fully engaged for the first time since Karter's arrival.

"I have no idea what his endgame might be. I had been confused about why he was so intent on getting this particular ship back, but I believe I now have my answer. It was never about the ship itself but rather that box and its sphere that had been stashed on board." Karter looked at Braedon. "I take it you didn't have permission to take his ship at the time?"

Braedon kept his mouth closed and crossed his arms over his chest.

"If he's willing to take down a ship with his son on it, then it must be something powerful," Cierra said. "Where does the map lead?"

"I believe that's something we need to discover before he gets his hands on it," Karter said.

"Why should we trust you?" Braedon asked, finding his voice.

"Valid question. You want to know what I want out of this venture." Karter smiled, still pacing. "We have a shared enemy in your father, which presents us with a unique opportunity. He wants to take down my inheritance. I will use my wealth and power to stop him using any means necessary. If that sounds like something you can use, then you'll want me on your team."

"We could involve the TSS or the local Enforcers," Jovani said. "They have an interest in both cases. The theft of the items at the Blue Hills Estate and keeping the artifact away from Mr. Arvonen."

Iza waved a hand in the air to dismiss the idea.

"I'd rather not. No offense, but the TSS and the Enforcers haven't done anything to help us lately. Let's see what we can find out on our own first," Iza said.

"Besides that, there's no guarantee that Arvonen doesn't have Enforcers working for him," Karter said.

Iza raised her eyebrows. Karter nodded at her unasked question about his cousin. Investigator Desiree Hyttinen could be involved. No wonder he looked so nervous; his cousin could be relentless.

The others nodded in agreement, though they stayed silent. Iza noted how quickly he'd swayed the others to stand with him. His power of persuasion was legendary and his ability to charm anyone is what made him such a good businessman. It was also obvious he wasn't going anywhere soon.

"I take it that means you'll be staying?" Iza asked.

Karter glanced around and shrugged like the place was hardly good enough. "At this time, the safest place for me is being on the move. However, when it comes to dealing with my almost-abduction, it would probably be best if I sat out."

"Agreed." Iza didn't want him anywhere near the artifact. Despite his grandiose speech about sharing an enemy, he neglected to reveal the fact that he had his own obsession with power. She wouldn't let either him or Mr. Arvonen have it. "I guess that makes us a team for now."

14

IT WAS LATE and everyone needed to get some rest, including Iza. Braedon put the ship on autopilot and Trix would be on overnight watch in case anything went wrong. Iza was hesitant to burden Trix, but her friend assured her that she had been functioning normally all day and wanted to return to duty.

As the other crew and passengers retired to their cabins, Karter was left standing in the middle of the flight deck with his bag. "Is there someplace I can put my things?" he asked.

"Yes, Trix will show you to your cabin. Give him the one on the end, next to Cierra," Iza said. "Maybe he can endure the smell of her incense and candles."

"Wait, you're sending me with the android?"

"Yes, don't piss her off or you'll have more trouble than it's worth. Follow her or get off," Iza said, dropping all professional pretense now that the others had gone.

"Do not be alarmed, Mr. Hyttinen, we can agree that I also would rather be doing something else other than finding you a bed," Trix told him.

"See? She's the best company you're going to find, and she

doesn't even like you. Welcome aboard."

Karter bristled, then seemed to think better of testing the limits of Iza's hospitality. He straightened his suit coat and followed Trix out.

Iza was left alone on the flight deck of her ship at last. Well, not entirely alone, as the dog chose that moment to place his two front paws on her knees, begging to sit on her lap. She scooped him up and lost herself stroking his long fur. Her eyes filled for the first time since coming back.

Losing the sphere gave her intense feelings of anxiety, fueling worries about what Mr. Arvonen might do with whatever power the map was hiding.

Then there was Jovani. How had she gotten to this point? To see the look on his face and having to say the words she'd practiced was the hardest thing she'd ever done in her life. Would he ever forgive her? Iza hoped it was possible, and that he intuitively realized that her engagement wasn't on the level.

Once they had the sphere again, she would focus on the important business of getting Karter married to someone else. The casual way he talked about their 'wedding next year' made her more than a little nervous.

She heard boots in the corridor headed her way and hastily wiped her eyes. Sniffing, she pushed the dog onto the floor, and he ran to greet the visitor.

"Oh, I'm sorry if I'm bothering you," Braedon said, coming onto the flight deck. He reached down to scratch the dog behind the ears, gaining his undying loyalty. "You dropped a lot of news on us tonight, are you okay?"

She wasn't, but she didn't want to talk about it. "I'm fine," she said.

"Yeah, let's just pretend you're not okay with all of this. I don't understand why you're engaged to Karter, but it's as obvious as anything that you're not happy about it. Which means one of two things: either he's getting something out of the deal or you are."

Iza didn't flinch.

"Ah, both of you are getting something out of it. Of course. But it's clear you have no intention of actually marrying him, so why the fake engagement? You're stalling."

Again she said nothing, but her eyes widened.

"No, he's stalling. His family probably wants him to marry the first suitable girl that comes along who can produce an heir, and you're his escape card. That's one problem with being an heir to the dynasty. One advantage of being born second is you don't have to worry about who you marry because no one cares."

Braedon sat down on the deck at her feet. He was resting his elbows on his knees and his chin on his fist, as if enraptured by her story. The dog, enjoying the game, pushed his way onto the new available lap and Braedon made room for him.

"I'm not telling you anything," Iza said. Then she added, "I couldn't if I wanted to."

"I see. It's probably part of the conditions. Fine, but you're not fooling anyone. Rather, you're not fooling everyone. I'm not sure about Jovani, but I'd wager he's going to reach into Karter's mind and find out the real reason you two are engaged. He probably already knows the truth. Whether you tell him or not, he'll know."

Iza huffed, biting down on her lip to keep from spilling the truth. She couldn't confirm what he thought he'd figured out even though it was correct. Karter didn't need any more leverage over her. The fact that Braedon had surmised the entire scheme in the matter of an hour gave her hope that Jovani would come to the same conclusion.

She wanted to be out of the deal, but she wouldn't be the one to break it. She had everything at stake. Her life. Her home. Her future. Iza kept quiet.

"All right, but you're missing out on something big with Jovani" Braedon continued. "I think you know it, that's why you're up here sniffling instead of in his cabin making it up to him."

"Leave it alone," Iza said, shaking her head with a chuckle. "I've got something else for you to do."

"Sure, you name it. I'm here for you Iz."

"I want you to reach out to your little gamer friend, Viper."

"Viper? Why?"

"Can you do it or not?"

"Not," he said shaking his head vehemently as if it were on fire.

"Don't lie to me. You coders always have a way of reaching out to each other if there's a tournament or whatever it is you all do on the Dark Net."

Braedon rubbed his chin thoughtfully. "Maybe there's a way, but I'm going to need a reason. I can't just be like, 'Hey, Viper, remember that time I beat you in a tournament and we all got picked up by the Enforcers?'"

Iza bit down on another laugh. "Fine, tell her you're attending an off-world auction while the rest of us are busy with something else and you want to meet up with her."

"She'd never believe it."

"Then be resourceful." Iza stood up to leave and the dog bounded after her.

Braedon pursed his lips.

"Inform me as soon as you have your meeting set up," Iza said.

He walked over to his work console. "By the way, when are

you going to name that dog?"

"He's not staying," Iza snapped.

"Do you have some kind of aversion of naming things? Your shuttle, the ship…"

"Just set up the meeting, Braedon." Psychoanalysis of her attachment issues could wait for another time.

— — —

Karter followed Trix to his cabin without a word. He had too much on his mind to engage in idle conversation with someone who wasn't even a person. However, the android had other ideas.

"No doubt this has been a trying day for you. How are you feeling?"

The question was spoken with more concern than Karter expected, and it took him several seconds to clear his throat and answer. "Um, well, with everything going on this evening, I hadn't thought about it."

"Your secret engagement announcement party was ruined and your guests were robbed. From Iza's account, the attempt on your life must have you worried. I can assure you, aboard the *Verity* you are perfectly safe."

It was as assuring a statement as he could imagine. He paused mid-stride and gave her a side-long look, taking in her appearance properly. Her makers had chosen a beautiful model to replicate, with chestnut hair falling in side-swept waves to below her shoulders, framing a refined face with high cheekbones and perceptive eyes.

Trix continued walking and Karter fell into step beside her. She was pleasing to look at and it bothered Karter that she reminded him so much of Becca. His assistant's matter-of-fact way of speaking and attention to detail often made others feel uncomfortable, but he'd grown accustomed to it. Thinking of her made Karter ask Trix something that had been bothering him since he'd first met her.

"You are always so straightforward in your speech. Is there a reason for that?"

Trix stopped to look at him. If he didn't know better, he'd think she was trying to think of an answer, but AIs were notoriously tellers of truth. It was one of the main reasons he'd chosen never to employ one.

"My language matrix is complete with thousands of word choice options. I choose efficiency over more elaborate forms of speech." Then, as if the conversation were complete, she kept walking.

Karter's interest was piqued and now he couldn't stop talking to the android. "Yet, you don't talk like a flesh and blood Taran. Is your preference to stand out?"

"I am different."

"Yes, but you don't have to be. It is only your mannerisms that give you away as an android."

"You believe that I am purposely distinguishing myself from you?"

He cocked his head. "Aren't you?"

"No, I am merely remaining true to who I am. Is that not the goal of every person?"

Before Karter could answer, Trix stopped in front of a door. "This is your cabin. I hope that you will be comfortable."

Karter slid open the door to peek inside the cramped room and then looked back to Trix. "Being true to who you are doesn't always come with as many benefits as being what others find more palatable."

"Perhaps, but I can see from your bio-signs that you are not happy pretending to be something you are not. May I make a suggestion?"

Karter's mouth fell open and he found himself without a response.

Trix continued as if he'd acquiesced. "Be pleased with yourself, and you will never have to justify the lies you tell others to make them happy today but know they will hate tomorrow."

Karter watched her leave for a moment before stepping inside and letting the door close behind him. Trix was extremely complex and had information processing capabilities well beyond an organic person, but that didn't mean she was right. All the same, she'd given Karter something to think about.

He stared at the bare-bones cabin and sighed. He dropped his bag on the bed and tested the lean mattress. It felt about as comfortable as sleeping on the floor.

After everything that had happened that evening, he couldn't help but wonder if his desire to please others wasn't what had got him in trouble in the first place. His engagement to Iza, the party, his mother's demands, his investor's demands. It was all too much. In the end, his business was in jeopardy and his personal life was a disaster. He'd have to avoid the Sensationals to keep from seeing how much of a failure the world thought him.

His life on board the *Verity* didn't have to be all bad. Iza was an ally for the moment, but she wasn't the only one. Jovani owed him a debt for keeping his identity a secret; an undercover TSS Agent could be very useful to him. Arvonen wouldn't get away with stealing from him and walking away. He'd have to pay for this, and stealing his grandmother's ring was beyond intolerable. Iza didn't know about the last time he'd run into

Arvonen and wound up in critical care. Arvonen had made his displeasure over letting Iza keep the H3X very clear.

The man was far more sadistic than any of *Verity*'s crewmembers gave him credit for, no doubt because of their friendship with his son. Karter wouldn't be fooled. The boy was more like his mother, but that didn't mean there was nothing of his father in him. Karter saw the way the boy looked at him when he'd been brought on board the shuttle. He'd have to watch 'Braedon' to be sure he didn't get any ideas about changing his mind and helping his father.

Karter sat on the foot of the uncomfortable bed and got to work.

Before the *Verity* had jumped into subspace, Becca had sent footage from the engagement party to a private onboard message inbox. Though the *Verity* was technically Iza's, being the leaseholder afforded Karter access to systems like the ship's onboard communications, and he had been able to have Becca arrange a means for him to securely stay in touch without having his handheld.

Watching the playback of the events, Karter was impressed with the job Arvonen managed to pull off with such a small crew, especially considering they had less than two days to plan.

He watched the mannerisms of the man who'd done all the talking during the theft. It seemed a little rehearsed after about the third time. He noted the way the masked man walked as if counting the steps and the slight tap of his left hand against his thigh, like he was beating out the rhythm of the words. It was a memorization technique he'd used himself in high-pressure situations.

He found the section of the video that confirmed Iza had spoken with Douketis and Reis at the beginning of the party. Karter tried to trace the interaction of the pair's conversations during the party with anyone else. There was what looked like a brief, polite exchange between them and Raquel before Iza and then nothing. He tried to find a sign of them after they spoke to Iza, but after that point they seemed to disappear.

Without planning to, he found himself watching the playback of his dance with Iza. They almost looked like a real couple, he was pleased to see. Then, he saw what everyone else at the party had seemed to notice.

Without a word, Jovani stepped out from the crowd with his hand out, inviting Iza to dance with him. The dance floor was filled with couples, but among them, Jovani and Iza seemed to take center stage. Those dancing nearby parted to make room for them. The hungry look in Jovani's eye was obvious and Karter was forced to wonder if it had gone unnoticed. No, Maeve and Desirae were standing off to the side frowning and pointing.

Karter caught a trembling in his right hand, and he clutched it with his left. He couldn't let anxiety get the better of him.

First thing in the morning, he'd get everything square with Jovani. Then he could focus on stopping Arvonen from breathing down his neck.

— — —

Joe wanted something to punch. The frustration had been building in him all night, and he'd gone to the gym first thing in the morning to find some release. The *Verity*'s gym was well-equipped, with four weight machines lining one wall and a large sparring mat in the middle. But it was the heavy punching bag where he decided to focus his attention first.

Engaged. Iza had spoken as casually as if she'd been

listing the ingredients of soup. Didn't she realize every word drove a knife into his heart? Now, Karter was on the ship, strolling around with a smug grin on his face, trying to bait Joe into a reaction that he could exploit. It was worse than the TSS training academy had ever been.

Joe had stood with the others on the flight deck the night before listening to Iza's matter-of-fact briefing about her engagement. At the time, he hadn't wanted to give Karter the satisfaction of seeing how much the news had bothered him. Instead, he'd nodded along while in the same breath trying not to leap over the console and pummel Karter's perfect teeth.

There was no joy in Iza's words. None of the light in her eyes, the way she brightened when she looked at Joe. Whatever had prompted the engagement, it wasn't genuine love. Karter had baited her into it in some other way. And Joe hated him for it.

Was she in trouble? Why didn't she come to me *for help?*

He'd thought they were on the same page with their feelings, and then Karter entered the picture and nothing made sense anymore. Joe was risking his career for Iza, but Karter was only in the business of Karter; he'd discard Iza the moment she wasn't useful to him anymore.

As if manifested from Joe's own imagination, Karter entered the gym. Even dressed in casual pants, black boots, and a loose-fitting shirt, Karter didn't fit in.

Joe ignored him. He moved from the punching bag to the leg machine and upped the weight before sitting down. With both feet on the platform, he pushed hard against it, imagining he was kicking Karter off the ship and out into space.

"I don't mean to interrupt," Karter said. "I hoped we'd get the chance to talk."

Joe didn't answer for a full minute. Karter refused to take

the hint and leave him alone, so he answered. "About?"

"Well, about Iza, to be exact. I'm sure as a TSS Agent you have certain connections, and I would like use of those services."

"I'm not your personal assistant. If you want help with something, speak plainly. I'll see what I can do. I realize I owe you for the arm and I'm willing to pay, but we're not friends or anything even close. You don't need to spare my feelings."

"This isn't about the arm at all. I don't double charge for services, and Iza has paid for your arm in full. You only have her and your delicious Healer to thank for that."

Then understanding dawned and Joe squared his shoulders. "This is about you knowing who I am."

"Let's just say, what you and I have is a mutual arrangement for as long as I deem it beneficial."

"Beneficial for you."

"Correct."

Joe held his gaze, unmoving, until Karter laughed like they'd shared a private joke.

"I see it now. You're mad about Iza being engaged to me. You're jealous."

"No, not jealous, annoyed. I may not be able to read Iza, but I've read you like a blip in the Sensationals. You don't have her heart, I do. The question is, why is she doing this for you, since it only benefits you?" Joe rose from the leg press machine and marched toward Karter until they almost stood nose-to-nose. Joe caught the scent of the fruit juice Karter'd had with his breakfast.

Karter didn't back down, but his eyes dropped to the floor while his wary smile froze on his face. "Iza and I have a complicated history. She's been wanting a ship of her own and a free life for as long as I've known her. Her obligation to me is one I plan to use to the fullest." Then his eyes hardened and his mouth turned down. "Cross me and I'll see you never have her."

Joe's heartbeat thudded in his ears. "What do you mean?"

"I think you already have an idea. Iza couldn't care less about being married to me, but she's obligated to serve as my dutiful partner. If you get in my way, I'll see to it that she's stuck with me forever. Do I make myself clear?"

Joe stood staring at him, mouth agape. *Why would Karter willingly attach himself to a woman who doesn't care two credits about him?* There was something else, something he was actively trying to bury within his thoughts. It wouldn't take much for Joe to discover the whole truth. In fact, he was ready to do just that when Trix came in looking for him.

"Are we all out of oats?" she asked, staring at Joe.

"Um, maybe." He took a step back from Karter and rubbed a hand over his forehead. "Why?"

"I am running inventory on supplies, and it seems we are out of oats. Breakfast will consist of Cierra's shakes if we can do no better."

Joe mentally groaned. Cierra's shakes were the worst. He'd never look forward to the galley again if he had to force down the green sludge.

"Fine," Joe said with a toss of his head. He continued to stare at Karter, ignoring Trix until she left the room.

Joe had no intention of being Karter's pawn. His job with the TSS was on the line every time he told another person about his mission. Karter's involvement had come accidentally and without warning. It didn't hold as much power over him as Karter had originally thought.

However, when it came to Iza, Joe was willing to do much more than he'd do for himself. Her happiness meant everything to him. She stuck to her word no matter what it cost her. He wouldn't let her sacrifice herself for him any more than she already had. Even if she never forgave him, he wouldn't let Karter force her into something that would eventually break her spirit. Joe needed to learn what Karter had over her and help her get out from under him. If he learned Karter's motivation, it would be a good place to start.

"What do you want?" Joe asked.

Karter nodded with another satisfied smile and sat down on the nearest machine bench. Joe sat opposite him on the next machine over, rolling his shoulders and neck to loosen up the tight muscles.

"I want you to reach out to the TSS and find out everything there is to know about that sphere and get that information to me directly."

Joe huffed. "It's not that easy. I'm not lying about my standing back at Headquarters. They're not going to want to hear from me about this thing."

"Regardless, this is what I require at this time. I believe your High Commander has access to more information about this sphere than is publicly known. Get it to me and I'll make sure to personally put Iza's hand in yours when the time comes."

Joe clenched his teeth together in anger. His fist was already closed, and he felt his nails digging into his palms. It was the only thing preventing the blind rage that was welling up within him. Karter was many things, but one of them was not a tease. He'd make good on his promise to ruin Iza's life if it meant he got what he wanted.

"Fine, I'll reach out to them, but I can't do that until we drop out of subspace. Even then, I won't hear back right away."

"Good, send them this." Karter passed him a small digital

reader the size of his thumb and Joe looked it over. "It's got all the information I've already gathered on the sphere and will hopefully put you on the right path to finding out the truth about its origins."

Karter rose from his seat and nodded to Joe as he left.

"Oh, and this information and my thoughts are my own. I'm counting on you to keep your little Healer friend from reading me. I'm sure that's well within your capabilities, Agent."

Joe's jaw ached from clenching his teeth.

"I'll take that as a yes. See you later, Agent, and enjoy the rest of your workout."

—

Joe had no intention of being Karter's informant. He'd submitted the information request to the TSS and hoped his superiors would be able to provide more information about the sphere and its origins—not for Karter, but for Braedon and Iza's sake. Joe only had to wait for an answer.

He was staring up at the ceiling of his cabin, planning how to get out from under Karter's plan, when a knock sounded at his door.

"Hey, open the door, it's me," Braedon said from the other side.

Joe got up to answer the door. When it slid open, Braedon didn't wait to be invited in. He barged past Joe and sat on the chair, kicking his feet up onto the coffee table.

"Why are you moping in here?" Braedon asked.

Joe threw himself back on the bed. It was more comfortable to stare at the ceiling and talk than it was to make eye-contact with Braedon. "I'm not moping."

"Yes, you are. Karter's an ass, don't get me wrong, but he's not a threat."

"That depends in what way you mean."

"Look," Braedon leaned forward, "let's forget about Karter's wealth and business influence. I'm talking about how they feel about each other, and when it comes to that, Iza's as engaged as I am. Haven't you read the comment sections in the Sensationals? There's more speculation about their relationship than whether or not we should eat organic or processed foods."

"That doesn't change that fact that she *is* engaged," Joe said. He tasted the ire whenever he said the word.

Braedon flourished his hands. "Psh, most of my gambling friends have placed bets on the fact that the engagement is a sham and the wedding will never take place." Braedon huffed when Joe didn't respond. "Hey, I may not understand much about women, but one thing is for certain, a woman who wants to get married doesn't act like that. Iza not only doesn't want to marry Karter, but I don't believe she will. You better not give up on her, or I'll pummel you myself."

Joe pulled away, shaking his head. "I'm not letting her go. I just... I don't know how to be there for her when every time I try to get close, she pushes me away."

He could hardly bear the stifling pressure on his chest every time he saw Iza and Karter together, the ache he endured every night when Joe saw Iza go one way while he had to go another. The link between them had only grown stronger in their time together, and it pained him every moment they were apart.

"Karter isn't going to win her over, not unless you give up. She's showed *me* more attention than Karter," Braedon said raising his eyebrows. "Don't act like you haven't seen it."

Joe had seen it. She was in the arrangement by necessity, not by choice. *But she won't tell the truth. If she doesn't, how can I help her?* Joe sighed and looked over at Braedon. "What do you suggest I do, Romeo?"

"Romeo? I thought I was Robin Hood. Who's this Romeo?"

"Never mind. What should I do?"

Braedon crossed his arms and stared at him. He seemed to be gauging whether Joe was worth advising. "You make her find you irresistible."

That's it? That's the best he can come up with? Joe rolled his eyes. "Why am I taking advice from you?"

Braedon only smiled. "I think you know."

True, Joe had noticed how Cierra's behavior around Braedon had changed. They still fought, but there was something underneath the fighting. Something Joe hadn't been able to put his finger on.

"Answer me this, what do I do about Karter?" Joe asked.

"Ah, yes, the insatiable, power-hungry starship dealer. My suggestion is you do what you'd do if you were still with the TSS. As I understand it, they're not known for taking orders from civilians." Braedon gave Joe a vicious little smile, which gave him an idea.

15

JOE HAD KEPT to himself for the last several days in transit, wanting to avoid further encounters with Karter. During that time, Iza had seemed on edge, and Joe hadn't thought the timing was right to reveal his position in the TSS to her. He knew full well that he'd already waited far too long to tell her and there might never be a 'right time', but he needed to handle it in a way that wouldn't make her feel more trapped with Karter.

Now that they'd reached Hubyria, he couldn't delay any longer. Iza needed to hear the truth from Joe directly before Trix, who seemed to be sporadically malfunctioning, or Karter passed on the message in a less delicate way.

He was about to head to Iza's cabin to talk to her when his TSS handheld went off. *Of all the bad timing.*

The message had an urgent notification signal and had been signed by Agent Ian Mandren. It read:

> Joe,
>   *Despite the lean content of your recent*

reports, your last correspondence—though not as detailed as I would have liked—got our attention. I have some news about that sphere. When you receive this message, I can only hope that you will respond immediately, as playing communications tag between subspace jumps will become cumbersome considering the urgency of my message. Believe me when I say this sphere needs to be your new priority.

The sphere is ancient and believed to be a remnant from an era of Taran history predating even the Aesir. What little we've been able to glean so far points to a species from outside known Taran space. In the ancient Aesir historical files, there's a reference to a forbidden region of space in connection to these aliens, but all it says is that we should avoid contact with them and their tech at all costs. Though I'm not sure what that means, usually when there's something to hide it's because people did something they shouldn't have.

I hope you can track down more information on the sphere from your end, as we have exhausted our search here. Everything points to this alien tech being extremely dangerous.

Whatever you do, don't let the sphere fall into civilian hands or tell anyone what you know. If your captain has it, you have permission to break cover and do what you must to retrieve it and bring it back here. Lives

are at stake, including your own, if you fail.
                                                            - Ian

Joe closed his handheld. The warning against involving civilians had been clear and the fact that the first thing he wanted to do was go straight to Iza meant he'd already been compromised. *When did that happen?*

Up until now, he'd been convincing himself he was still putting his mission first; now it was clear he'd be putting Iza's desires above his duty. Whatever hesitation he'd been feeling about it before was gone now. Despite her current status, whether the engagement was real or fake, he wasn't going to lose her to Karter. Not like this.

Jovani opened his cabin door, intending to head straight to Iza's room, but he found Trix standing in the corridor.

"Are you breaking the rules?" she asked.

He looked at Trix and wondered what she'd already overheard. A few seconds passed before he realized she was going to wait for him to answer.

"No, I'm doing the best that I can to protect Iza, but I'm not sure I can now that she's engaged to Karter. What am I supposed to do?"

"Are you planning on telling Iza the truth?"

"Um, yes, I was just going to tell her. She's been a little busy with other things until now."

"I do not think it is healthy for either of you to continue to keep secrets from each other. It is obvious that you love her, and she should know the truth."

It wasn't lost on him he was speaking to an android for advice on love. He wasn't entirely sure she wasn't malfunctioning again. Every time someone asked if she was all right, she said she was fine. He'd read in an article once by a notable psychologist that the classic warning sign that any woman was not okay was that very word: fine.

"You must keep your word, Jovani," Trix continued. "I have kept my word to you and everyone else who has asked me to. I told no one about all the things I had to do before Iza met me. She has no idea about all the lies she has been told. I kept my word and she trusts me. You must be honest and she will trust you."

It didn't all make sense, but he was sure somewhere in there she wasn't wrong. It didn't take a genius to recognize she was hurting, too, but he'd only worried about his own pain.

"I want to tell her the truth but, what if she doesn't understand?" Joe asked.

"Iza's understanding of the situation is irrelevant. The most important thing is that she be able to trust you more than she has anyone else in her life. You cannot abandon her again."

"I don't understand. I never abandoned her. Are you talking about her parents?"

"No, I am not talking about Iza's mother, she is dead."

Joe stared at her a moment, waiting for her to clarify her last sentence. She didn't.

Frustratingly, Joe lost the opportunity to find out what she meant because Karter strolled down the corridor.

"Ah, I'm glad I found you. Do you have news from your people?" Karter asked.

Trix walked away without a greeting to Karter. She seemed to dislike him as much as Iza did.

"Regarding what?"

Karted tsked. "Don't play coy. It's been days, and we've had plenty of stops when a message could have come through. What have you found out?"

Joe dropped his voice. "You better be careful what you say

out in the open."

"Trix knows, doesn't she?" Karter looked around him. "It's just us. So?"

"I haven't received any communications from TSS Headquarters, but I'll inform you as soon as I do," Joe said. He clapped Karter on the back as if they were old friends then turned back to enter his own cabin.

Iza would have to wait. He didn't want to risk Karter finding out anything before she did. As soon as he could get her alone, he'd tell her about what he'd learned.

— — —

Iza sat on the flight deck contemplating her next move. Since they'd been in orbit over Hubyria for at least an hour without any trouble, she figured they were clear to land the shuttle.

Once there, they would have a couple days before the auction to smooth things over with Yeaga. The woman had made it clear Iza wasn't welcome on the planet. However, to take care of Viper and get the sphere back, Iza would have to find a way to change Yeaga's mind.

Braedon had been on his handheld all morning, probably playing a game. Iza rolled her eyes at his lack of attention and slid out of her chair. She snuck a look over his shoulder just out of his peripheral vision. What she saw, though, wasn't a game. There were several images on the page, and one of them looked like a hand-drawn image of her own face.

"What's that?"

"Nothing," he said, trying to hide it.

"It's something." She snatched the handheld out of his hand and held it away from him while she balanced a knee over his crotch to prevent him from getting up. "It looks like you're making a cartoon. I haven't seen one of those since I was a kid."

"Braedon has been working on it for over a month," Trix volunteered from her workstation next to him.

"Sensationalist!" He glared at Trix while still trying to grab his handheld. "It's just a little something I do when I'm bored." He leaned back, guarding himself with one hand while stretching the other up to yank the device away from Iza. He dropped down into his chair in front of her with the handheld clutched to his chest.

"It looks like that job we pulled on Phiris. Are you writing some kind of story?" Iza asked.

"It's a comic," he mumbled.

"Let me see." Iza held out her hand for him to show her.

Braedon stared down at her hand. "You won't laugh?"

"No promises." Iza wiggled her fingers out in front of her.

Braedon's shoulders dropped as he handed her the device.

Iza studied the image. It featured a cartoon version of herself and Jovani on Phiris with a crate just before they got caught by the armed guards. Braedon had cast himself as some kind of superhero wearing a blue cape.

"I like to make up stories sometimes. I may even create a virtual game based on Captain Valterri's adventures," Braedon said. "I know it's amateurish, but I hand-drew the characters myself. The animation will be hard, so I'm creating the storyboard first and then I'll need to make 3D renderings of each of the characters. It's not easy."

"I understand. Can I give you one piece of advice?"

She watched as Braedon took in a deep breath as if preparing to take pulse fire.

"You should lose the cape. The whole thing would get caught in the force field fencing system they had on Phiris. The cape will only get you killed."

"Really?!" His voice took on a higher octave, matching his excitement. "I wondered if it was too much. I was going for a sort of retro thing with the cape, but I'm not set on it. Otherwise, though, you like it?"

"I don't hate it. For example, I like what you did with my hair, not bad. I doubt Jovani will appreciate being cast as the wimp, though."

Braedon's mouth hung open in surprise.

"What?" she asked.

"I thought you'd be mad."

"Should I be?"

"Well, I sort of exaggerated your features a bit. And I made you more of a sidekick character than the lead. I put you in a dress and everything."

"The story is made-up, and you used the crew as inspiration. I'm not mad. Although, if you're going to exaggerate anything, I'd think you'd give me more backside. The breasts are large enough." She shook her head playfully. "I'm surprised at you. Keep some semblance of proportion!"

Iza laughed as she watched Braedon struggle to avoid looking down at her chest. Poor thing, it wasn't his fault. He was sitting, and she was standing right in front of him. He pulled his handheld up to eye level and managed to turn in his seat without ogling her. Well done.

She returned to her seat at the center of the flight deck. "Braedon, have you heard back about our application to attend the auction?"

"Oh, right! Yes, gave us the option to buy in to two seats. I also got in touch with Viper and she's agreed to meet with me."

"Good, what did you say to get her to come?"

"I said while you were off dealing with the miners, I wanted to show her this new game I've been working on. It worked. Honestly, I didn't think she'd go for it."

"I'm not surprised at all. I knew you'd convince her."

"Hey, Iz, one question though," he turned in his seat to look at her.

"Sure."

"I thought she was your friend? I mean, we're doing this job with her. Why aren't we just inviting her over?"

"Yeah, well, when we met on Sarduvis, our friendship came with some stipulations. She seems to have forgotten what they were."

Braedon raised one eyebrow but shrugged.

"Whatever the reason, I'd hate to be on your bad side."

He was right, of course. She'd gotten Viper out of prison and given her a chance to straighten up. She'd made the young girl promise never to get herself in trouble again. Yet, she'd been at the party and with Captain Douketis and his people. Somewhere along the way, she'd forgotten her promise.

"Any trouble with Hubyrian border patrol?"

"No, they approved our codes. Why, are you expecting trouble?"

"Always. Trix, prep the shuttle. Braedon, you and Jovani get dressed for your buy-in at the auction. I'll meet you in the cargo hold for final instructions."

"Sure thing, Iz."

Braedon and Trix set about their tasks.

Iza looked down at the dog, who was already whining. "No way. I don't care how sad you can make your eyes, you're not coming."

On her way to the cargo area, Iza stopped in the infirmary to remind Cierra that they needed her.

"Yes, Captain?" Cierra looked bored.

"I need you on the flight deck, remember?"

"I had hoped to collect more oats. We're completely out. I realize the rest of you don't value real food, but it's important that we have something that isn't just processed food bars."

Iza started to tune her out after oats but maintained a neutral expression. "Noted. With the rest of us off the ship and Karter on board, I need you holding down the flight deck. Can you handle it? I'm taking the shuttle down to the surface with Braedon, Trix, and Jovani."

"You can't trust him."

"I don't, which is why you'll be on the flight deck. Don't worry, you don't need to touch any of the buttons, just be there."

"No, I'm not talking about Karter; that's obvious. I'm talking about Jovani."

"What?"

Cierra poked her head into the corridor and checked that no one was nearby. "Come on, we need to talk." She led Iza to her cabin and closed the door.

The aroma of Cierra's plants assaulted Iza while the humidity in the room seemed several degrees above normal. "Are you playing with the environmental controls in here?"

"No." Cierra shook her head and waved her hands. "They're already waiting for you. We don't have much time."

Iza pushed down the pit in her stomach and crossed her arms over her chest. Cierra wasn't her favorite person on board, but she tried to keep her imagination in check. *Listen, Iza, give her a chance.*

Cierra shifted from side to side, lacing her fingers together and then releasing them to rest at her sides. Iza couldn't ever remember seeing her so anxious. Her normally calm and casual demeanor had become like a comfortable blanket.

Seeing her like this made Iza's heart race and shift in her shoes.

"Out with it," she said, losing her patience.

Cierra took a deep breath and sighed. "Jovani, isn't who he says he is. He's a TSS Agent."

"He *was* a TSS Agent," Iza said with more conviction than she had.

Cierra shook her head, lifting her hands to ring them again. "No, Jovani is an *active* Agent. He's working with the TSS now."

Iza wanted to believe she couldn't possibly know. There had to be proof before she could let herself believe it. The doubt must have shown on her face because Cierra continued.

"I got it from Karter. Jovani's using his abilities to block Karter's thoughts, but he's not strong enough to block me from his own thoughts *and* Karter's. It took a while, but the truth slipped through."

"Why would he be blocking Karter's thoughts?"

Cierra shrugged. "I don't know, but Karter's trying to keep something hidden from us, and it's not Jovani's secret so it must be something else. Jovani's helping protect him, but I suspect he doesn't want to or he'd be more careful around me."

Iza nodded, though she wasn't sure she understood.

Cierra put her hands out to Iza's shoulders. "I'm sorry. It's not normally in my nature to get involved, but for the safety of all of us, I thought you needed to know."

Iza tried to reconcile all the conversations she'd had with Jovani up to now. He'd had ample opportunity to tell her the truth. She might not have even cared so much if he'd been straight with her. Then she thought of all the times he'd come through for them. It had begun on Sarduvis when he got them all released from Enforcer custody. That had got her attention, but the connection between them distracted her from focusing on how he got them all out. Him having active ties to the TSS explained how he'd pulled those strings, and it also went a long way to explain how the *Verity* had ended up with an independent jump drive.

"You should go. They're already in the cargo hold." Cierra turned Iza around by the shoulders and guided her toward the door.

Iza whirled around and looked Cierra in her eyes. Regardless of how painful it was to learn the truth, she was grateful. "Keep this knowledge between us. I don't want the others to know just yet and—" The words caught in her throat. After everything they'd been through, she was trusting Cierra over Jovani. Hadn't he told her *she* was holding something back? Whatever it was, it couldn't be worse than his secret. Now she had to do what was necessary to protect herself.

Cierra seemed to understand her hesitation and spoke in a gentle, soothing tone. She reached out to Iza, as if through the power of touch she could convey the truth in her words. "If I learn of anything else, you'll be the first to know."

16

IZA STUMBLED OUT of Cierra's cabin with incense smoke clinging to her clothes and her heart in pieces. *Why didn't he come to me and tell me the truth?* Instead, Jovani had let Cierra reveal his secret for him.

The others had the shuttle prepped by the time she arrived in the cargo hold. Trix had already boarded while Braedon and Jovani were standing outside the shuttle waiting for her. Braedon had chosen one of his expensive new suits to wear, dark blue with metal fasteners along one side of his chest. Jovani wore all black with black shades covering his eyes, looking his best to appear to be private security, but looking more like an Agent. It was so obvious now, she wondered why she hadn't noticed it before.

She must have been frowning because they mistook it for disapproval.

"Is everything okay?" Braedon asked. "Don't you think they'll buy it?"

Iza smiled. "No, of course they will, you both look perfect."

"Now, what do you want me to say to Viper?" Braedon

asked.

"Nothing, Trix and I will meet Viper at the coordinates."

"Oh, I thought I was—"

"No, we'll handle her," Iza told him. "Scope out the situation with the auction. I want to know exactly where they're keeping the items and everything about the security. If I know Captain Douketis, they're already here."

"Whatever you say, Captain." Braedon gave a mock salute and boarded the shuttle.

"Any word from Yeaga?" Jovani asked once Braedon was beyond earshot. He was so perceptive.

"No, which means she's got something else planned for me."

"Are you sure about this? Maybe I should go with you," he said. When he reached out and touched her, she had to fight not to flinch.

"No, she'll sense you. Trix and I are the only ones she won't see coming. Signal if you run into any trouble."

Jovani lowered his voice. "I wanted to tell you earlier, but I never got the chance. I managed to get in touch with someone who has TSS access."

"Really?" Iza asked raising an eyebrow. *I bet I know who that person is.*

"Yes, and it appears the sphere was made by an alien species that doesn't want any contact with Tarans."

Iza's mouth dropped open. *Aliens?*

"The TSS believes that using any technology connected to this species would be extremely dangerous. Though it wasn't stated to me directly, I got the impression that there may have been some sort of ancient agreement with these aliens that Tarans would leave them alone and never pursue research of their tech. If that hunch is true, then using this sphere might violate the treaty, assuming these aliens are still around." He ran his hand through his hair. "I don't know. I can't help but worry that if the sphere falls into the wrong hands, it could inadvertently drag the Taran Empire into a war with an alien race with superior technology and abilities."

If what Jovani was telling her about the sphere was true, then she had even more reason to get it away from Douketis and keep it from Mr. Arvonen.

"What kind of abilities?"

"I'm not sure, it's just speculation. But I know advanced telekinesis used to be a common trait in past Tarans, so whatever made our ancestors blacklist an entire region of space must have been a formidable enemy. I just wanted you to know what the stakes are walking into this."

Iza knew what was at stake. The question was, could she trust him now that she knew the truth? At the moment, she didn't have an answer, and going into something like this and not completely trusting her team was a dangerous move. She might get herself captured or killed; or worse, someone else.

—

Iza sat in the parked shuttle waiting for Viper to arrive. The agreed upon rendezvous location was near an abandoned factory, one of the few prominent landmarks in Hubyria's desolate landscape. Patches of lichen were the only visible vegetation to break up the dark rock stretching to the horizon.

The shuttle sat out in the open with no cover. If Viper had arrived early, she'd be able to watch them from the abandoned building. It was ten minutes past the arranged meeting time, making Iza agitated and anxious. Maybe Viper had been tipped off.

"Your blood pressure has increased by one-point-three percent," Trix observed.

"Don't worry about my vitals. Monitor the sensors and inform me the minute there's even a slight indication she's in the vicinity."

"You mean like a heat signature traveling at a steady speed of twenty kilometers an hour and headed for our location?"

Iza perked up. "That's a whole new level of funny even for you," Iza said with a side-long glance at her friend. "Where is she?"

"Coming in from the south. It looks like she's on some kind of hoverboard," Trix said.

"She'll be here at any second. Get ready. I want her to see you working around the shuttle."

"The shuttle is functioning normally."

"Look for some boulders to move. She only wants to know where Braedon is, so that's the only question she'll ask you." She pushed Trix toward the exit hatch.

Iza turned on the exterior cameras so she could watch the exchange on the holodisplay.

Viper leaped off the board and approached Trix with a relaxed smile. She didn't seem to be expecting trouble. Good.

"Hey, what did those boulders ever do to you?"

Trix dropped the boulder. "Are you looking for Braedon?"

Iza slapped a hand to her forehead. *She needs to work on her acting skills.*

"Yes, is he around?" Viper asked as she scanned the surrounding rock formations.

"No, he's not here," Trix said.

That's not what she was supposed to say! Iza leaped from her seat and headed out the hatch.

Viper must have heard her coming because she turned and

started to drop her board, intending to ride away on it. Trix anticipated the movement and held her with one hand. In a lightening move, Viper knocked aside the hand holding her and gripped it with her other.

Mechanical components whirred with strain. Viper had been augmented. There was no way she could match an android's strength and reflexes without upgrades of her own.

The two were locked hand-in-hand, dancing around each other while Viper struggled to get away and Trix held her steady.

"That's enough!" Iza's voice boomed, and they both stopped but didn't let go.

"Viper, I want to ask you a few questions. Can we sit down like civilized people?" Iza held out a hand toward the shuttle hatch.

Viper looked from Trix to the shuttle door and down to her hoverboard. Iza saw her decide a moment before the pressure building up in her cybernetic arm released and her other hand dropped.

Iza gestured toward the shuttle, inviting Viper to follow her inside. On board, Viper sat on the small bench with her eyes on the hatch. The bench had once served as Iza's cot, the bedding lay neatly tucked away in case of emergencies now. Iza sat in the seat behind the copilot's chair at an angle to face her. Trix stood at the hatch entrance, prepared to prevent Viper from escaping.

"So, let's omit the part where I ask what you've been up to over the last two months and we get to the real questions," Iza began. "What you were doing at Karter's party the other night?"

"What party? I didn't get any invitation to a party." She was trying to be coy. Brazen little thing.

"My engagement party to Karter at Blue Hills Estate. You recognized me, though you didn't offer your congratulations. Perhaps it was because you were leaving in a such a hurry." Iza waited for her to come up with another story or lie. She didn't.

"I was just taking care of some private business. It had nothing to do with you. It wasn't personal."

"It was personal to me. You took something of mine and I want it back."

Viper laughed. "You know I can't do that. The people I work with, they're not the kind that give back out of charity. It was a team score, and the profits were split equally among us."

Iza snorted. "So, you're trying to convince me they split their haul with you equally? I doubt that very much. You're barely a blip on the scales to them. They would just as soon turn on you as keep you."

Her jeering must have hit a nerve because Viper's smile instantly faded. There was a disappointed sadness in her eyes that Iza recognized. No doubt she'd already been explicitly told how little they cared.

Iza had run with a similar gang in her past. It had gotten her into loads of trouble. At the time, she thought she was evening the score, giving herself some kind of street credit. Instead, they were using her, just like they were using Viper now. Iza knew where this road ended. Viper would wind up in a juvenile detention facility, and the rest of them would walk free. They wouldn't even leave her cabin empty for longer than a day before getting someone else.

"I'm sure they've told you how replaceable you are," Iza said. She meant the words to sting. She would say whatever it took to get through to Viper. "They're all out for themselves. If you get injured, caught, or killed tomorrow, they won't give you another thought."

The tears welled up in Viper's eyes but her mouth remained sealed tight.

"Now me, on the other hand, I'm a different kind of captain. I've been where you are, I know these people. What they'll take from you, you'll never get back. Come with me today and I'll help you in a way they never will."

Viper's eyebrows shot up. "How's that?"

"A real home, with real work. You'll have your own cabin, a place to call yours. When we get work, you'll get a cut. It won't be equal, but it'll be fair."

"Nothing illegal?"

"I didn't say that," Iza qualified with a smile. "However, we don't leave our people behind to get caught by Enforcers so we can get away. If you're injured, we don't abandon you. We stick together."

Iza realized what she offered wasn't a false or unrealistic view of her crew. It was the truth. She and the others had stuck together. No matter their personal views or agendas, they'd looked out for one another and that was something she could depend on.

Iza gave Viper a moment to let the offer sink in. The option to have a real home. A place where she didn't have to look over her shoulder. A place where she didn't have to hide her stuff for fear that someone else would take it and sell it. Iza had fought hard to create that space on the *Verity*. Now, she was offering it to her young friend. The question: would it ever be enough?

"You think I have it, but I don't. They put everything we took that night into the hold. I don't have access to it now."

"You're lying. You have as much access as anyone else. I'm giving you a choice. Help me get my things back. I don't even care what else you grab, as long as you bring me what's mine.

Then you and I are square, and I'll give you place on my ship or drop you off at another desired location."

"And if I don't?" Viper's chin lifted in challenge.

"If you don't, I will sell you out to Captain Douketis and his crew faster than you can blink. I'll tell them you told me everything. Not only that, I'll convince them that you gained access because of me. He'll be forced to give me a cut, cutting your share to zero."

"You wouldn't. You can't do that!" Viper stared at her in shock.

"I can and I would enjoy doing it. Captain Douketis owes me one, anyway. You have no leverage, no standing, and barely any friends. I suggest you take me up on my offer. It'll be better for you in the long run."

"What makes you think threatening me will make me want to join your crew?"

"Oh, you're mistaken, I wasn't asking you to join my crew. I'm giving you a permanent way out. Their methods of dealing with traitors are painful at best. Their lifestyle will only get you either thrown in prison again or killed. Like I told you before, I've been where you are."

"I doubt that," Viper muttered. She worried her bottom lip, looking at Trix. "Is she on the level?"

"If you are asking if you can trust Iza, the answer is yes. I would trust her with my life."

Viper nodded then let out a sigh, dropping her shoulders and her last defense. "Fine, I'll do it."

—

Braedon and Jovani were already waiting at the pickup point when Iza landed the shuttle. When they boarded, they were both surprised to see Viper.

"Um, is she coming with us?" Braedon asked.

"Yes," Iza said. She smiled. "I made her an offer she couldn't turn down."

"Does she know what's going on?" Jovani asked.

"Yes. How did it go?"

Braedon met Viper's glare with one of his own. "I did what I was told," he said, reading her reaction.

"So did I." Viper crossed her arms over her chest, still glaring at him.

Iza waved a hand in the air. "Save your battle for the next underground VR tournament. Let's get back to your recon. Where are we with everything?"

Braedon rolled his eyes away from Viper and back to Iza. "We confirmed our buy-in with Karter's credits, and we have detailed notes about the entire operation."

"Did anyone suspect or recognize you?"

"No, we were discreet," Jovani said.

"In fact, Jovani got several job offers while we were there, he played his part so well," Braedon said, smiling at him.

He has no idea. Jovani's a skilled actor. Iza needed more time to cool off before she confronted Jovani about his deceit.

Viper laughed pulling Iza out of her disquieting thoughts. "Douketis will see you coming from a kilometer away."

"That's where you come in," Iza told her with a smile. "You're going to make us invisible."

17

VIPER SAT ON the bench with her arms crossed over her chest while Iza gave the others their orders.

"Braedon, Trix, secure the shuttle and meet me on the flight deck in ten minutes. Viper, we need to find you a place to sleep."

"I'd like a room with a view, if you don't mind," she said with a smirk.

"No promises," Iza said.

They walked off the shuttle and into the *Verity*'s cargo area, where the dog ran up to greet them.

Cierra descended the stairs from the upper deck of the ship. "How did it go? Any trouble?"

"No, everything went according to plan" Iza responded. "We need to meet about—"

"What is she doing here?" Cierra asked, her tone suddenly cold and sharp.

"I was invited," Viper said, her hands going to her hips. "I see you're still dressing like a barefooted gardener."

"You look like something living under a city bridge,

hoping for a scrap of processed food," Cierra shot back.

The two women stared each other down from a meter apart, refusing to look at anyone else. It electrified the air in the room. The crackle of it made Iza take a step forward, worried something worse would happen. She was about to separate them when Braedon caught sight of the standoff.

"Wait, do you know each other?"

"You could say that," Cierra snapped.

"Well, at least you're acknowledging that I exist."

"Don't play the innocent victim here! You abandoned your family and ruined your body," Cierra's voice rose to a shrill.

Viper was rounding up to do more than talk when Iza stepped forward, holding up her hands between them.

"How do you two know each other?"

"Captain, this is my sister, Abby Quetzali." Cierra's words came out like a hiss.

"My name is Viper. Not that you ever cared about being my sister before."

Cierra rolled her eyes. "Of course, I care. Mom and Dad care, too, for the record."

"Don't speak for them. They have their perfect little all-natural daughter to turn to. Why in the stars would they ever need me?"

"That's not true. They love you. Why won't you believe that?"

"I have no reason to believe it." Viper shook her head. "I spent most of my life competing for the things that are important to me without their help. Meanwhile, you all did everything you could to hold me back."

"I didn't know you had a sister." Braedon looked over both young women, trying to see the resemblance between the Healer he'd dated and his Dark Net gaming nemesis.

There really wasn't one. Where Cierra was exotic and bright in her choice of colors, Viper was hard-edged and dark. Viper's dyed green hair was cut in a short pixie cut that framed her heart-shaped face, and her wide blue eyes slanted slightly downward. In contrast, Cierra had all the curls and the gray eyes. But it wasn't just a matter of their looks, it was the way each of them moved, their manners. Iza had never seen two people more opposite. Having both of them on board would be a lot more drama than Iza had signed up for.

"Well, I'm so happy to have provided you with this opportunity for a family reunion, but it doesn't change anything," Iza said. "Viper is here at my request and has agreed to help us with our job tomorrow."

Cierra scoffed. "You're working with those criminals?"

"I could say the same to you." Viper looked around at the misfit crew. "I never would've thought you'd end up in space, so what brings you out here?"

Cierra didn't answer right away, glancing in Braedon's direction and shaking her head ever so slightly.

"Oh, I see. I had no idea that you and Little Lamb were acquainted."

"Blacksheep," Braedon corrected. "And your sister and I have known each other for some time. But don't let that get in the way of our future tournament. I still plan on beating you again. Not only do I have my reputation to protect, but I believe you owe me some credits." He crossed his arms in challenge.

"No chance, you'll get a proper beating and then we can put this to rest," Viper said. She moved to take a step toward him, but Cierra stepped into her path.

"That's enough, you've done enough posturing this evening."

"Are you going to try to get in my way, big sister?"

Iza could hear Viper's mechanically enhanced arm winding up. The dog let out a warning growl. He was right, things were getting out of hand.

"Enough. Let me remind you that this is my ship. I make the rules here."

"Sorry to disappoint you, Captain, we haven't seen each other in two years. Our relationship isn't like the ones from the story books," Cierra said, turning to Iza. "Abby—" she sighed, "*Viper* and I don't frequent the same circles."

"That's only partially true. Since I know both of you," Braedon said.

The coincidence seemed to defy odds, but Iza somehow wasn't surprised that Braedon would unwittingly find himself trapped between two feuding sisters. The guy was a magnet for trouble. She couldn't help noting that her life kept getting more complicated, not less, the longer he was on her ship.

"And how *do* you two know each other?" Viper asked.

"We—" Braedon started to say.

"That's a story for another time," Cierra cut him off. If her eyes held daggers, he'd already be bleeding out on the floor.

"You mean the two of you were— Ha! Stars, wait until your parents find out," Viper said. Her jeering made her older sister's mouth clamp shut.

"*Our* parents," Cierra corrected once she'd gained her voice again.

"I still can't believe it," Braedon said under his breath, still shaking his head.

"Have your domestic disputes elsewhere," Iza interjected. "I've got work to do. Cierra, if I recall, you have no interest in what we have planned this evening, so I suggest you keep to your cabin or the infirmary this evening. The rest of you, meet me on the flight deck where we can go over the plan." Iza looked around. "Speaking of, where's Karter?"

"He left," Cierra said, turning to leave.

"What do you mean he left? How? We took the only shuttle."

"How would I know? He told me he was leaving, and as you can see, he's gone. And before you ask, he didn't say what time he'd be returning." Cierra turned her back on them and retired to her cabin.

Fantastic. Iza didn't need any more problems. If they were going to pull off this job, they couldn't be also worrying about Karter getting captured and held for ransom.

She sent him a warning message, not sure if he'd be able to receive it: >> If you get yourself nabbed while we're here, don't think I'll shed a tear or waste valuable resources coming after you. You have until this job is complete to be back here or you'll get left behind. <<

She was patting herself on the back for making her point when she received notification of a new message. It was from Karter. *That was fast.*

>> Understood. -KH<<

Iza shook her head. Karter could take care of himself; he'd even been able to secure a new handheld, apparently. She had more important things to do than worry about him.

—

After two hours of deliberations and arguments over the plan, Iza was squeezing the bridge of her nose and considering dropping the whole thing. The sphere seemed impossible to reach. She felt close to contacting the TSS to see if they might handle the problem of getting it before Mr. Arvonen did something drastic.

The *Verity*'s crew had begun the meeting by standing around a three-dimensional holographic rendering of the auction hall, but after a while they'd all gotten tired and sat down to strategize. Iza's backside was beginning to ache from sitting on the hard flooring in the flight deck for so long.

All the ideas they'd come up with Viper had shot down. Every single one. There seemed to be no way in or out with the goods that didn't end in all of them being caught or killed.

"I'm telling you, what you want to do is impossible" Viper insisted. "The place where they're holding everything is next level. You need at least four players to reach all that treasure. Every security measure has a back-up. Not to mention, there's only one way in or out."

"We're running out of time. The auction is tomorrow. We've got to find a way in, and purchasing all the items you stole won't work," Iza said. "I don't want any more bad ideas. Let's go over our assets again and how we can use them."

"All right, between the five of us, there are two telepaths and two who are unreadable," Jovani said in a monotone voice, clearly sick of rehashing the same information.

"Two coders," Braedon said.

"Two with super strength in at least one arm," Viper said.

"We know what the box looks like and it's small enough that it can be easily hidden from most people, but not from me," Iza said, rubbing both hands over her face. "I think the only way to get what we want is for one of us to get caught."

Viper stiffened. "Who?"

"Me," Iza said. "I'm the most recognizable and I can be a bigger distraction than any of you."

"I don't like it. How will we get you back?" Jovani asked.

"They won't hurt me in front of all those people, and I have a legitimate reason for being there."

"You don't have a pass or a buy-in. You won't get a meter inside the room."

"It doesn't matter. All I need is for the video feed to pick me up and the rest will happen naturally."

"But how will we get you out?" Jovani asked again, this time enunciating each word for emphasis.

Iza turned to him. His protectiveness took her breath away. Her gaze dropped away when she remembered his role as a TSS Agent in disguise, his agenda still unknown to her. Maybe he wanted the sphere, too. *Does he plan to take it? What's his real mission?* She shook her head. It was making her brain dizzy trying to keep up with his duplicity.

"I'll get myself out. Douketis doesn't need to keep me, and if I'm with him, I can't be the one stealing from him."

"He'll never go along with it. Douketis will come after you, and when he does, he'll find me," Viper said, shaking her head. "No extra lives. Game over."

"Trust me, I'll distract them so you can all get out. It's the only way."

The others remained silent. Iza figured they were trying to come up with another plan, but this was the approach that had the best chance for success. They'd exhausted all other possibilities. There were no guarantees, but if she got caught, Karter wouldn't let her rot in a cell or on the *Iron Dog*. He still needed her, and that meant she had an emergency out. At least, she hoped he'd smoothed things over enough with his cousin enough to help her.

"That's all for tonight." Iza stood up and shook out her legs. "Go get some rest, and we'll meet in the cargo area for an 09:00 departure."

Braedon and Viper filed out and were already talking VR before they reached the threshold. Trix stood at the front of the flight deck looking out the viewport as she monitored the ship's systems.

Jovani hung back. "Did you consider what I said about the artifact?"

Iza had thought long and hard about his words. They had motivated her to try so hard to keep the sphere from Mr. Arvonen. It seemed that little object had the potential to shift the balance of power in the Taran Empire, and it was in everyone's interest that he not get his hands on it. However, Jovani hadn't been forthcoming about where he'd learned the information; more than likely, it was directly from the TSS. She didn't trust him with the sphere, either.

"Good night, Jovani. I'm tired."

Jovani looked at her with his head tilted as if trying to read her thoughts. Iza kept her face neutral and her eyes on his. *Those bomaxed brown contacts are covering his brilliant blue eyes.*

He squared his shoulders. "Sure, see you tomorrow."

Iza followed him to the threshold and watched when he turned into his cabin. She'd hurt him, but it remained out of her control. If she apologized for it now, it wouldn't change things, not with so much at stake. Though her pull toward him felt real, it might be an Agent trick—using his abilities to fool her into feeling connected to him. She'd heard of things like that happening, though she didn't understand how. Until he came to her with the truth, she wouldn't risk trusting him.

Iza turned and walked over to where Trix stood and spoke, keeping her voice to a low whisper. "Tomorrow, no matter what, make sure you end up with the box. I don't trust any of the others to get it back to me."

Trix nodded. "Yes, Captain."

—

The afternoon sun on Hubyria warmed Iza's skin under her jacket. The rocky terrain was difficult to traverse, but she'd done it enough times in the dark to be familiar with how best to avoid tripping and falling.

Jovani seemed the most comfortable hiking over the rocks, as well, while Braedon stumbled as if it were his first time, despite her firsthand knowledge of his previous outings. Jovani had to catch him from falling several times to prevent him from soiling his dress clothes. Trix and Viper carefully followed along behind Iza, quiet and focused in preparation for the task ahead.

The settlement appeared so much more welcoming than it had on the night her ship had been brought down by an EMP. Having the auction on Hubyria was ingenious. No one would think to pay much attention to a border planet with residual animosity for the local Enforcers. They had updated the former hotel restaurant, she noticed; a new face for the same old shady dealings. It fit with the information Viper had given them about the auction taking place in a large cavern underneath the miner's hangout.

Yeaga and the rest of the miners had broken free from their corporate employers a month prior. Their coup against the Enforcers included taking down hauling ships to bring the entire mining business to a halt. It had worked. Their efforts had forced the corporations to pay a fair price for the ore used in key manufacturing industries. As a result, the people of Hubyria now did business with whoever they chose.

Iza had heard rumors about groups on other planets rising up in a similar fashion. Since the leadership change on Tararia four years prior, there was a clear trend of the Outer Colony worlds turning their strong political opinions into action. In some cases, that manifested as voicing additional support for the central Taran government and a desire to be more connected to the rest of the Empire; in other instances, there were calls for greater independence and autonomy. If that trend continued, Yeaga and the miners on Hubyria might soon find themselves in the company of many others seeking to forge their own way.

Iza stopped in the narrow passage between two buildings opposite the town's old hotel. It wasn't much cover, so they didn't waste time. Everyone knew what to do. With a nod from Iza, they were on the move. Braedon, with Jovani providing private security, went in the front using his pass while Trix and Viper circled around the back.

As with many jobs, their success would come down to timing. Iza started the count on her handheld. She would need to wait until the auction started before she began her distraction. They didn't know in what order they would present the items—not that it mattered, since her people would cover both the front and the back.

Her role was to draw the attention of the security, and from the look of the two guards out front, it wouldn't be too hard. Both of them wore bored expressions on their faces and their pulse handguns were on their hips. Neither spoke as people entered through the door, only glanced down at their digital passes and either allowed them access or didn't.

Eventually, the stream of people stopped. The auction was underway.

Iza waited several minutes before she stepped out from between the two buildings and headed for the old hotel serving as the auction house.

As she came out in the open, she caught sight of a young

man dipping in between two buildings on the other side of the street. His broad shoulders and the way he moved was familiar. He looked into a window then knelt to avoid being seen. Something made him turn her way.

There was a bolt of electricity when his gaze met hers. Not the bond she felt with Jovani, but an electrical compatibility that she'd never experience before. He started to stand, and she took a step toward him. Before she could place where she'd seen him before, a voice spoke behind her.

"I thought I told you that you weren't welcome here, Captain Sundari." The soft rasp unmistakably belonged to Yeaga, the leader of the miners.

Iza turned to face her and smiled. Yeaga had pulled back her blonde hair from her face in a long ponytail segmented with brown elastic bands all the way to the end. Her brown eyes narrowed as she looked Iza over from head to toe.

"Yeaga, I assumed you'd be at the auction," Iza said with a glance at the front doors and the two apathetic guards. "If you'll excuse me, I'll be gone before you know it. It will be like I was never here."

"Like you were never here," Yeaga repeated. "That's not quite the same thing as never being here. I see you're trying to get into that auction. That's not going to happen, so whatever it is you were hoping to buy, they'll sell it to someone else. You're coming with me."

Iza pulled out her handgun from the inside of her jacket and held it up to Yeaga's small nose. "I'm sorry, I'm in a bit of a hurry. You understand," Iza said. Then, she felt the cold metal barrel of a gun at the base of her neck.

"You mistook it for a suggestion. You're coming with me. Now." Yeaga nodded, and the man holding the handgun on Iza reached around to disarm her. He grabbed her right arm, and a woman came forward and grabbed her other arm. They hauled her off.

"Look, you've got this all wrong, I swear," Iza said raising her voice and dragging her feet. It wouldn't be enough to cause a disturbance. Worse, this was much too soon. Her crew wouldn't have a way out of the building, and they'd all get caught.

Yeaga brought Iza into a small bakery next to the hotel. The bread-maker ignored them as they dragged Iza to the back. Hot ovens in the small kitchen, covered in baking flour, drew beads of sweat from Iza's brow. The aroma of cooking bread filled her nostrils, reminding her that she only had a light breakfast hours ago.

They dragged her through a set of glass doors into a storeroom beyond the kitchen. She was shoved into a chair and they cuffed her hands behind her back. She was facing a small desk, where Yeaga sat down across from her. The muscle who had dragged Iza took posts on either side of her, also facing Yeaga with their backs to the door.

"I warned you about coming back here."

Iza didn't respond. Yeaga loved to listen to herself talk.

"Our system works, no thanks to you. However, I'm curious if you brought the former TSS Agent with you."

"I did not," Iza said, looking the woman in the eye. *That's mostly true, since I actually have a current Agent with me.*

"Hmm, no doubt you're lying. I remember you going through a lot of trouble to come back for him. Have you had a falling out already?" Yeaga laughed to herself then placed her hands in front of her on the desk. "What are you doing here?"

"Just taking in the sights," Iza said with a smile. The man on her right punched her in the face. Her vision went from dark to bright and then dark again when she realized her eyes were now closed. Her jaw ached; any harder a hit would have dislocated it.

"Let's try again," Yeaga said, leaning forward over her hands. "Why were you skulking around the auction house?"

Iza worked her jaw, testing the feeling. It would be bad later but nothing her medical nanites couldn't handle. "I heard about the score and wanted to see if there was anything I could pick up. I've got a few more credits than the last time we met."

"Do you think I'm a fool?"

Iza tilted her head and raised her eyebrows as she looked down at the floor, indicating she didn't want to answer that one honestly.

"You're engaged to a Lower Dynasty heir who just specializes in selling the transport vehicles that haul the rock we mine. You're not here for the auction; you're here to get rock off of Hubyria behind my back."

"To be fair, I've been more help than Douketis. Instead, he's the one setting up an auction of illegal goods right now."

Yeaga glared at her. "Douketis knows how to pay his debts. He made sure we got paid for our work. You didn't glance in the rearview on your way off-planet. For that, I should chain you up and throw you in a mine to rot."

Iza realized her mistake. She had helped the miners, but not through Yeaga. From Yeaga's vantage, Iza was still in the red. She'd have to think fast if she wanted to get out of this one.

An alarm sounded in the building next door, followed by a loud boom.

Iza's stomach dropped. She'd missed her window. *Who set off the explosion as a distraction?*

Yeaga looked out the window behind her and shrugged as if it were just another day in the streets. She turned back to Iza. "When are you going to tell me the truth?"

A knock sounded behind Iza. She looked over her shoulder and was surprised to see Jovani standing beside Karter on the other side of the glass doors. *If Jovani's here, who's with Braedon?*

"Open the doors but don't let them through," Yeaga said. When the doors had been swung open, she settled back in her chair. "Gentlemen?"

The alarm stopped but people were still yelling next door.

"Yeaga, it's been too long." Jovani took a step forward and was stopped by the guards. He had a hum of energy around him that was even more intense than Iza typically felt in his presence. "What's all this?"

"Sorry, precautions," Yeaga said casually. "The last time you were here you left in a hurry, and we'd been having such a good time."

Iza kept still while Yeaga watched her face for a reaction.

"Understood, which is why I brought a friend with me," Jovani replied. "I didn't want you to think I'd forgotten about you. You must have heard I suffered an extreme injury."

"Yes, you lost an arm, if the rumors are true." Yeaga got up from the desk and moved around to stand behind Iza.

"I did, in fact, but it's obvious you've done well without me," Jovani said to her back.

With a nod of her head, Yeaga's people turned Iza's seat around so she could watch the exchange between them.

"What are you and your people really doing here?" Yeaga crossed her arms over her chest and tapped her right foot.

"I'm escorting these two love-birds into town. This is Karter Hyttinen, he was here hoping to get some baubles for his fiancée at the auction. But there was a problem over there."

"Why are you still following her around? I could have made you such a nice warm bed," Yeaga said with an appreciative glance up and down Jovani's frame.

"You still could, but at the moment I'm working," he responded with a pout on his lips that made Iza tighten her jaw. "I've got to get these two out of here before someone recognizes them. You know how unforgiving the Sensationals can be."

Yeaga reached out and ran her hand suggestively down his arm. "I can't let you just leave. What's in it for the miners? Times are hard you know," she said in a loud whisper.

Karter cleared his throat. "Perhaps I can help you with that." He pulled out a new handheld, angling the screen so only Yeaga could read it. Her eyes widened and mouth pinched. "Will that be enough to get my fiancée back?" Karter asked.

"Is he for real?" Yeaga questioned.

Jovani nodded, careful not to say anything. Though Iza thought he would glance in her direction, he kept his eyes off of her during the entire exchange. "Do we have a deal?"

Yeaga waved a hand and the two guards took a step back. The man took the cuffs off Iza and gestured that she was free to go.

Iza wanted to see how many credits had freed her, but there was no time to sneak a peek at Karter's handheld. If he and Jovani were there, it meant the shuttle had to be close and Douketis would spot them if they didn't hurry.

"Thank you, and I hope there are no more hard feelings," Jovani said to Yeaga.

"No, we're good. If you ever tire of trailing after her, you've always got a home here," Yeaga said.

Jovani nodded fell into step behind Karter, leaving Iza to follow them out. She hurried after them, trying to erase the sight of Yeaga stroking Jovani's arm.

"We need to hurry," Jovani said the moment they were outside the bakery. He turned left, away from the commotion at the auction house.

"Wait, you're going the wrong way." Iza stopped, and Karter took the opportunity to grab her arm and wrap it around his back. She was about to pull away but through better of it, realizing it was in all of their interest to pretend like they were a happy couple.

The three of them casually strolled down the settlement road, with Jovani playing up the role of private security once again.

"We're this way," Karter said.

"What about Braedon, Trix, and Viper?" Iza whispered to him.

"They're already heading back to the shuttle and will be on their way to the *Verity*. We need to get ourselves to safety. That little diversion of Karter's isn't going to last."

"What did he do?"

"I had to improvise," Karter said.

They walked until they were beyond the settlement's lights. As they approached a vertical rock face up ahead, Iza looked back and noticed they were being followed.

"They're on to us," Jovani said at the same moment.

Iza was about to break into a run to get ahead of their pursuers, but Karter pulled her back.

"Relax, we're almost there."

"Where are we going?" Iza asked him.

"Here." Karter led the way around the side of the rock face, which jutted up in a semi-circular ring just large enough to park a shuttle inside. Iza immediately recognized the sleek craft hidden behind the wall as being a similar model to the shuttle that had chauffeured her to Blue Hills Estate. The side hatch opened.

"Get in." Karter motioned her inside.

Seeing the unexpected shuttle was one thing, but the pilot was another.

"Hey, how are you?" Raquel asked.

Iza did a double-take. "Raquel, what are you doing here?"

"It's a long story. We need to bolt. Strap in, there are two shuttles headed our way," the archaeologist said as Karter seated himself in the copilot seat beside her.

"Can you get us out of here?" he asked.

"Of course, I can." Raquel entered coordinates into the front console as the shuttle lifted off the ground.

It darted toward space.

Iza needed answers. "Is this the shuttle you used to get down here?"

Karter nodded. "Yes. I arranged to meet with Raquel, since she was already in town. The *Verity*'s side airlock is equipped with an umbilical compatible with this vessel."

That part made sense. And it also followed that Raquel, a wealthy archaeologist, would attend an auction of rare and valuable items. However, none of that explained how Jovani ended up paired with Karter rather than Braedon.

She focused her attention on the TSS Agent next to her. "Did you go to the auction? How did you get out of there?"

"Karter sent Raquel inside to bid on some items for him while he waited outside. When he saw you get grabbed on the street, he messaged me, figuring we'd need some help. With a little impromptu coordination, he rigged up an explosion as a distraction so we could grab the artifact and escape."

"You're welcome," Karter said with a smug look at his fingernails.

"After we made it outside, Karter told me who'd grabbed you. I figured that Yeaga would agree to meet with me, since we left on good terms last time, so I went with Karter to get you back."

"You didn't really give her the money, did you?" Iza asked.

Karter was about to answer, when plasma beam fire hit the shuttle's shield and sent them spinning.

"What's going on?" Iza yelled.

"Someone's firing at us," Raquel called out.

"It's Arvonen," Jovani said.

Of course, it is. Iza tightened her flight harness.

Raquel dove the shuttle back toward the ground, seeking cover in the foothills and rocks.

"Is Mr. Arvonen here himself?" Iza asked.

"I'm not sure," Karter responded. "However, it was certain that he'd at least send a rep to bid on your item. That's why I thought it pertinent that Raquel represent me at the auction, since it wasn't wise to show my face."

"Did you get—"

"Incoming communication for you, Iza," Raquel interrupted.

"Arvonen?"

"No, a Captain Douketis."

How did he even know I was on this shuttle? Iza groaned. "Put it on."

The man's dog-like face appeared as a holoprojection in front of Iza. "Captain Sundari, it looks like you've got some trouble. Can we offer you any assistance?"

"You're not actually here to help me, are you?"

"You stole from me, Scrap Rat. You'll pay for that."

Iza flashed a challenging smile. "From one captain to another, you can't trust everyone you meet out here. Watch your back, Douketis. Next time, things might not end so well for you. End transmission."

"There's a third short-range shuttle showing up on our

sensors," Raquel said. "We need to get you out of here, Karter."

"Arvonen's after the box with the map. Where is it?" Karter asked turning to Jovani.

Jovani reached inside his jacket pocket and pulled out the box, holding it up for Iza to see before tucking it away again.

Iza's mouth tightened. "So, you did manage to get it." She'd given Trix strict instructions to transport the sphere herself. Apparently, the intensity Iza had felt when she saw Jovani in the bakery's storeroom was due to the sphere and not just their connection.. *What is he doing with the box?*

"The Douketis shuttle is also firing on us," Raquel called out.

"Arvonen knows we have it; that's why he's after us," Karter said. "We need to make a run for it."

"Has our other shuttle reached the *Verity* yet?" Iza asked.

"Yes, I got a signal from Braedon that they've arrived," Jovani confirmed.

"Good. Warn them we're coming in hot," she instructed. "Tell Trix to plot a jump to Phiris."

"Why there?" Raquel asked.

"It's close and there's no way they'll be able to track us. Just in case, I need a spot where Arvonen won't look for us right away."

"All right, hold on." Raquel once again pointed the shuttle on a steep upward trajectory.

Iza was pressed back in her seat as the racing shuttle acceleration began to outpace the effectiveness of the inertial dampeners. Though it was an uncomfortable few minutes, their pursuers were unable to keep pace.

"I had no idea you could fly like that," Karter said looking more than a little impressed.

"Once we're secure, give the *Verity* the signal to jump," Iza said.

They landed the new shuttle inside the cargo area next to Iza's old shuttle and the doors closed behind them. A second later, there was a momentary elongation of time as the *Verity* slipped into subspace.

The four climbed out of the shuttle to find Braedon, Viper, and Cierra waiting for them.

"You made it! I knew it. Didn't I say they'd make it? You owe me fifty credits," Braedon bragged.

"Yes, we made it." Iza pointed at Braedon. "No, gambling on board my ship."

Braedon raised his hands in surrender. "You've got it, Iz. You slid in here at the last second just like I imagined. Speaking of imagining things, this shuttle is a stunner. Where did you find it?"

"That would be mine," Raquel said, stepping forward. "Thanks for the lift."

"She's gorgeous," Braedon said, admiring the shuttle.

Raquel smirked. "Hands off. Now, time to tell me what you scored."

"We got you the box. It was sitting by itself, easy to reach," Braedon said. He looked over at Jovani, who stood unmoving. "Well?" Braedon prompted.

With obvious reluctance, Jovani lifted the box out from his pocket. Before he had a chance to put it away, Iza snatched it from him.

His eyes pleaded with her, but she stared back, daring him to reveal in front of everyone why he would hold onto it rather than returning it to her. He remained silent, but she could tell he was conflicted about how things were going.

Cierra stepped closer, focused on Iza's cheek. "You're hurt. Come to the infirmary and we'll clean you up."

"It's fine," she protested.

Jovani caught Iza's gaze. "I'm sorry we didn't make it there sooner."

"Don't worry about it. Thanks for coming to get me. Without you, I'm pretty sure Yeaga would have tossed me down a mineshaft."

"I'll always come for you," he said in a low whisper meant only for her. Iza wanted to believe him. Every fiber of her being wanted Jovani, but she didn't trust her feelings.

Karter turned to Raquel. "I believe you have something of mine."

Raquel pulled the engagement ring out of her pocket and handed to him. The blue and white gemstones looked out of place on board the *Verity*, sparkling in the overhead lights.

He looked it over and smiled before stepping over to Iza, forcing Jovani to move back as he placed it on Iza's finger again. "There, that's much better."

It felt heavier on Iza's hand than it had before, she noted. She glanced at Jovani, who was staring at it. She closed her hand into a fist to hide it away for now.

"Thanks," she said, her voice just above a whisper. Then louder, "Where's Trix?"

"She's on the flight deck," Braedon said. "Do you want me to call her down?"

"No, I'm on my way up there, anyway. Raquel, I think we've got one more cabin available. I'm sorry it's the smallest, but it's all we have left."

"Not a problem. I just need a place to sleep and change clothes. I'll grab the rest of my things from the shuttle."

"Cierra, can you help her find the empty cabin? I'll meet you in the infirmary."

Cierra nodded and Raquel went to retrieve her items from

the shuttle.

Iza turned to Braedon. "We outran your father, but I want you to keep an eye out, just in case they find a way to pursue us."

"Sure, Iz," Braedon said, running off to the flight deck. Viper following behind him. There was an invisible tether between them.

Raquel emerged from her shuttle carrying a duffle, and she followed Cierra up the stairs to the residential area.

"What are you going to do with it now that you have it?" Jovani asked when they were alone in the cargo hold.

Iza stiffened. *Is it him or a TSS Agent asking?*

"I'll hang onto it for safe keeping. Why, did you have a better idea?"

Jovani shook his head. "No, I think you're right to hold on to it. Our priority should be finding out what it can do."

His behavior surprised Iza. Despite her feelings for him, she doubted his motives and had wondered if he might try to steer her toward giving it up.

"I'll find out where this thing leads and if we need the TSS, I'll come to you," she said.

"Why?"

"Don't you still have connections with them?"

Jovani looked at her as if she'd said something in a language he didn't understand. "Not directly, just some third-party contacts. If I was still close with anyone in the TSS, I would have used them to get the scientists help when we picked them up. My connections ended when they kicked me out."

"That's right. Well, I'm sure once we have more information about what it can do we'll have tons of people wanting to help us." Iza rolled her eyes.

"True, but I wouldn't trust it with just anyone."

"You're right, we can't trust just anyone," she said, grateful her thoughts were her own in that moment.

Iza plodded toward the infirmary, hoping Cierra had something to numb the pain.

18

IZA LOOKED OVER her jaw, finding almost no trace of the cut and bruise. Cierra's healing methods were extraordinary. The telepathic stuff didn't work on Iza, but the telekinesis Cierra used made her one of the best Healers she'd ever come across. Her complementary work with herbals was exceptional, too, and Iza was grateful she had finally listened to Braedon about trying one of Cierra's healing teas.

Cierra was also discreet, which was even more invaluable than someone who was handy in an infirmary. Once Cierra told Iza what she knew about Jovani, she didn't bring it up again or harp on Iza about doing something drastic. Instead, they went on about their business.

"Did you and your sister always fight?" Iza asked, setting down the mirror she'd used to inspect her healing injury.

Cierra nodded with a smile. "Almost from the very start. Abby is only two years younger than me. Our interests were never aligned, but before she got her first handheld, she used to follow me around looking for trouble to get into. She's the reason I became a Healer."

"What happened?"

"Abby was small for her age. She always overcompensated for it by trying to run faster, leap farther, and climb higher than the rest. One day when we were young, she raced her friend up a tree and her hand slipped. I'll never forget the sound of her small bones breaking."

Iza flinched imagining it herself. "Did you heal her?"

"I didn't have my gifts then." Her features darkened in a way that made Iza believe she still regretted that she hadn't been able to help her sister. "I had healing instincts, though, and I did what I could, but it wasn't enough." Cierra gave her a wry smile. "Once I received my gifts, I learned how to heal others and vowed to do so for the rest of my life."

"What about your sister? Did she learn anything from the experience?"

Cierra's smile faded, replaced by a sad frown. "Not what I would have hoped. Her arm healed and was stronger than ever. Instead of rejoicing in what nature can do, she focused all of her attention on technology and cybernetics." Cierra shook her head, "She wanted an arm that couldn't break from a fall, or miss it's intended grasp. As soon as she'd earned enough money gambling on the Dark Net, she went out and bought herself that cybernetic arm."

Iza could see then how they both happened to meet Braedon. He was drawn to the Healer's gentle nature, a refreshing change from his demanding upbringing, while the virtual gaming world, where he felt at home, was the perfect place for someone like Viper. No doubt, he had been attracted to their passionate spirits—one thing they did have in common—though the way they fit into his life were as disparate as their personalities.

The two women seemed to openly acknowledge each

other's differences, and yet Iza didn't understand why they couldn't live and let live. "Why do you hold such animosity toward each other? Isn't it enough that you've each found a lifestyle that makes you happy?"

Cierra pursed her lips, "I'm a Healer; when someone is broken, I want to fix them. When Abby sees someone who's broken, she wants to turn them into a machine. We don't have a middle ground."

Cryptic and strange. Iza didn't understand it, but clearly it was something that would take more than a single conversation to resolve.

Cierra shrugged. "Family is a lot harder than it looks."

Thankful their conversation had focused on Cierra's life and not on her own, Iza slipped out of the infirmary and went back to her cabin to check on things.

The dog had missed her; he bounded onto Iza's bed with her and nuzzled himself under her resting arm. Iza would never admit it, but she enjoyed having him around. He seemed to know exactly what she needed in a way that no one else did.

Iza grabbed the artifact box and twirled it between her fingers. The constant hum in her mind had become a strange comfort; it had felt empty and quiet without it around.

Reflecting on the subject of family, she brought up the surveillance video Karter had provided of her mother and watched her roam the market. Iza had watched the vid several times already, cementing the image of her mother's smile in her mind. The carefree look on her face that said she had no other worries in the world other than what they would have for dinner. How easily she had shaken off her old life and her daughter. It made her wonder what kind of woman she really was. Perhaps she had the answers to Iza's past, but Iza didn't want anything her mother had to offer—not from a woman who didn't want her. Still, she hoped to someday tell the woman exactly how she felt about the situation.

Iza was about to shut off the video when she caught sight of someone in the background that she hadn't noticed before. He was a young man approximately her age with long, curly hair a similar texture to her own. He stood at attention, as if scanning the crowd for something. It seemed a second more and he would have caught sight of whoever had filmed the video.

He's the one from my dream. The one I saw on Hubyria. Who is he? While she pondered the questions, another thought surfaced. *Does he know my mother?*

A knock on her door sent Iza scrambling to turn off the viewscreen and rush to the door.

She cracked it open. "Yes?"

Trix was standing in the corridor. She glanced through Iza's door at the viewscreen as if expecting to find something there.

"Are you feeling all right?" Iza asked her.

"I am fine."

"Good, why did you come here?"

"During our time on Hubyria, I tried to get the artifact but Jovani reached it first. He insisted on holding on to it, despite my verbal protests. I was unable to get it back from him before the alarms went off."

"That's okay, I have it now, so it doesn't matter."

Trix nodded. "I apologize. I have failed you again."

"No, you haven't, I have the box." Iza reached out and touched her hand. The cold surface was a direct contrast to her own warm hands.

Trix nodded and walked away. She panned her head back and forth as if looking for something along the floor.

Concerned, Iza followed her out into the corridor. Just outside the flight deck, she ran into Raquel.

"Hey, I was hoping to see you before it got too late. Oh, wow, is that it?" Raquel asked looking down at her hand. Iza didn't realize she was still holding the box.

"Yeah. It's special, isn't it?"

"It is, do you mind?" Raquel asked, reaching out for it.

Iza handed it to her.

Raquel carefully examined, the box, looking at every marking. "It's like nothing I've ever seen before."

"That's what CACI says, too." Iza walked onto the flight deck, where Trix had gone to sit at her usual station.

Raquel followed, still admiring the box. "You've run an initial analysis on it, then?"

"Yes, it didn't reveal much," Iza said. "Jovani was able to get his hands on some classified information from a TSS informant. They claim the origins are with an alien race who had dealings with Tarans ages ago. Things didn't end well between them."

"I'm sure, if it had, we'd all know what this thing was and what it does."

Braedon looked up from his comic illustrating on his handheld. "That box is just a box. My father thinks there's a map inside."

"Really?" Raquel's eyebrows rose, and she shook the box and heard the satisfying *thunk* of the metal sphere inside. "I wonder if it's related to the gate mythology."

"What do you mean?" Iza asked.

"Well, there are stories, mostly legend, that say an alien race called the Gatekeepers traversed the universe using a gate technology."

Iza frowned. "If there's any truth to it, it sounds exactly like something a power-hungry Lower Dynasty ruler might want to get their hands on in order to elevate their standing in the Taran Empire."

Raquel nodded and smiled. "Exactly. If it's related to those gates in any way, it is a powerful thing that would be dangerous if it falls into ignorant hands," she added glancing at the box. "If only we could figure out how to open it, then we'd be able to study it. Once we learned what it does, we could use that power for good and also keep people like Arvonen from gaining too much control."

Iza stared at the box. In this case, it seemed the more she learned about the thing the better. Perhaps it was the alcohol talking, but she found herself wanting to open up. "Braedon said his father called it a map. The sphere inside has etchings on it. Do you think it will lead whoever has it to one of these gates?"

"Wait, what? You can unlock this box?" Raquel passed the box back to her and stared at it in Iza's hands. "There are rumors that this kind of technology might be genetically keyed. The only way to open it is if there are certain genetic markers present."

Iza shrugged. "I don't know. One day it was locked up tighter than an oxygen seal, and the next it popped open."

"That's remarkable!" Raquel shook her head. "Well, yes, it is most likely some kind of map leading to a gate. Whoever controls that gate would be able to decide who can and can't go through. Have you tried to navigate the map?"

"No, but I'm not sure it's that easy. Maybe you can decipher it," Iza rubbed her thumb along the edge and the lid opened.

Raquel jumped back with a gasp. Her hand flew to her throat as she stared at the metal sphere. She took a step closer and reached for it. She slowly turned it over in her hand, open-mouthed with awe at the sight of it. "Would you allow me to use the onboard computer system to run a few tests on the sphere myself? Nothing invasive, just to see if I'm right about its origins?"

"Yes, of course. I think of all the people on board, you're the only one qualified to tell us anything. The more we learn about the sphere, the better we can protect ourselves from whatever Arvonen has planned."

"Agreed. Whatever he wants to do with this thing, it's best you know now. I'm not going to lie, I think this might be well above my pay grade, but I'll do my best."

"Mine too," Iza said with a smile and they both laughed.

—

Three hours later, it surprised Iza to see they were in the middle of a jump when she went to meet Braedon on the flight deck. The green and blue shades of subspace swirled outside the viewports, tinting everything in cool light.

"Why aren't we there yet?" Iza asked.

Braedon looked confused. "It's a long way to go, but we'll be there by tomorrow afternoon, relax. And that's way faster than it would be without the upgraded jump drive, so I don't know why you're complaining."

"What do you mean? It should have taken three hours for a standard jump to Phiris from Hubyria."

"Uh, we're not headed to Phiris. The coordinates read that we're going to Tararia." Braedon brought up the flight path through the beacon network to show her. "Trix input the coordinates. I thought it was under your orders."

Iza's stomach dropped. "No, I would never head straight

for a central planet while we're being hunted." She turned to address the android. "Trix drop us out of subspace and input the coordinates for Phiris."

"I cannot do that," Trix said.

Iza looked at Braedon, who shrugged both shoulders and shook his head.

"What's going on with you?" Iza asked, placing a hand on her friend's shoulder. "Why did you change the destination coordinates?"

"You are in danger. You must learn the truth."

"Braedon?"

"Sorry, I can't lock her out or bypass her, she's integrated directly into the ship's systems. The destination is locked in. Wherever she's taking us, we can't stop it now."

Iza reached up and ran her fingers along the android's jaw. She always assumed Trix would outlive her, but what if this was AI degradation? There might be something irreparably wrong with her. She needed to get Trix back to Lynaeda. "We'll get help for you, my friend."

"I am functioning normally. I do not need any help. However, you are unhappy. Perhaps some time with Jovani would make you smile again."

"She's not wrong about that," Braedon mumbled.

"Enough about me. Trix why are we going to the new coordinates?"

Trix remained silent, looking straight ahead at the holodisplay.

So it's going to be like that. Iza crossed her arms, not sure what to do. At least Lynaeda was close to Tararia, though she didn't like the idea of remaining anywhere near the central planets.

"I can take a look at her operating matrix," Braedon

reached out to touch her, but Trix knocked his hand away. The unexpected force of it knocked him off-balance, and he fell to the deck.

The dog turned on Trix, barking angrily. Trix ignored him even when he tried to nip at her heels.

"Knock it off, you," Iza said with a snap of her fingers. "We're fine." The dog seemed to understand and took up a position behind Iza to wait.

"Speak for yourself," Braedon said, using his console to help himself up.

As much as Iza had wanted to believe that her friend was fine, Trix's handling of Braedon only confirmed that she was still acting erratically. When Trix had first started acting strange, the ship began malfunctioning soon after. Both Trix and the ship returned to normal at around the same time. It was looking like more than coincidence, and it didn't bode well for the ship if Trix was having issues again.

"Braedon, don't try to mess with Trix, but see if you can find a link between her and the problems we've had with the ship. Is that okay, Trix?"

The android didn't respond.

"Sure, I'll look into it," Braedon agreed.

"Disconnect Trix from the ship as soon as you're able to," Iza said. "You may as well bring Viper in on this, too."

"Viper?"

Iza nodded. "Yes, she's a coder, isn't she? We need all the help we can get."

"You don't understand," Braedon objected, "if I go to her and ask for help, she'll think I need her."

"What?" Iza waved a hand in the air as if she could erase away his drama. "I don't care about that, just do it."

"Fine, but I'm in charge."

"No, do not tell her that you're in charge, because you're not. The two of you are a team. If she comes to me saying otherwise, you'll have me to deal with, because *I'm* in charge."

"Yeah, I know," Braedon conceded with a huff. Then, he tiptoed over to whisper in Iza's ear. "Do you want me to continue monitoring ship's systems?"

"Ship systems are operating normally," Trix said in a normal voice.

There was no way to get around Trix's superb hearing, even if she was acting strange. "You've said the same thing about yourself," Iza told her friend. "Maybe when we arrive, you'll have more to say about what we're supposed to do there."

"We are going to Tararia. You need to learn about your past if you want to have a future," Trix said with a simplicity that made the hair on Iza's arms stand up.

"I have no reason to speak to my mother. I'm more concerned about you."

"She knows the truth, and the truth will protect you."

"From what?"

Trix's mouth clamped shut and she refused to say anymore.

This is getting creepy. Not bothering to whisper, Iza added to Braedon, "I want you to be on the lookout for any other abnormalities within the ship. Something is causing this, and I want answers by the time we arrive."

He frowned. "I don't know that I'll have it figured out by then, but I'll try. Just a heads up, the Enforcers at the border are going to have some questions for us, and I'm not sure I'll be able to get in there with codes while Trix is running the ship."

"I'll take care of that. Just keep an eye on my ship. If you manage to get manual control, you know what to do."

Braedon gave her a salute. "You've got it, Iz."

—

After her strange conversation with Trix, Iza wasn't sure what to do next. For whatever reason, Trix was bringing them to Tararia. The coordinates Trix input into the navigation directed them toward the Sixth Region in the southern hemisphere, near to the market that Iza had seen on the video of her mother and in her reoccurring dreams.

The only other mystery on board was the sphere, and she'd handed that off to Raquel. The archaeologist had been analyzing the artifact for hours. She must have some answers by now.

Iza made her way to the infirmary, where Raquel had set up a makeshift lab. Cierra seemed less than happy to have visitors, as most of her candles and other items sat pushed to one side to make room for the sphere and Raquel's equipment.

"How's your analysis coming along?" Iza asked as she entered. The dog bounded ahead of her, sniffing every corner of the room.

"Gross, don't bring your dog in here. It's unsanitary and disgusting," Cierra said with disdain.

"My ship, my rules. Besides, he's all natural; I figured you'd love that." Iza lifted one shoulder in a half-shrug.

Cierra was on one side of the room rearranging her things while Raquel was scanning the sphere and looking at more readouts. Iza hadn't formally thanked Cierra for telling her what she'd discovered hiding in Karter's mind. They'd gone on as if nothing had happened, mostly because Iza wasn't sure how to deal with the information. Jovani was a TSS Agent, but was he a traitor to her and the crew?

"This thing is amazing. The archaeological find of a lifetime." Raquel's voice pulled Iza out of her thoughts and back to the moment. "The research this will open up for Tarans in the fields of astronomy, metaphysics, astrophysics, and the like will be phenomenal."

"Glad to see someone's happy about the thing," Iza said. "Cierra, everyone is healthy. You don't need to stay in the infirmary all the time."

"I'm aware," Cierra said. "I'm here because I needed to grab a candle and saw that this person has taken up residence here in the infirmary with her analytical devices. If someone should need help, this would be the last place I would go. I'll go set up in my own quarters."

"That won't be necessary," Raquel said. "I'm finishing up here. All I have left to do is review the analysis. I can do that in my cabin. You can have this back." She handed the sphere to Iza.

Iza reached out and accepted the metal ball. Its heavy but the familiar warmth seemed to settle in her hand and the sound of humming returned.

"What's that expression on your face?" Raquel asked. "Are you nervous about having it back? You shouldn't be, it's not going to open up a wall on your ship or anything."

Iza shook her head. "No, that's not what worries me. It's humming again. I guess I keep hoping someone else can hear besides me."

Cierra put down her candle and stepped closer resting a hand on Iza's shoulder. Then she closed her eyes and seemed to be listening. Raquel stepped forward at the same time and left her hand hovering above the sphere while Iza held it.

"I can't hear it but I feel it." Cierra kept her eyes closed as if searching deeper.

Iza squirmed, uncomfortable not only with her touch but with her scanning her mind, or whatever she was doing. She started to back away, but Cierra held fast. Raquel also seemed to be listening to something. Was she telepathic?

"What is it?" Iza asked, looking at Raquel.

"Nothing." Cierra opened her eyes. "I just assumed if I could pick up on the humming, maybe I would sense something more. But I get nothing from you. Not from the first time we ever met. Strange, there are some who manifested that ability as a side effect from the neurotoxin deployed during the Priesthood's fall, but yours seems to be different."

"Yes," Raquel agreed, "It's less like a block, more fluid. As if the thoughts are too deep."

Iza didn't like the sound of that either. "I could ask my mother about it."

"Your mother? I'm sorry, isn't she supposed to be dead?" Cierra asked.

"Yeah, she Left, but may actually be alive."

"She abandoned you to die and then chose to live on without you?" Raquel gasped at Iza's nod.

Cierra reached her arms around Iza to hug her. Iza was already uncomfortable with Cierra in her space. What more did she want?

She pulled out of her embrace. "Yes, she was last seen on Tararia. It turns out that Trix is insistent that I find her. That she holds some answer to a question I didn't ask."

"You have to meet her," Cierra said.

"Absolutely," Raquel agreed.

"Why? She was never there for me. I practically raised myself. If she wanted to be a part of my life, she had her chance. What reason could she possibly give for abandoning me?"

"Mothers can be very mysterious," Raquel said. It was almost as if she was speaking from experience. "That doesn't mean she doesn't have a reason. You say Trix has been with you for a long time?"

"Yes, but I met her after my mother Left. She doesn't even know her," Iza said, trying to make sense of all the non-sense Trix had poured on her.

"That is strange, but you trust her?"

"Normally, yes, with my life."

"Then you have to seek out your mother. Perhaps your friend is serving as a guide for you," Cierra said.

"I don't know, she's part of my past. I'm looking to my future."

This time Raquel put a hand on her arm, and suddenly Iza felt the tension in her shoulders release.

"You cannot conquer the future without learning from the past," Raquel said.

"Where did you get that, an advertisement?"

"No, I'm an archaeologist; it's printed on all the T-shirts." She laughed, making Iza smile.

"You're both so immature." Cierra shook her head and left the infirmary.

They both watched her leave before Raquel turned to Iza and spoke in a low voice.

"What's with the bare feet?"

"I know, right?" Iza agreed, nodding. "She's like all of eighteen and she thinks she knows everything."

"She seems to know a lot about healing the body."

Iza nodded. "Yes, she does. She saved Jovani's life, and for that I'll always be grateful, so I'm stuck with her bare feet and green sludge."

They both laughed. As Iza left the infirmary with the

sphere in her hand, she came to a realization about Raquel. She wouldn't have minded growing up with a sister like her.

19

IZA HAD ANOTHER night of strange dreams.

This time, she saw her mother again, but not in the market as she had before. She was at home, in a small cottage with a warm fireplace carrying something in her arms. With a baby. The baby looked a lot like her, but—she didn't know how she knew—it wasn't her. Her mother was speaking, though Iza couldn't make out the words. Her mother looked down at the small smiling bundle in her arms and seemed to be rocking the baby to sleep.

Suddenly, the dream shifted, as though the image flipped in a mirror. The woman holding the baby was no longer her mother, but herself. And the child in her arms was her own. Iza felt a swell of joy at the sight of her child. In her mind, it didn't matter if he was a boy or girl, they were perfect.

Then, almost as if she'd heard something, she jolted. She felt it inside—something that made her afraid. She looked down at her child and knew she would do whatever it took to protect them. She didn't know who the father was, or what danger she feared. The only certainty was that she would protect her child with everything she had.

Before whoever was on the other side of the door came through, Iza morphed and became something else. Something she'd never seen before. It was like she had no physical substance, but she could be a barrier between whatever was at the door and her child.

Iza woke with a start in a cold sweat.

The sphere was back in her drawer where she kept it. The dreams were as they had been, disjointed pieces of something that felt real but had no basis in reality. She'd never had the desire to have a child before and didn't particularly in the cold light of day think she would want one now. Still, the dream had felt so real, she was left feeling a sense of emptiness at its absence.

Iza dressed for the day and to the flight deck, where she found Braedon and Viper working on the ship's navigation problem. Trix was standing in the middle of the room and didn't seem at all bothered by what they were attempting to do.

Iza greeted her friend first. "Good morning."

"Good morning, Captain."

Iza tilted her head to one side. Well, at least Trix was talking, that was something.

Braedon and Viper were bickering about something unrelated to the ship's navigation while they worked.

"You can't be serious," Braedon was saying. "There's no way, that a mech made of metal could be defeated by what is essentially a giant cat."

"The claws on this thing, you should have seen it. If they were in a ring together, my credits would be on the giant cat," Viper insisted.

How they managed to argue and work on the coding simultaneously amazed Iza.

"Where are we on all this?" Iza asked.

"I think we're making progress. We've identified multiple threads of a virus in our systems, and we're attempting a purge now," he said. "There, focus in on that." Braedon watched over Viper's shoulder while her hands flew over the console.

"Do we have any idea where it came from?" Iza asked.

"No, it's like nothing I've ever seen before," Viper said, still tapping.

"It's strange. The way it's infiltrated the computer system doesn't follow the patterns we'd expect to see. It's learning and adapting, which any good virus should, but it's behaving almost like it hasn't seen a ship operating platform like ours before—which is ridiculous, since everything here is pretty standard."

Iza crossed her arms. "So, it's a dumb virus?"

"No, it's *really* good. We're having a tough time eradicating it because our standard hacking techniques aren't working. So, either the person who programmed it is a crazy genius who found a way to disregard all normal logic, or..." His voice trailed off.

"It could be alien." Viper turned her head to face Iza then stood up and switched places with Braedon.

Iza's heart skipped a beat. "Could this have something to do with the sphere?"

Braedon shrugged. "There's nothing else that we've come into contact with lately that can explain how it got into the ship's systems and Trix. Not to mention that both the ship and Trix started behaving normally as soon as you left with the artifact."

That was all Iza needed to hear to confirm her suspicions. Even so, she had no idea what to do. Trix's AI matrix was among the most sophisticated Taran tech in existence, and the virus had influenced her behavior without her even knowing. Still, Braedon and Viper could see the virus and monitor its behavior, so there was hope that there was a solution to stop it.

"Maybe the Lynaedans can help us," Iza suggested. "Once we get to Tararia, Trix might let us set a new course to go there."

"It won't matter if she or the virus seize control again and take us out into the middle of nowhere, like apparently happened before," Viper said. "At this point, all we can do is create temporary blocks around certain systems, but the virus will eventually worm its way through."

Iza didn't like the implications of that statement. "Is this problem permanent?"

"Honestly, I think because the sphere is on board," Braedon said. "My guess is that it's going to continue to affect Trix and the ship regardless of what we do. The most straightforward solution is to get the sphere off of the ship."

Where could I keep the sphere so Mr. Arvonen can't reach it? Iza couldn't think of a place safe from the man.

"Come to think of it, we had some problems back on the *Iron Dog*, too," Viper revealed. "At the time, I didn't understand the code and what I was seeing. But, this foreign code, or alien virus, or whatever it is, was too similar to this to be coincidence."

"Iza, are you here?" Trix asked suddenly. Her eyes were unfocused.

"Yes, I'm right here." Iza ran over and took her friend's hand. Trix responded with a light squeeze.

"My people cannot fix this," Trix said. "What is happening to me now has happened to me before."

"Wait, have you been around a sphere like this before?" Braedon asked.

"No, not a sphere. Iza, your father."

Iza's breath caught in her throat. "My father? What do you mean, Trix?"

"I'm not supposed to tell you. I was never supposed to tell you. I made a promise, a solemn promise. It is dangerous for me to tell you too much. You will have to leave us, but you won't be alone." The desperation in her voice was real. Iza had never heard Trix speak this way before, so overcome with emotion.

Iza looked at Braedon and back to Trix again. She wasn't sure how to proceed. If Trix's own people couldn't fix her, they were in trouble.

Braedon sighed, sounding defeated. "We're doing the best we can, Iz, but until the sphere is permanently off the ship, this virus is going to keep popping up. And, based on what we've seen, the longer it's around, the worse the problems are going to get." He kept typing as he spoke, working as fast as he could.

Iza turned back to Trix. "Do you know about my mother?"

Trix's head tilted to one side. "I do not understand."

"My mother. She's alive," Iza said. "Karter found video of my mother. He believes—I think—that she might be alive. She was last seen on Tararia. Is that why you're taking the ship there?"

Trix seemed to be processing the information with a frown on her face. Then, she shook her head. "No, your mother is dead."

"That's impossible. The woman in the video that Karter showed me is my mother. She looks just like her."

Trix again tilted her head to one side. "No, your mother is not alive. Your father, he is dangerous."

What is she talking about? Her father was dead. It was her mother who was alive. Maybe the virus was taking hold again. "Then why are we going to Tararia?" Iza pressed.

"I will take you where you need to go. You can count on me."

Iza wished she could believe Trix, but she couldn't tell if the virus was taking or her friend. She turned to Braedon again. "Is the ship's memory compromised by the virus?"

"*Everything* is compromised," Viper replied without looking up.

"What's the current status of the ship? Do you have any control of the virus?"

"We're putting up temporary blocks around the core systems, and we're almost finished," Braedon said. "But, and I can't emphasize this enough, it is *temporary*. By the time we reach Tararia, though, I hope to have an idea of how much time it takes for the virus to reenter the systems."

"How long until we arrive?" Iza asked.

"Two hours, ten minutes, and four seconds," Trix answered.

At least Trix wasn't so far gone that she'd activated the independent jump drive, which could have brought even more unwanted attention to their ship. Iza would take whatever small victories she could. "Thanks, Trix. We're going to help you, don't worry, my friend."

"Once we've got the virus contained, we'll either need to get rid of the sphere or get to where we're going fast," Braedon as he switched places with Viper again. He rubbed his hands, and Iza realized they must hurt from all the work they were doing.

"You two going to be okay with this?" Iza asked him.

Braedon shrugged and smiled, "Sure, we've got this." His voice lowered and he added, "The kid is amazing, but don't tell her I said so."

Iza smiled. Viper was a welcome addition to the crew. Her skills, combined with Braedon's, made them a notch above the rest. She was happy to see the two getting along. If only Viper's sister would come around to accepting her.

— — —

>> Agent Anderson, why haven't you broken cover and returned? If something has happened to you and the independent jump drive has fallen into criminal hands, we'll be forced to take action. - Ian <<

It was the fourth message Joe had received from Agent Mandren, and each time it came with the warning that if he did nothing they would take things into their own hands.

One thing had become clear to Joe: he was more concerned with Iza than he was with his undercover mission for the TSS. He hadn't known for sure until he'd handed the ancient artifact over to Iza. It was a direct violation of his orders, and it hadn't phased him. He knew it would mean the end of his TSS career, but he didn't care. As long as he had Iza, any future would be bright.

The issue remained, she still didn't know the truth about him. They couldn't be open with each other until then. But the window had passed—saying the words now might just reinforcing her distrust of him instead of bringing them closer together.

I can't tell her. I need to show *her.* Actions would be the only way to assure her that it had been necessary to conceal his identity and that he would never betray her trust again. He wasn't sure how to go about that, only that he must.

I can't lose her. I'll do anything to keep her safe. He'd never expected to give up everything in his life for someone else. For Iza, though, he wouldn't hesitate. He'd find a way for them to be together. As long as they had each other, nothing else would matter.

— — —

When they arrived at Tararia, Trix relinquished control of the ship at last, allowing Braedon to deal with the final threads of the virus.

With the ship back under their command, they furnished their access codes to one of the planet's many spaceports. It was of the few times having two dynastic heirs on board paid off, negotiating better berthing than Iza would ever have been able to secure on her own credit. Karter had established his value back on Hubyria, but each time he helped them, it gave Iza a chance to see him in a new light.

"We should scout things out," Braedon suggested. "Start out by going down and do a little shopping, bring back some food, in case the Enforcers are tracking our movements."

His uncharacteristic volunteering to get food stuffs allowed Iza to see right through his ruse. "No, it's best that while the ship is malfunctioning, you remain on board. Especially since there may still be a warrant out for your arrest from Kinterin."

The day she'd met Braedon and she mistook him for a criminal holding up a tourist, they'd accused him of stealing nine thousand credits. They'd barely made it off the planet with the Enforcers out to arrest him. It had been about two months since then, but that was hardly long enough for it to be safe to let his guard down.

"Jovani, Viper, and Raquel will also remain on board, so you won't be alone," Iza continued. "Besides don't you have a project to finish?" she asked, trying to keep her tone light. The fewer people with her the better.

Braedon squared his broadening shoulders and nodded.

Iza smiled.

"I should go with you," Jovani said in protest.

Iza figured he might want to meet her mother, but she

didn't have high hopes for their future with his lie still sitting between them. Besides, she didn't want him there when things would inevitably go poorly. She shook her head. "No, I need you on the *Verity* in case Mr. Arvonen tracks us back here or the Enforcers come calling. I'd really appreciate it if someone would let the dog off the ship for a bit. He needs a good run."

"I'll see to it," Jovani agreed. The hurt was written on his face, but Iza appreciated that he didn't push the issue.

"Really, the only one who needs to come is Trix," Iza stated.

Karter had a smug smile plastered on his face. "I'm not giving up the chance to meet the mother of my fiancée. I led you here, I'd like to see it through. If this is some kind of ruse, you may need me," he said.

Now I remember why I don't like him. Of course, she couldn't deny their engagement in front of everyone, and that's why he'd done it. Even so, she didn't want him along.

Iza placed her hands on her hips. "This isn't going to be an engagement announcement. I have some things to say and she's going to listen."

"Your presence at this time would be a hinderance," Trix added.

"I insist." Karter gave Iza a warning look.

He had the power to make her life miserable and they both knew it. Iza conceded with a nod of her head.

She had enough to worry about, but if she ran into trouble, him being there might save her. On the flip side, the whole setup of her long-lost mother might be an elaborate trap, though Iza couldn't imagine why anyone would go to so much trouble. *Why would anyone want me? I'm no one.*

With the assignments made, Iza went to the cargo hold with Karter and Trix.

Cierra was waiting for them, wearing a sunny yellow shift with a sheer overlay. She had an empty satchel slung over one shoulder and her big hair was pulled back into a short, bushy ponytail. "You better give me ample time at the market. I need to replace all of the fresh goods after the malfunctioning refrigerator ruined so much of our stock."

"You should have plenty of time," Iza assured her as she climbed aboard the shuttle. She wasn't thrilled about Cierra coming along on such a personal excursion, but the shopping trip was a good cover for their visit—and Cierra wouldn't attract attention in the way Braedon would.

Trix piloted the shuttle to the surface. Tararia, the seat of the Taran government and home to the High Dynasties, had a beauty all its own. Unlike many of the heavily populated central worlds, the capital planet had intentionally limited development so there were still pristine natural areas outside the gleaming cities. The world illustrated a perfect balance between societal development and reverence for nature in a way few other places had been able to replicate. Much of that no doubt had to do with the immense wealth concentrated on the world; it was easy to make a planet into a paradise when one had the means to ship anything unseemly off-world and make it someone else's problem.

As soon as they passed through border patrol at the planetary shield, Trix directed the craft to Agnion, a town in the vicinity of Bael, capital of the less populated Sixth Region. The small continent in the southern hemisphere had large expanses of agricultural area, which furnished the fibers for the finest textiles produced by the ruling Baellas Dynasty's corporation. Consequently, much of the industry in the Sixth Region was centered around fashion and home goods, with expansive markets selling those wares—and cheap off-world imitations.

They set the shuttle down in the landing zone for the market where Iza's mother had been spotted in the video. When Iza exited the shuttle, she could see the tops of the buildings in the town center. She'd been to Tararia on business dozens of times; it was surreal to think she'd potentially been so close to her mother.

"Now what?" Iza asked Trix, crossing her arms over her chest.

"Follow me." Trix exited the shuttle.

Cierra ignored Trix, quick to make her own way to the market. Without a handheld, she'd learned to complete her business quickly in case they needed to leave in a hurry.

Iza and Karter followed Trix from the outskirts of the town toward the market. Just like the video, the outdoor bazaar was full of life and offered an array of textiles, produce, and other goods for sale, with each stall tended by a shopkeeper determined to find the right price. The smells of baked goods wafted in the air where they stood, and Iza hoped rather than believed Cierra would procure some.

"Doesn't that smell amazing?" Karter asked with his nose in the air.

Iza had her head down, as was her custom in large crowds, and caught sight of a young grifter making his way through the crowd.

She didn't say anything as the young boy made his approach but slapped at his hands when they went toward Karter's pocket. It was only then Karter noticed the pickpocket. He started to say something, but Iza waved a finger in his face.

"He's harmless, let him go. He didn't get anything," she said.

Karter didn't like it, but the incident was quickly forgotten when something caught his attention.

Iza followed his line of sight and recognized the young man from her dream. He'd dressed in dark green pants and a brown vest over a cream-colored T-shirt. His long, curly hair was pulled back in a band at the base of his neck and braided the rest of the way to the end. She was sure she'd never met him before, but when his eyes met hers a bolt of energy passed between them. His eyes widened in surprise before he disappeared into the crowd.

"Do you know him?" Karter asked.

"Yes and no. I think he's following me. I've seen him before, but I'm not sure I believe it."

"What do you mean?"

She decided against telling him that she'd dreamed about the young man.

"He was on Hubyria poking around before Yeaga grabbed me."

Karter stopped and stared at her. "Really?"

"I doubt it's a coincidence, but I don't really have time to worry about him. Let's find what we're here for and go."

Trix stopped suddenly and Iza almost ran into her back. She was staring at a small house beyond the marketplace in a row of similar homes in varying colors of blue.

"That's the one," Iza said. She'd reviewed the video at least a half a dozen times. The small house had two small green bushes out front that bore small white flowers, their fragrance not strong enough to overpower the market.

The woman she'd seen in the video had been carrying a small shopping basket, which indicated she might pass this way regularly. Still, they could be waiting for quite some time.

"Trix, what's the plan here?" Iza asked.

"She will be here soon. It is market day," the android replied. "Then you will see."

Iza checked her handheld and saw that it was indeed the same time of day as when the video was taken. Perhaps Trix had surmised a pattern to her activities based on information Iza didn't have.

For ten minutes, Iza scanned the crowd. It brought her back to the old days when she used to wait around looking for marks, trying to act casual.

Iza was just starting to get antsy when she spotted the woman the spitting image of her mother, with the same long, curly black hair. Almost every feature was just like Iza remembered; the biggest difference being the carefree smile on her face. Like in the video, the woman strolled through the market, waving and speaking to those she recognized as she passed.

Her mother passed within a meter of Iza but didn't take notice of her. *How is that possible? Wouldn't a woman know her own child no matter their age?* Iza found herself tense and turned toward her mother like she was a beacon of light.

Karter put a hand on Iza's shoulder to edge her forward when her feet refused to move. She shrugged him off and fell into step behind Trix, who followed Iza's mother without a word.

Her mother didn't seem to realize she was being trailed by Iza or her two companions as she strolled along the side streets. The small community that surrounded the marketplace was easily accessible. Each of the row-homes had a miniature garden of its own out front, enclosed by a small, gated fence.

The older woman's movements were relaxed and even as she entered into a small yard two blocks from the market, picked a flower from the garden, and walked inside. The home was modest and well-kept, with simple landscaping. Nothing about the place stood out to Iza.

"Go, learn what you must, to protect yourself from what is coming," Trix said, keeping her eyes on the door.

Trix had said something similar when she was malfunctioning before. With her eyes clear now, it seemed more of a warning. Iza wanted to turn around and run, not because she was afraid of the ominous future of which Trix spoke but because she didn't want to revisit the past. Suddenly knowing the truth seemed far worse than the lie. It was too late. She needed to know why her mother left her and came to Tararia to start a new life.

Karter and Trix waited on the small walkway leading up to the house while Iza forced herself to approach the door. She knocked twice. No matter what happened next, it wouldn't end well.

"GOOD AFTERNOON, CAN I help you?" the woman asked when she opened the door, still carrying a shopping basket in her arms.

The world around Iza faded to nothing. The sounds of the market and the birds in the nearby trees couldn't get through the buzzing in her ears. Iza gaped at her mother, waiting for some sign of recognition. Whatever Trix wanted from this reunion, it seemed they'd have to start with introductions first of all.

"My name is Iza Sundari." she waited a moment for the woman to recognize the name. It was obvious she had.

Her mouth dropped open, and she stared. "Oh my, I never thought I'd see you."

"Well, I hate to surprise you, Mother, but here I am."

The woman's face changed, her brow furrowing in confusion as she stared at her. "Mother? Oh." It seemed the realization that her daughter was standing in front of her had dawned on her all at once.

"Yes, it's been twelve years, but I thought you might still

recognize me. I haven't changed all that much. You haven't," Iza said.

"We have much to discuss. Please, come in. Your friends are welcome to step inside, as well," she said with a nod over Iza's shoulder to where Trix and Karter stood.

"No, that won't be necessary. They already know all they need to."

Iza followed her mother inside and noted the interior with some shock. There was nothing inside resembling the woman she had been. Her decorating style had changed from a hoarder of sentimental junk to an absolute minimalist. Iza had played as a child among tons of what her mother called 'collectables' that covered almost every surface of their home. It was akin to living in a small shop, where nothing was for sale. This home was different. It was obvious by the care she took to place each item that they had meaning, but none of it was connected to the life Iza had known as a child—no trace of herself or her father. It only drove home the point that her mother had moved on with her life and Iza needed to do the same.

The older woman evaluated Iza. "I can understand your confusion. It's been many years, but I should be clear with you now, I'm not who you think I am."

"You're right," Iza said. "Why don't we start from twelve years ago when you walked out the door and end around the time you got here." She kept the emotion off of her face but not out of her voice, which quivered with unshed tears. Iza clenched her teeth, adding as much bite as she could to the words as she spat them out.

"Oh, this is so awkward. She was so headstrong, and stubborn. I wish you had known about me before. If I had known, we wouldn't be meeting this way," she said, shaking her head. "I'm not your mother."

She waited a beat for Iza to register the words. 'Not your mother.' They rang back and forth between her ears.

"I'm her twin sister, Reagan Sundari."

The room shifted, and Iza felt herself sway. The woman who claimed to be her aunt moved fast, sliding a chair beneath Iza before she crashed to the floor. Iza sat down hard on the wooden surface, grateful for the support.

"What do you mean?" Iza asked. "My mother never had a sister."

"I believe my face speaks for itself. We are—were—identical twins. We grew up together, fighting, making up, and fighting again. To be honest, we always had a very tumultuous relationship right to the end. However, when we met the brothers, we..." Her voice trailed off.

"What brothers?"

Reagan took a seat on the edge of a couch across from Iza. "Are you saying your mother didn't tell you about your father?"

"No, she'd been too busy mourning his death and planning her own."

"How old were you when she died?"

"Ten, and she didn't die, she Left. She had a choice, and she chose death like a coward."

Reagan's lips tightened in a straight line. Something her mother did when she couldn't decide what to say next. Iza didn't want to look at her aunt anymore. There were too many similarities between them, too many differences.

"You must remember your father, then, if you were ten years old."

"No, she didn't tell me anything. Only that he died when I was younger. She removed every image of him from our house after his death. I remember her struggling to get out of bed sometimes and not a day went by when she wasn't crying. Then, one day, she wasn't there at all."

"Oh, dear, I'm so sorry."

"My question to you is, where were you?" The tears burned behind Iza's eyes now as she spoke.

"Of the two of us, your mother loved hard and almost never forgave."

"Don't tell me about my mother. All those years, when I didn't have anyone, why didn't you come for me?"

Her aunt stood up and paced the room.

Iza's eyes fell on a picture of her aunt standing with a young boy with similar features. His eyes stared out at her from within the frame. A crackle of recognition filling her thoughts. *The guy I keep seeing... he's my cousin.*

Reagan was still pacing. "I didn't know about you. Not exactly. I reached out to your mother when I got pregnant. Considering our unique situation, I realized she might be pregnant, too, and that we might need to talk about it. But she never answered me, I assumed she was still angry." She looked at Iza, the desperation in her eyes. "We didn't part on the best of terms."

Nothing her aunt said made any sense. It was as if her mother had died all over again. She'd gone without telling her daughter about her aunt or any of her people.

For what purpose did Trix bring her here? Had it only been to steer her from the idea that her mother might be alive? Iza stood up on shaky legs and moved to the door.

"Where are you going? We need to talk." Reagan followed Iza to the door.

"You claim to know your sister and what kind of woman she was, so you should have known. You could have searched me out. But you didn't. Instead, I grew up on the streets of backward colony worlds where no one had more concern for me than an abandoned shoe. There's really nothing more to say." Iza opened the door and walking out.

Reagan raced to the door calling out from behind her. "Wait!"

Iza wasn't willing to wait any longer. She'd been waiting her whole life for someone to save her from the mess her mother had left her in. Now, to discover she had an aunt the whole time—an identical twin to her mother—was a cruel twist of fate. Whatever happened to them, Reagan hadn't tried to track down her sister whom she'd know might be in trouble. It wouldn't have taken any digging at all to find Iza from there. Iza didn't want to, and wouldn't, make time for a woman who'd so easily walked away from her family. Iza needed to deal with more important and pressing matters.

Iza stomped toward the shuttle while Trix and Karter raced to follow her. No one said a word.

Once on the shuttle, they sat in thick silence for twenty minutes while they waited for Cierra. A couple of times, Karter looked like he wanted to ask about the conversation, but he wisely thought better of it. Annoyingly, Trix didn't volunteer any explanation for why she'd felt the need to rip open Iza's wounds from her youth.

Voices sounded outside as Cierra thanked two young men she had enlisted to help her carry the crates of food back to the shuttle.

When the provisions were secured, she sat down in the seat behind Iza. "Are we headed back to the *Verity* now?" she asked.

"Yes." Iza started up the shuttle.

Her tone must have made it clear she wasn't ready to talk, because Karter quickly seized the opportunity to find a new topic for discussion. "Did you find what you were looking for?"

he asked Cierra.

"I did, I got lots to hold us over until our next planetside visit." Cierra, however, chose to ignore Iza's less than subtle hint. "What about you, Iza? Did you find your mother?"

Her stomach knotted. "She's not my mother. She's my aunt."

"Oh." Cierra looked at the others, not sure where to rest her concerned expression.

"Don't ask," Karter advised in a low whisper.

Trix reached over and put a gentle hand on Iza's shoulder. "Families can be difficult. However, you have a home and you have surrounded yourself with people who care about you. Do not concern yourself anymore with the past."

Wise words from an android. Her timing was terrible, but that might be due to the virus.

Still, Iza's emotions were too raw. She hadn't yet had the time to deal with the pain the way she always did, by pushing it down and ignoring it. Until she'd done that, the others ventured near her at their own risk.

"I hope you got what you wanted," Iza grumbled to Trix.

The android turned her head to look at Iza but didn't respond.

"Once we get back to the ship, I have some business to see to," Karter said. "How long can we stay docked at the spaceport?"

"With the berthing fees they charge?" Iza scoffed. "I'll give you an hour. Plus, if Mr. Arvonen has a presence on this planet—and he probably does—it won't take them long to find us. We should be on our way as soon as possible."

As soon as they docked in the *Verity*'s cargo hold, Cierra launch into an explanation of the goods she'd bought while the others filed off the shuttle. Iza hung back. She told herself the reason wasn't because she was avoiding them.

After giving the others a head start, she disembarked the shuttle only to find Jovani and the dog waiting for her. The pain in her chest eased at the sight of them.

The dog bounded up to her, and she reached down to scratch his head, avoiding Jovani's concerned expression.

"It didn't go well," he stated.

"Don't ask."

"You don't have to talk about it if you don't want to. I'm just—I wanted to be here for you," Jovani said. He reached out a hand to touch her shoulder, but she turned away from him.

"I'll be in my cabin. When Karter finishes his business, we'll be leaving the system."

"Are you upset with me?" Jovani asked.

Iza stopped but didn't turn around. He was a TSS Agent on some kind of mission that he hadn't told her anything about. How hypocritical for him to stand there and act like she was the one being unreasonable. There was a fight coming, but at the moment she didn't have the energy in her to hash it out with him.

"I'm tired and I want to be left alone," Iza said. The dog pranced along beside her as Jovani's eyes bored a hole in her back. She plodded to her cabin without another word.

—

When an hour had elapsed and they were still docked at the Tararian spaceport, Iza wanted to be anywhere else. She stewed for another ten minutes before calling up to the flight deck. "What's going on, why haven't we departed? Isn't Karter back yet?"

"No, he's not," Trix replied.

Iza swore as she prepared to drop the ship on Karter's head.

"Not that it would matter," Trix continued, "since we're not going anywhere."

Iza pinched the bridge of her nose. "Is there something wrong with the ship again?"

"The same problem we've been having," Braedon chimed in. "Like I warned you, we were able to temporarily wall off the virus, but it's found a way through again."

"So Trix is still at risk, too."

Braedon sighed. "Yeah, I wish I had better news for you, Iz. Since the two are linked most of the time, the virus could easily pass from the ship to her and back again. But here's the thing—I severed those connections while you were gone, so Trix shouldn't have had anymore contact with the ship's systems. Except, the virus in Trix and the virus in the ship are behaving like they are still linked. I've checked, and it's not using the *Verity*'s built-in interface; that connection is cold, like it should be. So there's some other kind of communication going on that our tech can't detect. Until we understand what's going on, I suggest we stay put."

"I understand the issue, but it's not realistic to stay here," Iza said.

"You're asking if we can risk a jump. To be honest, we'd be taking a huge risk. If we lose something like propulsion or nav control again, we could end up stranded in the middle of an asteroid field."

Iza ran two hands over her face. This was the last thing she wanted to deal with now. "Can you fix it?"

"Like I said before, getting rid of the sphere is the easiest solution. But I also get why we can't do that. Viper and I are still trying to figure out a solution. I'll let you know."

"Until then, we're stuck here?"

"For now, yes." He dropped his voice. "But between you and me, Viper is almost as good as I am. We might have a more permanent work around before you know it."

"Tell me as soon as you have something, not a minute later."

"You've got it. Hey Iz," Braedon began, "take it from someone who knows; family is a real mixed bag. You might be related to them, but you don't have to be like them."

Iza disconnected the comm link.

She climbed back into bed, where the dog curled up next to her. He tilted his head back and gazed up at her expectantly, but she still wasn't ready to deal with him. Instead, she thought about what Braedon had said.

A knock at her door pulled her out of her thoughts. The dog bounded to the door to greet whoever disturbed her peace. Iza took a deep breath and answered it, prepared for the hurt look in Jovani's eyes.

Instead, she found Raquel's smiling face. She held up a bottle and two glasses. "You look like you need this." She eased herself inside.

Raquel didn't bother with the chair or the small table. Instead, she slipped off her shoes and climbed onto Iza's bed, using the wall to prop herself up. She poured two glasses of the pale pink concoction and held one out to Iza.

Iza climbed up beside her, not bothering to undo her boots, and took the glass. *When is the woman not drinking?*

Balancing the bottle between her knees, Raquel took a drink. "I never told you how I got into archaeology," she began. "It's an interesting story, because I come from a family of inventors and opportunists. My parents consider themselves forward-thinking people."

Raquel gulped down some of her drink and smiled. "They thought I was out of my mind to be digging in the dirt, looking for ancient artifacts left behind by civilizations long dead. They didn't take it seriously until I made my first major discovery." Raquel paused, as if reliving the story instead of telling it.

"What did you find?" Iza asked.

"I was out on a dig in the desert fields of Phiris. If you've been there, it's miserable heat during the day. I mean, three showers a day became the norm. I was out there by myself one evening when the others had gone off to bed and I found a stash—that's what we call a small treasure of items buried together. The black box had several antique pieces, but the most important thing I found inside was an old subspace comm relay, the sort you'd use if you want to keep your messages off the grid. It had an external data backup drive with it. I brought it to my brother, who's into electronics. I helped him clean it up, and we used old specs and rebuilt the thing. It was the most time he and I ever spent together. Then we turned it on for the first time."

"What was on it?"

"Most of the data on the drive was encrypted by a cypher we'd never be able to crack, but we were able to pull a few files. The data linked to a file server with access codes to something much bigger. Though the communicator's original owner was long gone, one of his beneficiaries had left their entire inheritance under encrypted code. As a result, all of that wealth was subsequently lost to the family. It turns out, that fortune belonged to old Wohali Terrades."

"Of Terrades Transports?"

"The fastest hovercraft on the market until a few years ago. The very one. The files led us to his inheritance, which had been under constant debate since his death and the plans he'd written for future transports."

"What happened to it all?" Iza asked as Raquel refilled their glasses.

"Funny thing, when the old man died, his kids went berserk about all the funds and they got tied up in the judicial system. Turns out he'd left them all a huge amount of money that he'd hidden away on Beurias, where he'd planned to make the Hyttinen's an offer."

"Is that how you two know each other?"

Raquel nodded. "When we discovered the plans had been meant for Karter's father, we figured he might want to see them."

"Of course, he did. I'm sure he didn't mind putting those plans to good use, either."

Raquel raised her glass and laughed. The dog took their combined giggle as a party he was missing and hopped on the bed at her feet. When they both calmed down, he curled himself up into a ball, resting his head on his paws.

"So the two of you never?" Iza asked as she and Raquel shifted to face each other.

"Oh, Karter. He's such a quandary, isn't he? No, the two of us never pursued anything. I considered the possibility, to be honest, but he already had someone in his life." She raised her eyebrows at Iza.

"I wouldn't stand in your way if you wanted him." Iza finished her drink. She hoped her hint at the possibility was enough.

"I didn't mean you," Raquel said, downing hers too.

Iza perked up, put her glass down, and sat up. "What do you mean? There's someone else?"

"I can't believe you haven't noticed. You are in trouble, aren't you?"

"Tell me. Who is she?"

"His assistant."

"Becca?"

"The very one."

Iza considered it. "I thought the only thing between them was efficiency and respect."

"Sometimes that's enough. Sort of like you and that brooding little ex-Agent you've got following you around."

"Jovani and I are complicated." Iza looked away to hide the flush in her face.

"Not too complicated." Raquel raised her eyebrows. "He's loyal to you and respects your leadership. He's a lot like Becca, in his own way. Efficient too, I'm sure in more ways than one."

Iza laughed giving Raquel a friendly shove.

"No, he and I have something," Iza searched for the word, "more. But it's nothing I can pursue as I'm already engaged."

Raquel made a sound in the back of her throat that said she had her doubts. "Regardless, I'm not so interested in Karter that I'm willing to fight for him. Becca is patient and the woman that Karter will eventually see, if he doesn't already."

"Why didn't he ask her to marry him, then?"

"No doubt he had his reasons for asking you, but that aside, marriage for a Lower Dynasty heir isn't the thing you can just jump into without connections. His family was no doubt surprised he chose you over the many eligible women in his class, but I suspect his reasons are more political than emotional."

Iza wasn't sure what Raquel was getting at, but let it go.

"Can I see your sphere again?" Raquel asked.

Iza reached into her bedside table for the box and offered it to Raquel.

Raquel turned the object over in her hands, looking for the

latch to open it.

"It's weird, I know. No obvious way to open it." Iza rubbed her thumb along the edge and lid hissed opened.

Raquel closed the box again and tried to replicate what Iza had done, but failed. "Well, that's interesting," she said, passing it back to Iza to open again. "Can you still hear the humming?"

"Yes, it's low at the moment, but sometimes it's louder. I'm not sure what makes the difference, but it's annoying."

"I can imagine." Raquel turned the sphere over in her hands. "How did the box open the first time? Were you doing anything different than normal?"

Iza looked down at the far corner of the room. "I'd been crying."

Raquel placed a gentle hand on her shoulder and gave her a sympathetic smile. "Well, that might explain it. I've heard of old tech that's genetically keyed, though saliva would be a more common transfer method."

"Why me? Why was I able to open it and no one else can?"

"Did anyone else try spitting or crying on it?" Raquel laughed, then shrugged. "I don't know. It's possible genetic material needed to get into the hidden seams, so it needed a liquid to get in there rather than dry touch alone. Maybe you were the first to handle it under the right conditions, and so it imprinted on you and now you're the only one who can open it." Raquel handed the box back to Iza, and she returned it to her nightstand drawer.

"Maybe. I guess that's a little reassuring, for if it somehow ends up in the wrong hands." Iza took a hearty gulp of the pink drink. Her toes were feeling tingly.

Raquel looked her over. "I take it you didn't get any answers from your aunt today?"

Iza shook her head. It had been an utter disappointment.

Without planning to, she told Raquel about the whole thing. She revealed her expectations and even the part about her cousin seeming to follow them.

"Maybe he just wants to get to know you," Raquel said.

"Then don't skulk around creeping me out. Besides, why is he hopping ships between planets like that? Hubyria isn't exactly a tourist destination."

Raquel threw her head back and laughed. "Oh no," she said, grabbing her head. "I've had a little too much." Then she looked down at the empty bottle as if surprised to find it empty.

"I better go before I pass out here." Raquel stood up and leaned to one side before catching herself.

Iza slid off the bed, tried to stand, and fell back down again. "I don't think I can walk you to the door, sorry."

They broke out into hysterical laughter as Raquel slid to the floor to roll around. She eventually gathered herself again. "That's okay, I got it."

The dog played host by following Raquel to the door.

"What's his name?" She scratched his chin and the dog's tail flew back and forth, pleased with the attention.

"He doesn't have one yet."

"He's cute. You know, this breed was popular among the Aesir in the early years. I'd call him Sniffers, if I were you."

"Okay." Iza's mind relaxed into the name as she mouthed it a few times.

Raquel opened the door and then turned back to Iza. "Hey, leave a little room for complication in your life. If you don't, you might regret it someday."

Raquel gave her a formal wave before stumbling out the door and down the corridor to her cabin. Iza was about to tell her she was going the wrong way when Raquel doubled back just as the door automatically slid closed. Iza waved her goodnight from the bed.

"Sniffers!" Iza called out to the dog. He bounded back to her. His curly tail wagged as he waited for her next command. "How do you feel about that name, Sniffers?"

His head tilted to one side before he huffed and lay back down, resting his head on his paws as she settled into bed.

"Okay, you can stay just this once. But only because I'm here and I say so. Got that, Sniffers?"

He whined, and she took that as consent.

Iza leaned back into her bed and her thoughts retreaded the day's events. She had learned next to nothing about herself from her visit to Tararia. Her aunt said Iza hadn't been told the truth about her father. No surprise there. Iza already knew her mother had been a selfish woman. How else could she walk away from a ten-year-old child? Not that it mattered now. Iza didn't want to get caught up in her aunt's reminiscence over the past.

So why was she crying into her pillow?

Iza tried to dry her tears by focusing on the future. Wherever the sphere led, Mr. Arvonen would use it to gain more political power. His own son had warned them of that danger.

The artifact still hummed lightly from inside the box in her drawer where she kept it hidden. Some nights like now, she pulled it out and stared at the etchings on the outside. *Where does the map lead? It has to be buried treasure. It's always buried treasure.*

—

Iza didn't remember falling asleep, but she realized she was dreaming. The rhythm of time and her sense of touch seemed heightened, electrified.

Her mother sat behind her, brushing Iza's hair. Iza smiled up at her before turning back to her game. Her cousin sat beside her and hooted with laughter as he picked up another piece of the game, waving it at her. Iza reached for the piece, but he pulled his hand away out of reach. Her movement yanked her hair free of her mother's hands and she scolded her. Though Iza couldn't hear the words, Iza felt the emotional pain of it.

Her aunt said something to her mother that made her sad. The two of them argued. Her mother stormed out of the room, letting the door slam and bounce on the hinges behind her. For the first time, Iza recognized the house as her aunt's on Tararia. Her aunt had a sad look on her face when she sat back down; she was still shaking her head when she fell to the floor. Her eyes still on Iza, her lips moved but made no sound audible over Iza's own screams.

Her cousin came into the room. He was a man now, with an angry expression. He took her hand and led her away from her aunt on the floor.

Iza sat up gasping for air, finding her face wet with tears. The light snoring on her floor meant she hadn't woken up the dog. Instead of activating the lights, she slid back down between the sheets with her eyes wide on the ceiling. They filled again, sliding to either side of her face and pooling near her ears. The unsettling dream sat heavy on her chest for some time before she let sleep drag her under again.

21

AFTER A FITFUL night and half the morning, the ship was running smoothly, Trix was recharging her systems, and Karter was still out on his business.

Iza had reached the end of her patience. Every minute they were there was another day they might run into Mr. Arvonen or someone who worked for him, on top of the ridiculous docking fees stacking up. Karter better be willing to foot the bill, since he was the one holding her up.

After her late night with Raquel, Iza had lost track of the time, but now they couldn't afford any more delays. When she'd arrived late that morning onto the flight deck and still had no other messages from Karter, it was clear he wasn't coming.

"Prepare for departure," Iza ordered.

Braedon turned to stare at her. "You want to leave him?" he asked.

"He'll be fine. Trix has waited long enough. This virus thing is messing up everything and I want full control of my ship again."

"Starting up the engines," he said.

"The virus is still showing up in random places within the systems, so we could still lose control of navigation, not to mention other critical systems," Viper cautioned, exchanging a worried look with Braedon.

"I understand," Iza acknowledged with a nod. "Plot a course for Lynaeda. They may be our only hope of permanently purging the systems."

"Hold on, we just received a priority message," Braedon said.

Iza swore, slapping her hand against the arm of her chair. "It's Enforcers, isn't it?" Iza said before he identified the call sign.

"How did you know?" Jovani asked.

"Because it's the only way this day could get any worse."

—

The Enforcer ship sat off their nose while two shuttles flanked the *Verity* on both the port and starboard sides.

"This is Investigator Desirae Hyttinen requesting that you stand down and prepare to be boarded."

So that's why they didn't come after us right away yesterday when we docked; the locals were waiting for Desirae to get here and do the honors. Iza held back a sigh. "What's the charge this time?"

"You are being held on the suspicion of illegal smuggling."

"Haven't you already tried this tack before?" Iza needled.

"Yes, it seems we have been here before. However, you didn't learn your lesson the first time. Now, prepare for our arrival, or I will have the port authority impound your ship while I drag you to the nearest prison. Once you're in custody, we can sort out the details. Your choice," Desirae said, keeping her voice sickeningly sweet and pleasant.

"What are we going to do?" Jovani asked when Iza cut the comms.

"We don't really have a choice, do we?" Iza said, dropping her hands. "Enforcers have the right to search any ship under the suspicion of smuggling. That includes ours, so let's all put on our best behavior and prepare to receive the Enforcers."

As they turned to leave, Braedon called out from his console. "Wait, I've got Karter bringing back the other shuttle."

Why would Karter choose this opportune time to arrive? "Let him know what's going on," Iza said.

"He already knows, and he's got his comms open. Do you want me to play the audio?"

"Yes, let's hear it."

Iza and the others listened to the exchange while Karter docked his ship on the *Verity*.

"Cousin, I'm surprised to see you out here. How is your mother?" Karter asked.

"Save the pleasantries for later. I'm bringing the *Verity* in on suspicion of smuggling. If you don't want to share in the arrest, you're free to go."

Figures, she'd let him go.

"No, I'll be sticking around. It will be good to see you in your element."

"Be sure to stand aside," Desirae warned. "I would hate for you to get swept up at all of this." Her voice razor sharp.

"As you wish," Karter said with the same calm as if they were discussing tea.

"I've heard enough," Iza stated. "Let's go line up in the cargo area. I'd hate for them to think we were evading."

Within minutes, Desirae had strolled onto the *Verity* like

she'd been there a million times. In Iza's mind, she had been.

Iza, the crew, and passengers were all waiting in the cargo area when she arrived. Karter's shuttle had docked, and he was also waiting in line to receive the Enforcer contingent.

Iza was pleased that Braedon had cleaned up the equipment he'd been using to run his diagnostic on Trix; there was no need to draw further questions. Having everyone gathered in the cargo hold would make things easier, since Desirae would start her inspection with the cargo hold and she would want to see all the passengers and crew as early as possible in the process.

Iza kept her features neutral and her body still as Desirae approached. This time, Desirae wasn't wearing the makeup or the soft ballgown. She was in a rigid Enforcer uniform, her face bare and holding her helmet underneath one arm. There were twelve Enforcers with her as if she expected trouble—or maybe just because she wanted to put on a show of force.

The dog, unhappy with visitors for interrupting his naptime, decided he should step up. He stood between Iza and Desirae, barring his teeth.

"Well, here we are again. I thought you'd cleaned up since the last time you were under investigation, but I guess old habits die hard. And, it seems you've also picked up more strays." Desirae strolled down the line of crew and passengers.

When she reached Iza and the growling dog, Desirae pulled out her multi-handgun and activated its sonic emitter at low intensity.

The dog whined and retreated at the disturbing sound of the device.

Desirae sneered at Iza. "Are you running some kind of charity?"

"No, just honest people doing honest work." Iza gave a

significant look to the masked Enforcers over Desirae's shoulder. "I take it the standard six Enforcers wasn't enough for you?" Iza eyed Desirae up and down and added, "However, you don't look as good as you did the last time I saw you."

"Hilarious," she said with a nod to an Enforcer on her right, who step forward. "This will be fun."

"Aren't we a little out of your jurisdiction, Officer?"

"Not in this case. We've been investigating the Blue Hills Estate robbery, and it's led us to you."

"It was *my* engagement party," Iza said, sounding incredulous even to her own ears.

"The perfect cover for someone trying to procure enough credits to escape an unwanted engagement."

"That's a reach, even for you." Iza didn't try to hide her disdain. Fake though the engagement might be, it was hardly a cover for smuggling.

"Arrest everyone and put them into the detention cells while we search the rest of the ship," Desirae ordered her people.

"What about the dog?" one of the Enforcers asked.

"If it doesn't follow its master, then put him in restraints."

"Why would you arrest us?" Iza asked as they placed stasis cuffs on all of their wrists, including Karter's, she noted. While being dragged off by two Enforcers, Iza kept her head tilted to one side so she could hear the response.

"Standard procedure when we're dealing with suspicion of smuggling. I don't want to have any passengers or crew in the way. It's just easier," Desirae said. There was a hint of laughter in her voice as she turned away from them.

Thankfully, the dog was smart enough to follow Iza off the *Verity*. They dragged Iza and the others onto the Enforcer's ship while the remaining officers searched the ship.

Iza sat with the others in a holding cell. The dog decided the only decent place to rest was on her lap, where he snuggled while she lightly stroked his fur. The dog's comfort did little to ease her worries about Trix. Braedon and Viper had been able to contain the virus enough to risk a jump to Lynaeda, but it would no doubt overrun the *Verity*'s systems again without their constant upkeep of their security patches around the key systems.

There was nothing Iza could do about it now. They were under the jurisdiction of Investigator Hyttinen and her Enforcers. The offense of hauling illegal cargo was the most common and most regrettable of charges levied on a ship captain. Iza had learned early in her career that it wasn't worth it.

"What's her deal with you, anyway?" Braedon asked. "She's always got it out for you."

"We have a history," Iza said, not really wanting to talk about her sordid past in front of everyone.

"They've arrested you before?" Raquel asked. "I knew I liked you." Sitting on Iza's left, she nudged her with an elbow.

Iza cracked a smile. "Don't be so excited. We could be here for some time," she said. Then she caught Viper's agitated pacing. "Relax, this kind of thing happens all the time. We have nothing she wants; the sooner she figures it out, the sooner we can be back on the *Verity*."

Today, Iza wasn't overly anxious. Desirae didn't hide her feelings for Karter or her hatred for Iza. They'd been in a cat-and-mouse game for years. Iza wasn't even sure it bothered her anymore. Her engagement to Karter only made her more of a target for her jealous rival.

"Doesn't your second cousin sort of have a thing for you?" Raquel asked Karter.

He waved away the sentiment as if it were nothing. Karter stood leaning against the wall with his eyes on Iza from across the holding cell. "She's a second cousin by marriage, and as my engagement to Iza proves, I have no interest in Desirae Hyttinen."

Jovani sat on Iza's right with his legs outstretched toward her, making it impossible for Karter to sit down beside her even if he deemed it appealing. Jovani seemed lost in his own thoughts as did Cierra. She sat on the floor near Karter with her legs crossed and eyes closed.

Braedon was lying flat on his back in the middle of the cell staring up at the ceiling. "Do you mind?" he asked with a glare in Viper's direction. "You'll wear a hole in the floor."

"You deal with getting arrested your way, and I'll deal with it mine," Viper spat back while she continued pacing.

"You'll only tire yourself out. Use one of the meditation techniques I taught you and you wouldn't feel so anxious," Cierra encouraged her sister.

"I'm not anxious, not that it's any of your business. So, the both of you, leave me alone."

Their bickering came to a sudden stop when an Enforcer returned.

"Iza, Investigator Hyttinen will see you now," the guard said to Iza as he released her from the cell.

Ever loyal, the dog tried to follow Iza, but she held out a hand for him to stay. He sat down and let out a huff.

Iza was led to a small office where Desirae sat behind a desk. Iza was directed into a seat facing her. An Enforcer remained in the room; perhaps that meant Desirae would be more civil, even if unfair.

"Captain Sundari, for the record, I need you to be perfectly honest with me. Have you been involved in any illegal hauling activities?" the Investigator asked.

Iza just stared at Desirae, trying to make her eyes blank. "No, I have not," she said.

"Have you or any of your crew ever been under suspicion for illegal activity in the past?"

"You'll need to be more specific than that." Iza flashed her a smile. If she wanted to entrap her, Desirae would need to do better than that. Everyone on her crew had been in prison, of that much Desirae was aware. For Iza to lie and say that none of them had ever been under suspicion for any criminal activity would invite her wrath and Iza knew it.

"Let me be more specific. Have you or any of your crew been involved in any illegal activities while on board the *Verity* in the last four weeks?"

"No, ma'am." Iza sat back in her chair with her arms crossed over her chest, waiting for the questioning to continue.

Instead, Desirae stood up from her chair and gestured to the door. "That is all."

Iza stared at her for a moment, unsure whether she was being serious or facetious. She knew Desirae like to play mind games, but this was something brand new. "Aren't you going to ask me where I was or where I was headed before you dragged me in here?" Iza asked, baiting her.

"At this time, any such information would be irrelevant. However, you could answer me one question. Where did you get a military-class jump drive?"

"It was a gift, from a friend."

"An expensive gift. I hate to think what you must owe them to keep it. We haven't found any information indicating that the jump drive is stolen, so for now you get to keep it."

"Okay," Iza said, letting her confusion show. *What is she up to?*

"We're still in the middle of searching your ship for other potential contraband. If we don't find any, you'll be free to go about your business with no further interference from me." Desirae gave her version of a smile, which looked more like a sneer.

The Enforcers escorted Iza back to the holding cell.

One-by-one, the others were called in to speak with Desirae. Most meetings were as short as Iza's. Viper was the first to return after an extended time with Investigator Hyttinen.

"You were with her for over half an hour, she said nothing to you?" Braedon asked.

Though she seemed calmer, Viper's eyes shifted back and forth in a way that made Iza uneasy, though she couldn't imagine why. She glanced at Jovani, who gave the slightest shake of his head. He couldn't read her. Viper, like her sister, was telepathic and had admitted to having several cybernetic enhancements. If she didn't volunteer the information, it would be hard for anyone else to get any information out of her. Iza made a mental note to speak to her in private. Perhaps she didn't want the exposure of sharing with the entire group.

"Karter Hyttinen, you're up," the guard summoned the last of their group to be questioned.

"Try not to miss me too much," Karter called over his shoulder with a wink toward Iza as the guard escorted him out of the cell.

Iza crossed her arms. Somehow, the day kept getting worse.

— — —

Karter sat facing Desirae from across her organized desk.

With one leg crossed over the other, he sank down into his chair, twisting so he could stare out the viewport on the starboard side of her office. From the look on this cousin's face, he gathered she was still angry at him for getting engaged to Iza. He understood what it meant for her to lose out on a potential marriage prospect, but that wasn't his problem.

Despite Maeve's and Desirae's attempts to elevate their social standing, they'd remained on the fringes of high society. Their adopted Hyttinen name didn't carry anything more than superficial clout, and even that was fading with time. Worse, Desirae's unfortunate dismissal from the TSS Agent training program and subsequent enlistment in the Tararian Guard had left a dark mark on her reputation. To wield true power, Desirae needed to marry someone with real influence—and a pairing with Karter had always been her mother's plan.

Still, none of that explained the craziness Desirae seemed to exhibit whenever she was around Karter. She couldn't offer anything to tempt him into sharing a life with her. He'd rather be single.

"Cousin, what brings you out our way?" Karter asked, knowing how much she hated the reminder of their familial connection.

"As I mentioned, you're being held on suspicion of smuggling. Your captain has a reputation for such illegal activities; however, there has been no specific indication of the *Verity*'s involvement. Unless you'd like to shed some light on it, in which case I would hold you in much favor. You would also likely avoid any repercussions that the rest of the passengers and crew will face," Desirae said. She peered up at him, beating her eyelashes in quick succession.

The game already bored him. However, he'd spent enough time with her to know he'd better play along. Her mother had made her feelings clear at the engagement ball. She was not at all pleased with his choice of a wife. She and his mother seemed to be in complete agreement about that fact.

"I wish I had something to give you. I have no knowledge that there has been any illegal activity involving the *Verity*. However, I would be happy to assist you in your investigation." He spread his hands wide as if offering himself.

"That won't be necessary. We have the investigation well under control. I would be more grateful if you could offer me some information about the other passengers on board," she hinted.

"Sure, who would you like to know more about?"

"Let's start with Raquel. What can you tell us about her?"

"She's actually a fairly new addition, being a friend of mine. After my unfortunate incident at Blue Hills, we thought it best that we maintain some mobility to avoid further danger. Raquel is an old archaeologist friend of mine, who was helping me with a little project that I'm working on. Is she under some suspicion?" Karter asked, knowing that Desirae would not admit to attacking one of his people directly or indirectly.

"No, Raquel herself is not under any specific interrogation or investigation. We found her records clean like yours. We assumed if all goes well today with our search, she'll be free to go."

Karter was getting tired of the fake pleasantries. "Let's drop the act. Why are you really here? Who sent you?"

Desirae smiled in a way that made Karter uncross his legs and lean forward in his seat.

"Your mother." Desirae raised an eyebrow as if waiting for his reaction.

Karter kept his own features unreadable. "Why?

"She knows someone on board has an artifact that she

wants to give to her new business partner."

"An artifact?" Karter felt the hairs on the back of his neck rise. The only person he knew who wanted that thing was Victor Arvonen. If Arvonen and his mother were somehow working together... He shook his head at his own thoughts and Desirae misunderstood the movement.

"Yes, an artifact. I'm surprised she didn't mention it to you earlier. Apparently, someone stole it during the party at Blue Hills Estate. A little green-haired hacker girl just like the one on board the *Verity*. She's already given it to me, so it won't be necessary to arrest anyone. Your mother wants it delivered promptly to the *Arvonen One*."

"Arvonen?" Karter stood up quickly, pacing the room. The guard he hadn't noticed standing next to the door tensed at the movement.

"Oh, so you've heard of him?"

"I have. Are you some kind of bomaxed fool? Arvonen isn't working with my mother, he's working for himself. The artifact belongs to Iza; they stole it from her. He's been doing everything he can to take it from her. Now, he's got you doing his dirty work for him through my mother. I'm here trying to keep it out of his hands."

Desirae's smug smile faded as he spoke, but he watched her fight against the idea taking hold. "That's not true. Your mother said the artifact had been in her suite the night of the party."

"Who do you think sent the crew who raided the party? It was Arvonen. The man you're helping now. If my mother is working with him, that means she was in on it the whole time. They stole nothing of my mother's other than this alleged artifact, am I correct?"

Desirae's lips tightened. "I don't believe you."

"You've played right into his hands. My mother has no clue he's using her to bring me down. Don't worry, when you deliver the artifact you'll find out exactly how little my mother and Arvonen care about you." Karter turned his back on Desirae, facing the door. "I'm ready to go back to my cell. There have been enough mistakes made today."

22

SOON AFTER KARTER was returned to the holding cell, the Enforcers came back to release Iza and the others. Iza let her friends return to the *Verity* ahead of her while she held back to glare at Desirae.

The Investigator stood with her people at the hatchway connecting to the other ship. "Until we meet again, Scrap Rat," she said, wearing her usual sour expression.

"Oh, can't find any friends of your own?" Iza taunted.

"Don't worry, I found what I was looking for this time, thanks to your friend."

Iza didn't have time to ask what she meant by it before the guards prodded her through the hatch. It occurred to her that there was only one thing everyone seemed to want from her lately. She raced to her cabin without a word, leaving the others' questioning looks behind in the cargo hold.

When she opened the door to her room, it surprised her to see it looked untouched. Enforcers normally liked to trash the place just to show they cared. Iza scanned her things. The bed sheets and pillow were as she'd left them, not even the table and chair were out of place. The Enforcers hadn't searched her room at all.

On her original hunch, Iza went to the bedside table and opened the drawer. The box with the sphere inside wasn't there.

That's what Desirae meant by finding what she was looking for. Iza swore under her breath. Mr. Arvonen had sent Desirae after the sphere, and now that the map was in his hands, there was no telling what he'd find.

Iza left her cabin to find the others milling around the corridor outside the galley. Only Trix was absent.

"Was anything of yours taken?" she asked them.

"No, nothing," Jovani said.

"Didn't even step foot in my cabin," Braedon said. As they all stared at him questioningly, he added, "I have my ways."

"Well, they took the box with the spherical map inside," Iza revealed.

"What? Is that what they were after the whole time?" Cierra asked.

"Yes, I believe so. Someone told them where to find it." Iza glared at Raquel. She'd been the last person in her cabin, not to mention fact that she'd been drinking. She was the last one to see her place it.

"You think I told her?" Raquel asked.

"Yes, your interview was a lot longer than mine," Iza said, taking a step toward her.

"I wasn't the only long one. Besides, if I'd wanted it, I would have held on to it instead of returning it to you before you'd asked for it."

Iza read the sincerity in her eyes, but perhaps Raquel was a skilled liar.

"She's blocking her thoughts," Jovani said, stepping

forward.

"What are you hiding?" Iza asked, eyes narrowed.

"Nothing," Raquel backed away toward her own cabin.

"Then why are you playing hide and seek with your thoughts?" Jovani asked.

"I don't understand what you're saying, but I didn't take the sphere or give it to the Investigator. She only asked me a bunch of questions about Karter and me. How we met, stuff like that."

Karter took Iza by the arm. "It wasn't her."

"What?" Iza's vision blurred with the haze of her anger.

"She didn't betray us to Desirae." Karter leaned against the bulkhead staring at his nails.

"Did you?" Iza clenched her teeth around the question.

"Don't be ridiculous. I'm the last person who'd help Arvonen. However, it seems my mother sent Desirae to retrieve the sphere."

"Why does your mother want the sphere?"

"She doesn't, really. She probably believes she's working with Arvonen. However, as you've seen the man, it's obvious he's just using her."

"How did she know where to find it?"

"They had someone on the inside all along."

He lifted his eyes until they rested on Viper. Iza followed his gaze and recognized the guilt on Viper's face before he finished his explanation.

"The person who gave it to them is the same person who took it."

Iza lunged for Viper but Braedon and Cierra stepped between them.

"How could you do this?" Cierra asked her sister.

Braedon looked at Viper with understanding. "What did

they offer you?"

"They didn't give me a choice," Viper said, her voice trembling. "I was working for Douketis, but Victor Arvonen is the mastermind. It's tough to trace anything to him directly, but I'm good with computer systems, you know?" Iza nodded for her to continue. "Anyway, Douketis was hired for the job, since he'd have a legitimate reason to be at the party. That's why all the other haulers who work for Apex were invited, for cover. Karter's mom is in on it, too, I think. All I know for sure is that we were explicitly told to get that box from Iza's room during the party. Everything else that was stolen was ours to keep.

"They were counting on Iza to recognize the crew at the party, and me specifically. I didn't know that they'd set me up until it was over." She briefly met Iza's gaze before looking down again. "They wanted you to bring me in a gallant effort to 'save' me, and you did. After I got here, though, and found my sister was on board, I changed my mind about working for Douketis—the old creep.

"I'd planned to turn on them, but I didn't realize that the Investigator was involved until she pulled me aside. She said if I didn't turn over the box with the sphere inside, she'd put me back in Sarduvis. I'd be locked up for the goods Douketis stole from the party, since she could prove I was there. At that point, I had to do what she asked." She hung her head. "I'm sorry."

Iza fumed, but she heard the fear in Viper's voice. She understood what it was like to be a pawn in an elaborate game of strategy.

"What do we do now?" Braedon asked.

"First we get help from the Lynaedans for Trix and the ship," Iza said. "Where is she?"

"Charging in the cargo hold," Braedon replied.

"All right, that's the best place for her right now." Iza nodded. "Braedon, run a diagnostic. Figure out if we'll be able to complete a jump."

"I'm on it, Iz." He started toward the flight deck, then stopped and motioned to Viper. "Try to go easy on the kid. she's the smartest dummy I know. We've all found ourselves backed into a corner before." He dashed down the corridor.

Iza wasn't ready to be so forgiving. "Viper, go to your cabin for now. The sight of you angers me."

"What are you going to do with me?" Viper asked while she backed away.

"I don't know yet. The important thing is, if you want to survive, do as I say."

Viper's head hung low as she made her way to her cabin.

"Karter, you said they involved your mother in all of this from the beginning?" Iza asked.

"Yes. It seems she was the one behind the engagement robbery and is working with Arvonen. Though, I doubt she realizes that her part in his grander plan isn't as an equal partner."

"No doubt," Iza agreed. "The question is, once we get to Lynaeda, who do we need to inform about Mr. Arvonen? This is beyond us now. Someone needs to be warned about what he's up to besides us."

Karter's lips formed a straight line as he pressed them together in thought. Jovani rubbed at his chin.

"Yeah, I've got nothing at the moment myself," she said. "We can hardly trust the Enforcers after this. From what I understand, the TSS won't go after a Low Dynasty lunatic on my word alone." Her eyes met Jovani's, and he confirmed her suspicions with a nod.

Braedon returned to where they'd gathered in the corridor

to give her the update. Although, from the way he searched the area, he was looking to make sure Viper was still alive. When he saw Cierra standing there calmly, he jumped into his message. "You're not going to believe this."

"What is it?"

"There's nothing of the virus left in the ship's computer systems."

Iza started back at him incredulously. "How is that possible? A couple of days ago, we couldn't keep it purged."

"All I know is there's no trace of the virus now. All of our ship's systems are working normally."

"What about Trix?" Iza asked. "Is she clear of it, too?"

"My guess would be yes. At the moment she's recharging, but I can run a diagnostic on her, as well, if you'd like."

"If she allows you, please do." It would seem Braedon's assessment that removing the sphere would solve the problem had panned out. All the same, Iza wished it had been on her terms. "I still want to head to Lynaeda, just to make sure. We can find someone there to look Trix over, and maybe they'll be able to tell us more about the virus."

Jovani frowned. "When the Enforcers docked with us, do you think it migrated to their systems?"

"I can't be sure," Braedon replied. "Our shuttle doesn't have it, and Trix was also linked with that system. I don't know why it didn't jump to there. Without understanding how it got from the sphere into the *Verity* and Trix in the first place, I can't rule out any possibility."

"Should we warn them?" Jovani asked.

Iza shrugged. "I suppose that would be the decent thing to do. Though Desirae doing Mr. Arvonen's bidding doesn't endear her to me."

"No, but what sort of people would we be, if we infected

her ship and didn't warn her?" Jovani gave her a raised eyebrow in question.

Of course, he'd want to help them. He's bomaxed TSS Agent, after all. "Fine, warn them if they're experiencing any problems on board that we had a similar thing happen to us," Iza said. "Maybe they'll get their technicians on it and figure out how to keep the sphere from messing with things."

"If I couldn't figure it out, there's no way they will," Braedon said shaking his head. "But they can try."

"Let's set a course to Lynaeda as soon as your message is sent."

Iza turned to Raquel next. She'd accused her of being a traitor and now Iza felt like a traitor herself. How was she ever going to keep friends if she suspected them all the time? "I'm sorry, I shouldn't have questioned your motives," Iza apologized.

"You have a strange way of treating your friends."

"Trust doesn't come easy or fast. Just ask everybody else here. I'm a work in progress." Iza lifted one shoulder and let it drop.

Raquel seemed to search her face for something.

"What?" Iza asked.

"I'm trying to decide if I should punch you now and get it over with or what." Raquel balled her hand into a tight fist.

Iza could see by the smirk on her face; she wasn't serious, but she deserved it. "Sure, I'll let you hit me. Once."

Raquel dropped her fist and gave her a pinch instead.

"Ow." It stung a lot more than a punch from her would have.

"That's for doubting me. When we get to Lynaeda, you owe me a bottle of the good stuff." Raquel grinned.

"Not sure Lynaeda will have much to offer but I'll do my

best."

—

After she'd had time to cool off, Iza made her way to see Viper in her cabin. There was heavy-metal music blaring from inside. Iza took a deep breath and pounded on the door with her fist.

Viper called out from inside, "I'm coming."

When the door slid open, Viper was standing barefoot in a tank top and pants. Her music continued to blare. Instead of competing with the sound, Iza just raised a finger and pointed to the room's built-in speaker until Viper realized what she wanted. She raced over to the table and turned off the music streaming from her handheld. Iza's ears rang in the sudden silence.

Viper turned back around. "Sorry about that. Just enjoying what may be the last night of my life."

"I see," Iza said, taking in the room. Despite only having two bags in her hands, Viper had found enough to make the space her own. She had her handheld and tablet on the small table in front of a lounge chair, and a few items of clothing were spread out over the bed.

"I hope you're aware you might have doomed us all if Mr. Arvonen figures out where that map leads," Iza began. "He's a man hungry for power. For people like that, nothing is ever enough. This is no doubt only a stepping-stone along his quest for supremacy."

Viper nodded as if she understood and then looked up at Iza, the fear back in her brown eyes. She flopped down on the edge of her bed and dropped her gaze to the floor, letting the tears spill out. "Game over, I understand. I didn't want to do it.

She had proof of what I'd done."

Iza pulled the chair over and propped her feet on the bed frame. "I'm sure. Mech Neck did the same to me once. Look, you made your choice, and it means I can't trust you. Whatever work you were doing for Douketis turned around and bit you in the butt, and now it's become my problem."

Viper nodded keeping her head down.

"How did you know where I keep it, since you'd never been in my cabin before?"

Viper gave a weak shrug as if that were answer enough. Iza waited for her to answer.

"Your cabin isn't much bigger than the rest of ours. There are only so many places something like that can hide."

Iza didn't bother to ask how she'd bypassed the biometric lock on the door; that was nothing for someone with the coding abilities to access the ship's root systems. "How much do you owe Douketis?"

Viper's head flew up in surprise.

"Don't give me that look. You owe him something. If you didn't, you wouldn't have sold me out so fast. He helped you out of a jam and now you're paying him back?"

Viper nodded. "He said I had to work on his crew for six months before he'd consider us square."

"That's only if you don't take another thing from him. That means no food, no goods. You accept your cut of any jobs you do and that's it. He'll tally up everything he gives you and he'll own you for life if you're not careful."

Viper's jaw went slack. "Did you run jobs for Douketis?"

Iza shook her head. "No, someone just like him, though. Douketis is a hauler. He might be as crooked as Mr. Arvonen in some ways, but he functions like most captains. He'll respect you if you pull your weight and give him the time you promised. Are you willing to go back there to pay off your debt?"

"Do you think he'll take me back?"

"A smart dummy like you? Yeah, he probably would. He could use a coder. I'd also prefer to keep him from breathing down my neck about you, so it's probably best you reach out to him when we reach Lynaeda. He can pick you up there and you can go your own way."

Viper nodded her understanding.

Iza stood up and brushed her hands down the front of her pants. "I don't have to warn you that if you cross me again, I'll do more than send you on your way with a warning. Are we clear?"

"Yes, Captain," Viper said, pulling back her shoulders.

"The only reason I'm allowing you to walk this time is because you're just a kid. Your sister's also my Healer. I've met your parents. I don't want to make your mama and baba sad."

Viper's eyes filled again. Iza was about to leave but decided to add something she hoped might motivate the young girl. "You think they don't care about you, but they do. I wish I had one parent still alive to worry about me. Keep that in mind the next time you brush them off."

Iza left Viper behind her. Maybe something she said might stick with her this time.

23

IZA WOKE WITH a start, listening for sounds of unrest, but the ship seemed quiet. The light snoring coming from the floor revealed the dog was asleep, too.

She sighed as she untangled herself from the sheets and climbed out of bed. She needed a warm bath and a decent night's sleep, neither of which would happen tonight. Instead, she elected to patrol the ship as she did on nights when sleep evaded her.

The dog whined to come with her.

"No, you stay here and protect my bed. I know you've been sleeping on it when I'm not here, anyway." Iza scratched his chin before slipping out the door.

She'd start in the cargo hold and make her way back to her bed. The corridor creaked under her footfalls, familiar and comfortable.

The cargo hold held no cargo. Most of the compartments and cubbies remained empty. She hadn't had a haul in over a week, since the sheep. She hadn't felt comfortable taking on any kind of work with her ship and android friend malfunctioning, not to mention she now had passengers occupying every cabin on board.

She'd been losing control since the announcement about her engagement to Karter. Having him on her ship made their relationship even more irritating, and Iza didn't like others seeing the two of them together in close quarters; she needed to find him a new fiancée so she could be rid of him. Though Karter and Raquel got along well, there wasn't a love connection there. To Iza's dismay, she realized finding him a wife might be harder than it looked. She'd already stuck with him a lot longer than she had planned.

As much as she disliked Karter, his side of the deal still offered her an advantage she couldn't get elsewhere: the opportunity to own the *Verity* free and clear. That would only be possible if he was alive, and that meant keeping him safe by being on the move.

Something caught her eye in the cargo hold's rear port corner. "Hello? Who's there?"

No answer. Whoever it was might be hiding or playing a game. Neither seemed likely on board the *Verity.*

Iza pulled out her pulse handgun. She crept closer to the stacked empty crates where she'd heard the sound. Keeping her steps light, she approached with the weapon in hand charged and ready to fire.

She sighed with relief when she stepped around the crates and found no one standing there. *I'm as jumpy as a newborn kitten. I really need to get some sleep.*

There was something shiny on the floor that shimmered even in the dark. She reached down to pick it up, wondering who'd dropped it, when someone hit her from behind. The black overtook her before she could let out a sound.

—

It was cold and pitch black when Iza came to on the floor of an unfamiliar room. She couldn't see the hand she held out in front of her face. She tried to grasp her last memory through the throbbing at the base of her skull.

What had I been doing? She couldn't sleep. That's when she'd gotten up to wander the ship. Someone had been behind her.

Iza's eyes flew open. However, she still couldn't see anything. There were no identifiable smells in the place beyond the familiar scent of recycled air, too sterile to be an Enforcer cell. She felt the subtle vibration of an engine radiating through the decking.

That's when she realized the hum of the sphere was still there. It grew louder now. It seemed to be all around the room.

Iza gingerly touched the side of her head, finding a tender spot where she must have been struck. She didn't seem to be seriously injured, thankfully. Feeling more confident, she reached out to find the nearest wall. Her hand brushed a solid bulkhead behind her. She inched herself up to a sitting position and leaned against the smooth surface. It was too cold. She shivered.

A blood-curdling scream echoed down the hall outside the room. A loud, shrieking, desperate cry. The scream cut off as abruptly as it came.

Iza shivered again, but this time not from the temperature.

She began creeping along the wall until she reached the corner and buried herself into it. This was not the *Verity*. Whoever had attacked her had brought her to another ship.

Iza lost track of the hours as she waited. She wasn't sure if her eyes were open or closed when the knock sounded. Her head snapped up.

The door opened, letting in light from the corridor. It was bright and harsh, and she had to cover her eyes until they adjusted to the brightness. There were two figures in the doorway and one of them approached, gruffly hauling her to her feet and pushing her forward. Iza stumbled into the corridor and saw that it was four times the width of one on the *Verity*. The three of them walked shoulder-to-shoulder and still didn't reach the sides.

Iza was still trying to gain her bearings when they stopped outside another room. The door slid open and the humming of the sphere intensified.

Inside the room, the sphere was housed in some kind of amplifying device. It hung suspended in the claw-like mechanism, turning it in increments. Light emanated from the etchings in the sphere's surface. A wide beam of light extended from the device to the wall of the ship. At its center was a circular portal of swirling light suspended in midair.

"Where did you get this?"

The humming in the room was so loud Iza could barely focus on what was being said to her.

She recognized the man in the middle of the room as Victor Arvonen. He was directing this show. There were two other people wearing white lab coats she recognized—the man and woman from Galminus, Elyse and Natanael. He must have caught up to them. They glanced nervously in her direction and to each other before turning back to their viewscreens.

"Do you understand what this sphere does?" Mr. Arvonen asked, changing tactics.

The guards who'd brought Iza from the holding room urged her to answer by jabbing the points of their rifles into her back. She glared at them from over her shoulder before turning her attention back to Mr. Arvonen.

"No, I don't." Iza had to grit her teeth together to keep them from resonating along with the sound of the humming that permeated the room. It was obvious she was the only one who could hear it. *How did they get that box open?*

"It's a map of sorts," Mr. Arvonen explained. "But I think you've already learned that. Otherwise you wouldn't have enlisted the help of Karter and his archaeologist friend. Although, they don't understand where it's actually capable of taking us."

"Is this the part where you ramble on and tell me what it does?" Iza asked, sure to roll her eyes and look as unenthusiastic as possible.

Mr. Arvonen only laughed. Then, he motioned to a guard, who nodded and turned to the door. Someone new entered the room. It was a young man wearing a white coat like the others. His face, however, changed when he caught sight of the sphere. He seemed nervous to be there with the others.

"Let's get you prepped, shall we?"

The man who'd entered was still hesitating at the door. At Mr. Arvonen's words, he moved toward the other people wearing lab coats.

"We're on the brink of an amazing discovery," Mr. Arvonen continued. "This device unlocks new worlds we had no hope of seeing in my lifetime."

"You have your sphere. What do you want with me?" Iza asked.

"This sphere is much more than it appears. At first, we thought it was just a map—a way of locating the originators of the technology. Then, we learned it was capable of much more. Look at it," Mr. Arvonen gestured with one hand to the portal, "a gateway to other worlds. But we can't see to the other side by just standing here. The only way to know what's over there is to enter. That's where it gets interesting." The brightness and over-excitement in his voice was something that Iza recognized in unstable people.

Here we go. This is the maniacal plan of a crazy man. She took a steadying breath. "This is all very enthralling. However, I have somewhere else to be, if you wouldn't mind returning me to my ship," Iza said, keeping her gaze squarely on the old man.

He squinted at her, evaluating. It didn't matter if he was telepathic; he wouldn't get anything from her. She'd learned that much from Jovani and Cierra and any other telepaths that made the attempt.

"You're a very," he seemed to search for the right word, "independent sort of person."

"Yes," Iza said, unable to keep the question out of her voice. *What is he getting at?*

"It surprises me, is all. Why is my son traveling with someone like you? It's obvious you survive well enough on your own. Yet, you surround yourself with a rebellious dynastic heir and a TSS Agent. What possible use would they serve?"

"Well, if you knew your son the way I do, you'd understand."

"I'm not so sure about that. Devon is too much like his mother."

Iza squared her shoulders. She was careful to keep her features neutral. "Why do you care how I conduct my business and with whom?"

"Yes, I see the evidence in your eyes now. Emotional attachment fogs the mind at times," he said waving his hand as if dismissing the idea altogether. "That's probably why you didn't realize your TSS Agent has been communicating secretly with his superiors. I don't know what he's doing in our sector, but I'll put an end to his spying soon enough. I'll deal with all of you accordingly."

His last words had an ominous tone like he'd already made up his mind about what to do about them. That didn't bode well for her leaving the ship.

Iza glanced around the room again, looking for a possible escape or a weapon. The smooth consoles and lab equipment afforded nothing to help her. Neither did the two guards pointing pulse rifles at her back. Getting out of the room would be hard enough, but finding a way off of the vessel would be even more difficult.

"I'm sorry, are you planning to bore me to death or what?" she asked.

Mr. Arvonen shook his head and sighed. "Such beauty and yet so filled with venom. Frivolous matters fill the minds of the young with nonsense and they have no patience for the drama of reality." He turned his back on her to face the young man who entered after Iza. "Let's prepare the device. Step forward, young man, don't be shy. This is a chance of a lifetime. You're privileged to see something no one else has. With your help, we will bring in a new age of control and power that we've never experienced. Witness how the Arvonen Dynasty will come to rule the known universe."

He had a flair for the dramatic, Iza noted.

The young man they'd brought in had listened to this speech before and clearly wasn't a believer. His eyes grew wide with terror, and the guards had to force him toward the pulsing portal. He stood to one side of the opening between the sphere and the wall.

"There you go, step right into the light. It won't hurt you,"

Mr. Arvonen said.

The young man seemed less than convinced. Electrified tension built in the room, making Iza wish she could step back. She guessed the screams she'd heard earlier had probably come from a previous text subject. Everyone braced themselves, except for Mr. Arvonen.

"Don't forget now, take a quick peek around and come right back," Mr. Arvonen instructed like he was speaking to a child about to cross the street.

The young man visibly swallowed, closed his eyes and took in a deep breath before he stepped forward. His eyes opened and he squared his shoulders. Head held high, he strode into the portal. After a quick electrical pop, he disappeared into nothing.

Mr. Arvonen and the others held their breaths in anticipation.

What are they waiting for? Obviously, the guy had disappeared, but still they waited.

Then the odor of death filled the room. Whatever they had been waiting for, they received confirmation. The smell of charred meat gone bad permeated everything.

Iza's stomach churned and heaved to empty the contents of her stomach. She was thankful her last meal had been hours ago as there was nothing left to vomit. The guard behind her coughed conspicuously. The two scientists on the other side of the room held up small square towels to their faces, covering their noses and mouths.

Even Mr. Arvonen had a small square of material he held to his face, breathing in deeply before he spoke. "How many is that?"

Elyse answered. "That's twelve, sir."

"Begin decontamination."

"Shall we bring another subject?" Natanael asked.

"No, she's already here."

WHEN THE ALARM sounded, Joe leaped from his bed and raced to the flight deck. He hadn't bothered to put in his brown contacts; it wouldn't matter in an emergency.

"What's going on?" Joe asked.

Trix was standing alone on the flight deck. "Iza, they have taken her."

"What?" Joe stared down at the console and read the signature of a shuttle and then a much larger ship leaving the system, where the *Verity* had stopped for a decoy cooldown stop on the way to Lynaeda.

The others arrived a minute later, roused from sleep by the alarm.

"It seems someone deactivated the ship's security systems and boarded the *Verity* while I was still running my diagnostic," Trix revealed. "They escaped in a shuttle."

"Who took her?" Braedon asked.

"It was the *Arvonen One.* They took Iza."

"We need to go after her," Joe said.

"She told us to go to Lynaeda," Viper pointed out.

"That doesn't matter now. Joe shook his head. "We're not going without her. Why would Arvonen take her, anyway?"

"Wait, where's Raquel?" Karter asked, looking around the group.

"She is not on board the ship. It appears the Arvonen shuttle also took her," Trix said.

"Cierra, take Trix and do a quick check around the ship make sure she's not lying some place unconscious."

Cierra stared at Joe open mouthed then back to Trix in horror. "I don't think that's a good idea. I'd prefer to take a real person with me." Then to Trix she added, "My apologies."

Trix looked back at her in confusion but didn't get a word out before Joe spoke up on the android's behalf. "Trix is as real as you and I. Besides, she will be able carry her to the infirmary if she needs help." Joe considered the discussion over and turned to Braedon next. "Find a way to track that ship."

"There's not much of a trail to follow," the young man said.

"Doesn't matter, do you what you can. Karter, can you reach out to Investigator Hyttinen?"

"Yes, but I doubt she'll help us."

Joe nodded. "Leave that to me. Get her on the comms and I'll do the rest."

"I'll see what I can do," Karter agreed. Though he no doubt hated taking orders from Joe, he had a vested interest in Iza's well-being; that put them on the same team.

"Viper, get a hold of your old crew," Joe continued his instructions. "I want to talk to Douketis."

"Not sure he'll go for that, but I'll try. Most likely he'll want to yell at me so I can buy you some time, if you hurry."

"Good enough."

Joe went to Iza's cabin to look for clues regarding her abduction. Being a small, private vessel, the *Verity* wasn't equipped with surveillance cameras, and there wasn't any log about docking with another vessel. Whoever had taken her had sophisticated tech for covering their tracks.

The dog greeted Joe at the door and didn't hide his disappointment when he discovered Iza wasn't with him. Joe reached down and rubbed behind the dog's one brown ear. "Sorry, I miss her too, but we'll find her."

Joe searched around her cabin. There was nothing obviously out of place. It appeared that she'd been asleep and got up, judging by the night clothes she'd left on the floor and the absence of her boots. Her handgun was also missing. He knew she patrolled the ship on nights when she had trouble sleeping, so she'd likely been taken while she was wandering.

Joe sensed he wasn't alone, confirmed a moment later by a short bark from the dog.

"She's not much for personal items," Karter said from the doorway.

Joe kept his back to him. "No, but what she keeps are things she cares about."

Joe ran a hand along her shelf of keepsakes. He picked up a ship part and remembered her telling him about her very first ship one night when they couldn't stand to be apart. Karter had changed the nature of that closeness, and it made seeing the man even more difficult.

"Any word from the Investigator?" Joe asked to keep his mind off the engagement.

"Yes, I would like to be there when you speak to her."

"No." Joe said with a shake of his head. "This is a conversation for her and me alone. If that's a problem for you, well, then it's your problem."

Joe turned and looked Karter square in the eyes. The man had tried to use him, and Joe had found a way around it, but that didn't mean Karter wouldn't tell Iza his secret, eventually. He was already on borrowed time.

"It's your choice. Would you like the call routed here?"

"Yes."

"Fine, I'll leave you alone." Karter slipped out the door.

Joe waited for the viewscreen on Iza's wall to illuminate with the incoming call. He smiled when Desirae's face appeared. She seemed more disappointed than usual.

"Investigator Hyttinen, thank you for speaking with me," Joe said, keeping his tone as TSS business as possible. "Victor Arvonen has taken our captain Iza Sundari against her will. I hope that you'll render us some assistance."

"Is that your hope?" Desirae laughed and then sobered when she he didn't smile or blink. "Well, as it happens, I'm done with Victor Arvonen. He's preoccupied with getting his little box at the moment and doesn't have time to see to his other commitments through."

"So, you're aware of his side project?"

Desirae's mouth firmed. "More than I care to be."

"He was also involved in the kidnapping of several distinguished scientists on Galminus."

That got her attention. "Are you saying he ordered the abductions?"

"Yes."

"Do you have proof?"

Joe thought back to the two scientists they'd rescued and the henchmen they'd fought and shook his head. "No, not yet. But I could get proof. I need to get on the *Arvonen One*. I can get Iza off and get the proof needed to prosecute Arvonen for his crimes."

Desirae gave it some thought. "You're an ex-TSS Agent. You expect me to go in waving guns around in the face of a dynastic mogul to appease your girlfriend?"

"She's not my—"

"Spare me, it's like she's got some kind of magnet attached to you, it's so obvious. I don't understand how Karter tolerates it."

Joe let out a long-suffering sigh. He didn't want to waste time on her petty jealousy. "Can you take us to the *Arvonen One* and provide armed support?"

Desirae looked him over, measuring him up. "Perhaps, but you'll need to make it up to me. Isn't there some kind of alert out on you?"

Joe glanced at the floor and then met her gaze again. He knew what he had to do to get help, but Iza wasn't going to like it.

—

Viper's conversation with Douketis went as poorly as she'd predicted, much to Joe's disappointment.

"You stole from me, kid. Then you took off without so much as a thanks," Douketis blustered. He kept lifting his hat off of his head and slamming it back down in a comedic way that made Joe snicker. When he couldn't handle it anymore, he interrupted Viper's tongue lashing.

"Sir, I recognize that you and Iza have some bad blood between you, but in all fairness, you set her up to be captured and now Arvonen has her. She's in extraordinary danger. Do you have any idea what it was you stole for him?"

"I stole nothing for him. I work for credits, Agent Pretty," Douketis said with a smirk as he crossed his arms.

Joe ignored his insulting reference to the TSS and focused on the problem at hand. "That device he has is an alien artifact, and he's planning to use it to shift the balance of power in this region of the galaxy. I can't appreciate the difficulties of running a hauling business, but they must be bad when you have to dump your problems on a kid. The great thing about helping others, even if you don't want to, is that they can owe you one. If you do this for us, we'll owe you one."

Reis bristled in the background, her spiked pink hair shaking from side to side. Joe ignored her, as did Douketis.

"The kid owes you," Joe continued. "She's willing to pay off her debt with time, if you'll take her back. The *Verity* crew will also be in your debt. In the days ahead, having another crew to call on might come in handy."

"A payback is only good if there's someone left alive to pay it. You can't be sure you'll survive to make good on that deal."

Reis stepped forward and whispered something in Douketis' ear. He nodded twice before turning his attention back to Jovani. "You expect us to run at the Arvonen armada with only you for backup? I suggest you give up the drink and take honest work for a change and keep your nose out of politics."

Joe took in a deep breath. He'd hoped that the concession of taking back Viper would be enough. He didn't want to tip his hand too early, but it looked as though there was trust needed on both sides.

"We won't be alone. An armed Enforcer escort will be joining us."

"Enforcers?" Douketis raised his eyebrows. "Why in the bomaxed worlds would I want to get mixed up with them?"

"You won't be. I guarantee if you help us, you'll be free to take Viper and go your way."

Douketis rubbed his chin in thought. "This job is risky, I can't just send my people in there without some compensation."

I should've known. Joe's jaw tightened. He was dealing with a shady businessman, and a businessman made money. "What's it going to take?"

"It seems you've acquired a new shuttle. The sleek one."

"That's doesn't belong to us," Joe countered.

"Makes no difference to me how you got it as long as you turn it over to us when we come through for you. Whether or not you get your captain, by the way. If we help you with this, you'll need to hand it over."

Joe sighed. He'd need to clear it with Karter, which meant more even more debt. "Fine, I'll get you the shuttle. But only if we get our captain off that ship. That's my final offer."

Reis bent her head to whisper something to her captain but Douketis already knew his answer. He held up a hand to prevent her speaking, while keeping his eyes trained on the screen in front of him. Douketis was measuring him to determine if he was worth trusting. Joe kept his features neutral, but he felt a light twitch in his cheek where he bit back the stress. Then, the older man touched two fingers to the brim of his hat.

Joe let out the breath he didn't realize he was holding. "I'm sending you the coordinates. Meet us there and proceed with caution. You don't want the *Arvonen One* to see you coming."

"He won't."

Now that his external players were on the field, it was time to sit down with the quarterback and make sure he knew all the plays. It couldn't be easy for Braedon going up against his father like this, but Joe knew they'd need him to pull this off.

Braedon was working on his comic in the galley when Joe entered and sat down beside him. He'd started a new page and seemed to be focused more intently on it than any other page he'd worked on.

"Got a minute?" Joe asked.

Braedon sat back in his seat and gave Joe half a smile. "Sure, Captain."

Joe must have given him a strange look because he let out half a laugh and continued. "We're taking our orders from you now. I figured calling you 'captain' just made more sense."

Joe took in the statement and made a mental note to let Iza know she should assign someone to be her second. If she was gone, like now, they needed someone to step up to make the decisions. In this case, he'd taken on the job himself, but considering how she'd been acting lately, she might not be interested in having him be captain. Though, truth be told, he was pretty sure he was the most qualified.

"I came here to talk to you about your father," Joe said, keeping a close eye on Braedon's reactions. He was surprised to see that there was no shock or surprise.

"You want to know if I'm still going to be loyal to the crew or if I'm going to try and save my dad," Braedon said without taking a breath.

Joe raised his hands to protest, but Braedon pressed on.

"No, I get it. I'm the son of the megalomaniac. Of course, my loyalty is in question."

Joe had heard enough. "Let me stop you right there. Your loyalty is not in question here. You and I have been through enough to know where we stand."

Braedon nodded at this as if he'd already come to the same conclusion. "Then what do you need to talk to me about, with this most serious of expressions on your face?"

Joe tried to relax. As soon as he did so, he realized he'd not only been frowning. "With what we're about to do, going up against your father, things could get a little intense. Are you sure you want to be a part of it? No one would blame you if you said no."

Braedon shook his head. "I made my choice when I went against him and his agenda and stole the H3X out from under him. You know I'll help you any way I can."

"I'm counting on it. We'll need to hack into their systems if we have any chance of getting Iza out alive."

"Of course, I'm ready for anything they try to throw at us. I'll get you into my father's computer network and I'll keep them busy, but I'm going with you."

"I don't think that's wise. Rebelling against your father's agenda is one thing, fighting him hand-to-hand is another. It's better if you stay behind."

"No, it's not," Braedon insisted. He took a step closer to Joe and squared his shoulders to gain a couple more centimeters of height. "You need me to gain access to the *Arvonen One* and you'll want me there to hold down the shuttle so there will be a way for you to escape off my father's ship. Sorry, pal, you're stuck with me."

Joe stood up to leave the galley and clapped a hand on the teenager's shoulder. Braedon was eager but he was also young. Losing one parent did damage to a kid, but losing two could be detrimental, of which Joe was living proof. The anger could drag you under and pull you away from anything resembling a family.

Strange that it had taken boarding the *Verity* for him to realize he was home. He thought about his TSS handheld in the nightstand drawer. There were half a dozen more messages from Mandren demanding he report in. Now that he'd put the plan into place, he knew he'd made his own choice about his loyalties. Nothing mattered except getting Iza back. Whatever reprimand waited for him would keep until he returned.

— — —

Mr. Arvonen shoved his handkerchief into his pocket and turned toward Iza. Now she saw it; he was looking at her the way he'd been looking at the young man who'd entered just after her.

"Well, as you may have noticed, we haven't yet mastered the technology. But we will. We have plenty of subjects, and you're here now. Why waste perfectly good scientific minds when a nice independent spirit like you can go through the portal and tell us exactly what's on the other side?" He said the words as if he was asking her to sit down at the dinner table and pass the bread.

Iza choked back the bile burning her throat. This would be the end of her life. *Fantastic! This is going to be a great day.*

"Bring her forward," Mr. Arvonen said to the guards behind Iza. They jumped to attention, pushing her forward toward the portal.

"The Gate holds the answers to all kinds of mysteries we've never been able to figure out. But if we can harness its power, we can rule the Taran worlds." Mr. Arvonen made it sound like he was offering her up as a sacrifice.

He's crazy. She wasn't about to willingly go through that thing, not when a dozen people had previously stepped through and none ever came back. The scent of burned flesh still lingered in her nose, telling her everything she needed to know about their fate.

However, Arvonen had no illusions about her freely stepping through the portal. That's why the guards were there.

Iza needed to figure out a way to show she was more valuable alive than dead. "Wait, you don't want to send me. If

I go through, I'm not going to tell you anything. I'm useless to you."

"That's not entirely true, my dear. With each new subject, we learn a little more about the Gate. I'm certain you will be remembered in the years to come as one who aided my ascension."

"No, you're making a mistake. Killing me won't get you any new information that you haven't already gotten from the other twelve," Iza said trying to sound convincing. "I won't tell you anything if—"

"That's enough of your talking! Bring her into the light."

25

THE GUARDS PUSHED Iza forward using their pulse rifles to get her in line between the sphere and the Gate, as Arvonen called it.

The hum of energy traveled along her skin in a wave. It had swelled to a loud resonance that seemed to shake her to her bones, making her teeth chatter.

A scream bubbled up from her chest. The last man to go through the gate had been willing; he'd gone quietly and died at peace. Iza couldn't imagine such a fate. She was going against her will, and she would scream until she lost her voice.

"Wait, what's that?" Mr. Arvonen asked.

The pressure of the guards pushing at Iza's back eased, and she realized she'd closed her eyes.

Mr. Arvonen pointed at Iza's chest. "Her necklace, why is it doing that?"

The scientists turned to observe the phenomenon. Iza's necklace had lifted off her chest and was pointing toward the gate. They stared, speechless.

Mr. Arvonen approached her, hand outstretched. He

pushed the metal down with his finger and then watched it rise again. "What is this metal made of? Where did it come from?"

Iza shook her head. She didn't know, nor was she inclined to tell him. Instead, she clamped her mouth closed.

"Bring me the archaeologist."

Iza realized something in that moment. Mr. Arvonen didn't call anyone by name. Either he didn't bother to learn their names, or he didn't want to grow attached to anyone he might want to throw through the Gate. It was probably a combination of the two. Iza had her back to the door when the archaeologist entered.

"You wanted me, sir?" the woman asked.

Iza stiffened when she heard her voice. *It can't be. She's here against her will. She wouldn't work for someone like Mr. Arvonen.*

"Yes, come look at this and see what you can make of it."

Iza struggled against the guards at her back, but they held her fast. Then, Raquel came into view and looked Iza in her eyes.

This had to be some kind of trick.

"Well, this is interesting," Raquel said without acknowledging Iza.

"What is that symbol?" Mr. Arvonen asked.

He leaned in so close Iza had to turn away from his hot breath on her cheek. She tried to pull further back but ran into the chest of the guard behind her.

"It's the symbol of truth," Raquel said, examining the necklace. "The metal is like nothing I've seen before. Iza got it from her parents."

"Why are you doing this?" Iza asked her. She let the hurt and bitterness come through in her tone.

"I'm an archaeologist, you know that," Raquel answered

matter-of-factly, then turned to Mr. Arvonen. "At first I thought it was coincidence, but then she told me about her connection to the sphere."

Iza glared at Raquel's face, searching for any sign of duplicity. *Why would she tell him what I told her in confidence?*

"Can you still hear the humming?" Raquel asked.

Iza refused to answer any of her questions.

"I'm sure if you did a biometric reading we'd be able to know for sure, but I wouldn't doubt it. She might be the key. That's why she was the only one able to open the box."

As Iza looked at the sphere suspended in the machine, that particular point concerned her. "How did you get it open again?"

Raquel arched an eyebrow. "You don't need to be conscious to open it. All we had to do was run your finger along it after you were knocked out."

I guess having that box coded to me alone wasn't such a safeguard after all. "So I imagine I have you to thank for the lump on my head."

The other woman gave a non-committal shrug.

Iza was trying to make sense of Raquel's betrayal. She'd genuinely thought they were becoming friends.

As she thought back over the past weeks, though, Raquel's timely and coincidental appearance on Hubyria. How she'd made her way onto their ship. Her interest in the sphere and her analysis. Jovani said she'd been hiding something, but they hadn't pressed to find out more. She'd been working for Mr. Arvonen all along. She'd been planning to get at the sphere all this time, feeding Mr. Arvonen everything she learned. When they realized the sphere wasn't doing what they wanted it to, they grabbed Iza. She was just another piece of the experiment.

"I thought we were friends. How could you do this?" Iza

spat.

"We are friends, at least we would be if you felt the way I do about our history. This artifact is more than a gateway to another world. It's a look into our past. A view of races we may have encountered but are lost to us now. We're on the brink of discovery here, and Mr. Arvonen has the means and the will to see it through when others would just give up." Her eyes were shimmered with emotion, and Iza realized in that moment Raquel was willing to kill her for the sake of discovery.

"You're murdering people to do it."

"I know," Raquel said with a bow of her head. "It's a shame we've lost so many resources to see this to the end."

"Is that what you're calling the twelve before me? 'Resources'?"

"When they write history, you'll be so much more."

"Enough," Mr. Arvonen said, snatching the necklace from Iza's neck.

Iza glared at him as he fondled the metal between his large fingers. She was about to say something more when the ship shook from a blast.

Everyone in the lab fought to keep their balance. Raquel, who'd been closest to the Gate, screamed when her arm got too close. Natanael and Elyse fell from their chairs and lay sprawled on floor.

"What's going on?" Mr. Arvonen asked.

Natanael scrambled back up to his monitoring station and tapped at the console. "Someone's firing on us," he said.

"Do I look like a fool? Who is it?"

"It looks like her ship, the *Verity*. They followed us."

"How? That's impossible."

Natanael turned with eyes wide toward Mr. Arvonen. "However they did it, they're not alone."

"What do you mean?"

"There is a freighter-class ship, the *Iron Dog*, and an Enforcer ship," Natanael replied.

Mr. Arvonen's face flushed. "How are they getting through our shields?"

"I'm not sure, it's like they have the codes."

The ship rocked again from a blast powerful enough that the stabilizers were unable to compensate, and the artificial gravity shifted too far toward the port side. Everyone went sliding across the lab.

Iza dropped to her belly and started to crawl toward the nearest thing bolted down. She reached a stationary desk and grasped one of its legs. She smiled. *Braedon must have hacked the codes.* He was probably more familiar with his father's *Arvonen One* than the crew themselves.

"Get me the flight deck," Mr. Arvonen said from where he was awkwardly straddling the deck and port bulkhead. He wouldn't leave the lab; that was unfortunate.

Iza hoped to get past everyone with all the distraction. She figured she might be able to manage the two guards and scientists, but not with Mr. Arvonen and Raquel still in the room.

"This is the flight deck, we're a little busy, sir," a man said over the comm. He was trying to keep his voice level and respectful but was barely succeeding.

"Fire on that ship and blow them away!" Mr. Arvonen ordered.

"Sir, we cannot fire on an Enforcer ship. They are requesting we stand down and hand over Captain Iza Sundari."

"Then return fire on the other two."

"Sir, your son is on board the *Verity*."

Mr. Arvonen roared. His face turning from pink to red

then purple. "I don't care if the Head of a High Dynasty is on that ship, blow it up!"

There was a light rumble, and the ship steadied. They were firing back. Iza only hoped that the *Verity*'s shields would hold. They had Jovani, who was good at tactical. Braeden and Viper had the skills to break into anything. If Trix held on, they could use her to—

Another volley of plasma beams struck, and the ship rocked back and forth again. Iza stayed on the deck clutching the table leg; it was safer than standing and further from the Gate.

"Sir, the flight deck is reporting that they've breached the shields," a guard warned.

Another explosion ripped through the ship, causing the monitoring stations to short out. All the lights in the room turned off, leaving only the illumination of the sphere, which seemed to power itself.

"We've lost communications," the guard said. He helped Mr. Arvonen get back to his feet.

As soon as he had his footing, Mr. Arvonen sprinted across the room toward Iza faster than a man of his age should be able to move. Two pulse rifles pointed at her face when he reached her. He hauled her up to her feet and pushed her toward the Gate.

Red lights illuminated above the door.

The guard tensed. "Sir, those lights only come on if there's been an airlock breach. That means they're boarding the ship."

"It doesn't matter. We have an experiment to continue."

"But, sir, the flight deck is recommending we evacuate immediately."

"Not yet," Mr. Arvonen said between his teeth. His grip on Iza's arm was like a vise. Despite her kicks and struggles he held fast. With the weapons at her back and Mr. Arvonen gripping her arm, she barely registered when the door slid open and Jovani stepped inside firing.

Jovani aimed at everything moving like something out of an action movie vid. Both guards dropped in an instant. He telekinetically flung the two scientists back against the wall, an invisible force capable of leveling everyone and everything in his path.

Mr. Arvonen was yanked away from Iza, and he howled and kicked in protest. One of his legs caught Iza, tripping her forward so she bumped into Raquel. A brief look passed between Mr. Arvonen and the archaeologist. Raquel heaved with everything she had to keep Iza's momentum moving toward the Gate.

Iza heard Jovani calling her name, but his voice along with everything else disappeared as she flew through the portal.

—

Iza closed her eyes. She had no idea what awaited her in death, but she wouldn't go through with her eyes open.

She fought the kind of queasiness in her stomach she always experienced when looking down from a great height. After a few seconds of feeling like she was falling, she hit the cold ground on her backside with a thud.

Iza cracked open her eyes to see a cloud of blue-black dust settling around her. She patted the front of her body. One thing was certain, as she stared up at the Gate she'd just come from: she wasn't dead.

The cool, dry air felt distinctively different from the sterile environment she'd left. Iza dusted the dirt off her pants as she stood up to examine her surroundings.

A natural light source in the distance seemed to illuminate the end of a tunnel leading away from her. No sounds reached her other than the humming from the sphere, which seemed amplified here. Iza's eyes adjusted to the dark and she gazed up.

Stone walls towered above her into the shadows so far she mistook the cavern roof for night sky at first glance. Though the stone appeared to be natural, the configuration of the space had to have been constructed, carved right out of the rock. The cavern spanned at least thirty meters wide, by her estimation, distinguished only by several rows of metal railings running horizontally along one side of the room. Based on the dark dust in the room, the space hadn't been used for some time. She couldn't fathom what purpose the room served.

The sound of chatter or applause, like the snapping of fingers, broke the serenity of the space. It seemed to be echoing from an adjacent cavern or perhaps outside, but she couldn't be sure.

A break in the humming behind her drew her attention to the portal behind her. She recognized a voice called her name. As she stared at the Gate, she could see Jovani in the lab with Mr. Arvonen, where she had just been—where Raquel had practically pushed her through. Iza tried to spot Raquel but she was nowhere to be seen. Jovani was fighting off the guards to get to Mr. Arvonen, who was still screaming Iza's name.

"Hey, I'm right here. I'm fine," Iza called out.

They didn't look up. Her voice seemed to get drowned out by the loud humming and snapping noise around her.

She took a step closer to the Gate, and the humming energized the air all around her, lifting the hair off of her scalp and skin as it had done with necklace before. Whatever this place was, it wasn't Taran in design.

There was a swoosh of wind behind her. She whipped around to see if she could catch whatever it was.

"Hello? Is anybody there?"

No one answered, but someone was watching her. She was sure of it. Iza peered into the shadows, unable to shake her uneasiness.

I need to get back before it's too late. Panic gripped her chest. *What if going back through the portal doesn't work?*

She took another sweeping view of the room, trying to memorize what she saw, then stepped back through the Gate.

—

Returning through the portal was not the same experience she'd had going through the first time.

Iza kept her eyes open, expecting to see something while she felt like she was falling through space. But there was nothing, just a bright flash of light as she passed from one side to the other.

She stepped through and could feel the deck beneath her, but then it took more energy to pull the rest of her body toward the Gate—like something was dragging her back into the cavern.

"Somebody, help me!" she screamed.

Elyse was the first to see her struggling when Iza started to emerge from the portal. The scientist scrambled across the floor toward her and grabbed Iza's hands while bracing her feet against the base of the contraption housing the sphere.

"Should we remove the sphere?" Natanael asked when he came over to help her.

"No, it could rip her in half. We don't know what it would do to her," Elyse answered.

"Agreed, I like my legs," Iza yelled.

Jovani sealed the lab door to keep out the other guards and ran to assist the two struggling scientists. He grabbed Iza by the waist of her pants and the three yanked her through. They all stumbled backward, away from the Gate.

Iza realized she'd lost one boot. *How did that happen?* She had laced up her boots, she was sure of it, but now one foot was bare, not even covered with a sock.

She glanced over her shoulder to look back through the Gate. This time, rather than the portal being amorphous light, it had a mirror-like finish, reflecting the scene in the lab. *What does that mean?* She shook her head, not sure what to think of it.

"You're alive," Jovani said, clutching her to his chest. She inhaled the familiar scent of his soap.

"I'm fine. Let's get out of here." Iza tugged him toward the door.

"You passed through the gate. It's you," Mr. Arvonen murmured, pointing a shaky finger at her, the necklace he'd snatched from her dangling in his hand.

Iza's head still buzzed from her travel through the Gate. Arvonen's words meant nothing to her. Either way, she wasn't going to leave the sphere in his hands. Whatever he had planned, keeping the sphere guarded was the key to stopping him.

The moment she snatched the artifact from its cradle, the portal closed. The humming no longer encompassed the room, fading to a dull background resonance like Iza was used to. She slipped the sphere into her pocket.

Mr. Arvonen lunged for her. "No, you can't take it!"

Jovani telekinetically threw the old man back with a flick of his wrist. He crashed against the rear wall and collapsed into a crumpled heap on the deck, his face lifeless.

Iza's eyes flashed to Jovani.

"He's not dead, only unconscious," Jovani said with his mild tone.

Iza strolled past the white-coated scientists, picked up the necklace where it had fallen from Arvonen's hand, and slipped it into her other pocket.

"You came back. How did you come back?" Natanael asked.

"I don't know." Iza shrugged.

She was telling him the truth. She didn't understand how she'd been able to go from one side of the Gate to the other and back again. More concerning, though, was whatever had tried to keep her from returning. Without the aid of the scientists and Jovani, she might not have made it all the way back. She shuddered to think what would have happened if she'd been trapped only halfway through.

"I want to go home," Iza said.

"Take us with you," Elyse cried out, grabbing her companion.

Natanael eagerly nodded. "Please. I'm so sorry for what we did to you. He would have killed us, we had to play along."

Jovani looked them over. "All right, everybody grab a pulse gun. You're going to need it."

Iza hobbled along cold floor, one foot covered and the other bare. She grabbed a pulse rifle from one of the disabled guards.

When everyone was armed, Jovani led the way into the corridor.

The ship had been turned into one giant lab, from what Iza could make out from the rooms they passed. Mr. Arvonen seemed to have focused all of his attention on getting the sphere and figuring out how it worked. Sadly, it appeared his obsession was stronger than his attachment to his own family.

When they reached the cargo hold, Jovani led them to the waiting shuttle. The engines ignited the moment they climbed on board.

"What in the stars happened back there?" Braedon said from the cockpit. "You took so long I figured they caught you or something."

"We had some trouble. Take us out of here," Jovani ordered while he helped Iza into the chair behind Braedon.

Elyse took the seat beside her and Natanael rode in back of the shuttle on the bench seat.

The shuttle lifted off the deck and slipped through the force field into space.

"You hacked the system, thanks for that," Iza said, patting Braedon on the shoulder. "You're a real hero."

Braedon's ears turned pink, but he kept his eyes on the stars in front of him as they raced away from the *Arvonen One*. "Wait, what happened to Raquel?" he asked.

"She's with them," Iza said with her lips tight. "She got away when the fighting started."

They didn't ask her anything more about it.

26

IZA COULDN'T STOP replaying the events leading to her travel through the Gate and back again. Something a dozen others before her had been unable to do. What made her so different? Something Raquel said stuck with her: maybe she was a kind of key.

Jovani had stared at Iza as if she had done something miraculous. He'd been there to help her when it really mattered. In her heart, his hidden identity wasn't enough reason to toss him off her ship anymore. He'd proven his loyalty to her.

She settled into the passenger chair on her shuttle, trying to decompress from the harrowing experience. "How's everyone else?"

"They're back on the *Verity*. We didn't want to risk the entire ship, just in case. We weren't sure you were alive." Jovani glanced over his shoulder at her again. His eyes were bright blue—her favorite—but there was a sadness she didn't understand. He'd got her back, and despite her own shock, he should be happy.

"Is there something wrong?" she asked him.

"Nothing, it can wait." He turned back around in the copilot seat.

"How's Trix?"

"Actually, she's better," Braedon said looking from Jovani to her and back again. "As soon as we arrived, something happened to her. We're not entirely sure what."

Iza didn't know how to take the news, but she gathered that she had no need to worry. As long as her closest and longest friend was okay, she could relax. After her recent experience on board the *Arvonen One*, she still had some questions that maybe only Trix could answer.

"As soon as we get back, gather everybody together in the galley," Iza instructed. "I've got some news to share. Also, Natanael and Elyse need a place to crash until we can get them someplace safe." Iza didn't make eye contact with Jovani, as part of the news involved him.

When they got near the *Verity*, Iza was surprised to see her ship was waiting alongside an Enforcer ship and the *Iron Dog*.

"What are they doing here?"

"We'll explain everything," Jovani assured her.

The shuttle slid into its berth in the *Verity*'s cargo area and they disembarked. When Iza hopped down, the others greeted her with cheers and applause. Braedon threw an arm around her shoulders. Even Cierra seemed to need to be close to her. Iza wondered what they'd think if they'd seen her go through the gate like Jovani had.

She looked back and found him watching her. There was something wrong. The way he kept avoiding her eye put her on edge.

"Are you all right? Did they harm you?" Trix asked, stepping forward from the crowd. The android seemed to be back to her regular self.

"No, I'm fine. You seem well," Iza said.

"I am. All of my systems are functioning normally."

"Okay, so what're Douketis and his people doing here?" Iza asked. She watched as Jovani nodded to Viper.

"I called them in and told them I wanted to come back if they'd help me get you off the *Arvonen One*. They agreed, so they're waiting for me."

Out of nowhere, Viper threw her arms around Iza and squeezed.

"Ow, too tight," Iza complained, wiggling against Viper's artificial arm.

"Oh sorry, I just wanted to thank you for everything."

"Don't forget when you're done with him, you can always come back here," she offered.

Viper nodded as the tears filled her eyes. Iza dabbed at the tears coming to the corners of her own eyes. Then, in a strange twist, Viper went to her sister, and the two embraced each other. Cierra was murmuring something in her hair that the others couldn't hear. Iza wondered if that was how it was sometimes. Even if you fought, family were the people you forgave. It made her think of Raquel. She'd thought her a potential sister once, but she'd never make the mistake of trusting her again.

"That explains the *Iron Dog*, but why is Desirae's ship here? Isn't she working with Mr. Arvonen?"

There was an uncomfortable shift as the others quieted.

"I'll make sure we're prepped and ready," Braedon said, turning to leave.

"Let's go get your things," Cierra said to Viper, who was clutching her at the waist as they walked off together.

Trix didn't offer an excuse as she followed the others out,

leaving Jovani to answer the question. She turned to him and saw something in his eyes. Was it regret?

"She's here for me," Jovani said, raising his arms a bit before letting them fall to his sides. "I made a deal with her. She'd help us, and in exchange, she'd bring me in to the TSS."

"Why would she agree to do that if she was working with Mr. Arvonen in the first place?" Iza asked.

"That was before she found out Arvonen wasn't working with Karter's mother but she was working for him. Desirae didn't like the look of her part in things and made things right."

"No way. She's corrupt. What would it matter?"

"She may have done some favors, but she's rigid when it comes to the law. When she learned about Arvonen kidnapping those scientists and their subsequent disappearances, she wanted to take him down. I've collected everything she needs to prove it."

"Yes, but why is she still here?"

He swallowed hard and looked her in the eyes. "I'm a TSS Agent on active duty. I haven't obeyed my direct orders for weeks. I've taken part in unauthorized criminal activity, and I've forsaken my primary mission to continue living here with you. By turning myself in, Desirae gets two wins instead of just the one."

Iza reached for him, putting her head on his chest. She'd been angry for him keeping that truth from her for so long, but now, hearing it out loud after everything they'd been through together, she couldn't care less about his deceit. Everything he'd done, he'd done for her.

After a few seconds of quiet embrace, he pulled back and searched her face.

"You already knew," Jovani said, staring at her with confusion. "How long?"

"I found out before we met up with Viper the second time."

"Karter told you." He bared his teeth.

"No."

"Trix?"

"Why would Trix— Did you tell her?"

Jovani waved a hand. "Who told you?"

"Cierra. She read Karter discreetly and told me, since she thought I might be in danger."

"You'd never be in danger from me," he said.

"I know."

He sighed. "I had every intention of telling you the truth. Things got complicated once Karter came on board."

She couldn't argue with that. Karter *had* complicated everything. "What was your mission?"

Jovani shifted on his feet. "I'm supposed to be looking for general unrest in the outer colonies."

"Like on Hubyria. That's why you were so interested in Yeaga," Iza realized.

"Yes."

Iza stepped forward, needing to touch him now. She ran her hands down the front of his chest until he grasped her hands. He let his head drop until it rested against hers.

"So, you're going back." It wasn't a question just a statement of fact.

"I have to. If I don't, it might go worse for me. This way, they'll revoke my status for real and send me back to Earth," he whispered.

Iza tilted her head up and kissed him hard on the mouth. There was a long moment where he stared into her eyes before he spoke again.

"It's going to tear me up to be away from you."

Iza leaned into him, pressing her lips to his.

"If there's a way, I'll come back to you," Jovani said. "For now, I need to answer some questions, so don't go anywhere near the TSS. They're not looking for you at the moment, but that may change. I have to tell them everything, including what I saw today. You understand."

Iza smiled. "Tell them. Maybe they can make sense of it. I sure can't."

"This is serious. I can't promise they won't come after you. It won't be safe."

"Tell them the truth. I don't have any more information than you do. But regardless, we'll keep a low profile just in case." She dug into her pocket and pulled out the sphere. "Give them this."

"Don't you want to keep it?"

"No, it's playing havoc with the ship and Trix. Take it with you and maybe they'll go easy on you."

"You're the most fascinating woman I've ever met, Iza Sundari," Jovani said. He ran his hands up and down her arms, staring at her face as if trying to remember every feature.

Braedon announced his return by clearing his throat. "We should go before the Tararian Guard find another bogus reason to arrest us."

Iza turned back to Jovani. "Tell me something, what's your real name?" she asked.

"It's Joseph Anderson. Joe."

"Joe," she said, trying the name out on her tongue. She didn't mind it.

"Everything else I told you was the truth, and I promise I'll never keep anything from you again." Joe pulled away.

Viper was back and headed for the shuttle with her bag in hand.

With everyone ready to go, Braedon stepped forward and

extended his hand. Joe ignored it, pulling him in for a hug instead.

"Thanks for everything, and take care of them," Joe said.

"I will. You know how resourceful I can be."

Iza tried to laugh but her emotions got stuck in her throat. When they parted, Joe brushed his fingers along her jaw. "Viper will drop me off on the Guard ship, so I guess I'll see you."

Iza grabbed him by the front of the shirt and kissed him hard again. "That's a promise."

As she watched him walk away, a few tears escaped and she let them slide down on her face. *Stars! I think I've fallen for him.*

She watched the sleek shuttle clear the bay before she wiped her eyes and called up to the flight deck.

"Trix, set a course for Beurias. Gather everyone in the galley."

"Aye, Captain."

—

Iza sucked in a cleansing breath before she walked to the galley to meet the others. As she approached the doorway, she spotted Karter coming from his cabin.

She called out to him without stopping, "Oh, you're still here?"

"I could say the same about you," Karter replied with a raised eyebrow. "What's with the bare foot? Are you trying out Cierra's style?"

"I can't wait to drop you off," Iza said as she entered the galley.

Cierra and Braedon sat at the far end of the table with her head resting on his shoulder as he stroked her hair. Life without both Viper and Joe would be tough. After what Iza said next, they might not want to stay on board themselves. She hadn't realized it until now, but if they wanted to leave, Beurias was as good a place as any to find new accommodations.

Iza took the chair on the end and sat down. "Thanks for coming. I don't want to repeat the story a million times, so let's get it all over with," Iza said. "You probably have a ton of questions, and I'm going to ask you to hold them until I'm done telling my story. It's a lot to ask, but if I'm going to get through this, I need your patience."

She told them everything she'd seen and heard from the moment she'd woken up on the *Arvonen One*. The sounds of screaming followed by being dragged out of a dark cell and into the lab of Mr. Arvonen. Seeing Elyse and Natanael and realizing they were being forced to work for Arvonen.

"We wanted to help you," Natanael said breaking her rule by interrupting.

"We both did. We thought he was going to kill you," Elyse added. "But then the Gate—"

"Don't get ahead of me," Iza said, raising a hand.

She continued the story, explaining how Mr. Arvonen and Raquel pushed her through the Gate.

"What was on the other side?" Elyse asked.

"It didn't look extraordinary. It was a dry place, not unlike something you'd see on a Taran world. I think I was in a large cavern, but it had weird railing things on the wall unlike anything I've ever seen before."

"It's amazing you could even breathe out there," Braedon said.

"How did you feel in the foreign atmosphere?" Natanael asked.

"Yeah, good thing it was breathable, or I might not have

made it back. On top of that, I felt like I wasn't alone. So I saw the Gate behind me, and from my side, I could see everything happening on the ship. The lab technicians Mr. Arvonen, and Jovani. I figured, after what happened to the other twelve subjects, they'd think I was dead, too. But I didn't want to risk losing my way back, so I stepped back through.

Cierra spoke up. "You walked back through? Like it was a door?"

"Yes. The only difference was coming back was not as smooth is leaving. I came through, but it was like trying to pull myself through tar or molasses. These two had to pull me through," she said, pointing to Elyse and Natanael. "That's how I lost my shoe." Iza lifted it in the air and wiggled her dirty toes. "Well, Jovani helped, too. Or maybe I should start calling him Joe." She looked down, forcing back a wave of emotion at his absence.

"Yeah, when he made his deal with Investigator Hyttinen he told us," Braedon said. "You had to be mad at first. I don't know why he'd keep it from me, because I always figured we were friends."

"Yeah, well, it seems we were the last to know," she said giving Karter glare.

Braedon turned to Karter. "You knew he was still working for the TSS?"

Karter smiled, but he didn't deny it. He only lifted one shoulder and let it drop.

"Why didn't you tell us?" Braedon asked.

"Because you can't exactly blackmail someone with information you shared with someone else. It becomes less powerful that way," Iza said with a wink. "Isn't that right?"

"You've figured me out," Karter said. "Are you sure you don't want to marry me? I promise your life would be interesting."

"Not a chance. Besides, from what I hear, you already have a devoted woman in your life. I'm going to make it my mission to get you two together."

Karter raised his eyebrows but Iza wasn't going to elaborate today; there was too much to discuss.

"Anyway, it did upset me at first," she continued. "Then I remembered all the good that Joe did for this crew and this ship. He's a good man, and he put his career with the TSS in jeopardy for us."

"He did." Braedon fell silent.

"So, what are we going to do now?" Cierra asked.

It surprised Iza that she'd been the one to ask the question. With her sister gone, she figured Cierra would be tired of living on board.

"Yeah, aren't we going after Jovan—I mean Joe? We can't just let him get shipped back to Earth," Braedon said.

"Actually, that's exactly what he asked us to do. I'm not inclined to leave him, but we can't do anything until he leaves the TSS officially. So, for now, we head to Beurias as planned and drop off Karter. He has a location where Natanael and Elyse will be safe. Isn't that right?" Iza asked with a look to Karter.

"Yes, I can arrange something for them," he confirmed.

"Then we go and get Joe!" Braedon said with a fist pump in the air.

Iza cracked a smile. "Is this going into the comic?"

"Of course, it is."

"Fine, then it's settled. Any questions?" She passed her gaze around the faces at the table.

"Just one," Braedon said, looking up with a smile, "what's the dog's name?"

Iza didn't hesitate when she answered. "Atano."

Cierra groaned.

Braedon laughed. "Guess, that means he's staying. You might regret it."

"Don't I always?" Iza said.

When they all stood up and filed out, Iza held up a hand for Trix to wait. "I need to speak with you for a moment."

"Yes, Captain?"

"You also knew about Joe and his real reasons for being on board."

"Yes, I was aware of his current designation as a TSS Agent," she said in her monotone voice.

"You didn't consider it pertinent enough to tell me?"

"At the time, I approached Agent Anderson about his involvement with the TSS and his role on our ship. He assured me he only had good intentions for us as the crew and the ship. He had proven his allegiance to us, despite his former allegiance to the TSS. I did not see a conflict in that. However, not telling you sooner may have had something to do with my malfunctioning systems while the sphere was on board, though I have no way to confirm my hypothesis. Is it gone?"

"Yes, I gave it to Joe. He may need it more than me. Besides, it will be safer with the TSS than here."

"You do not trust yourself?"

Iza thought for a moment. *How can I trust myself when I barely know who I am anymore?* "Do you think my aunt can be trusted?"

Trix tilted her head to one side, thinking before she answered. "I believe you should have listened to what she had to say. Perhaps she can tell you more about who you are than you can learn on your own."

Iza raised her eyebrows. It was probably one of the most

insightful things she'd ever heard from Trix. "Next time, I'll have to bring you along. You can keep me from making things worse."

Trix nodded. "I believe you are right. However, you are not out of danger."

"What makes you say so?"

"It is in your blood."

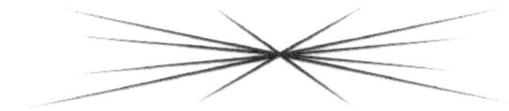

THE STORY CONTINUES IN *ON THE RUN*...

Sometimes the past is best left buried.

Breaking the rules got Joe Anderson kicked out of the TSS and shipped back to his primitive home planet, Earth. Captain Iza Sundari is left on the *Verity*, struggling to keep the crew together.

When the environment of an outer colony planet begins mysteriously transforming, Iza and her crew are faced with a puzzle that only they can solve. Unfortunately, the mission soon puts them on the radar of the TSS—but Iza's learned a thing or two about how to circumvent the law.

To avoid capture and find Joe, Iza will have to come to terms with her family history to save her future. If she fails, not only will Iza lose any hope of reuniting with Joe, but she'll ignite a galactic war.

ADDITIONAL READING

Cadicle Space Opera Series by A.K. DuBoff
Book 1: Rumors of War (Vol. 1-3)
Book 2: Web of Truth (Vol. 4)
Book 3: Crossroads of Fate (Vol. 5)
Book 4: Path of Justice (Vol. 6)
Book 5: Scions of Change (Vol. 7)

Shadowed Space Series by Lucinda Pebre & A.K. DuBoff
Book 1: Shadow Behind the Stars
Book 2: Shadow Rising
Book 3: Shadow Beyond the Reach

Mindspace Series by A.K. DuBoff
Book 1: Infiltration
Book 2: Conspiracy
Book 3: Offensive
Book 4: Endgame

Dark Stars Trilogy by A.K. DuBoff
Book 1: Crystalline Space
Book 2: A Light in the Dark
Book 3: Masters of Fate

AUTHORS' NOTES

From T.S. Valmond:

You know that feeling you get after you've been on an amazing roller coaster ride? When it's over you want to get in that crazy long line again? That's what I was going for with this second book and I hope it was worth the wait. I had so much fun returning to this world for another adventure, especially being stuck at home.

The characters in this story are special to me. They'll be a permanent part of my life, and it's my dearest wish you'll continue to make them a part of yours. Every detail that makes these characters unique exist for me. It's the main reason I brought a page from Braedon's comic into reality and made it available to you. Each character has way more story than can fit into one book, so I'm glad you've stuck around to see how things unfold.

I couldn't have done it without Amy and this amazing universe she created. During my ups and downs, she's been there. She brought along an amazing team to review and proof the books for us, and I thank each of them for their input and feedback.

In these uncertain times, my husband, Matthew has been my rock and confidant. His artistic soul allows me to pursue the dream of my heart and I'm ever thankful.

The ride isn't over yet! Get ready for the next story in the chronicles of the *Verity* crew.

An additional note from A.K. DuBoff:

Thank you for reading this second book in the Verity Chronicles! I hope you enjoyed it.

I must admit, I wasn't expecting to bring in another alien race to the Cadicle Universe. However, when Shelina pitched me on this story concept, I realized it was a perfect fit. I've always loved 'ancient alien tech' as a sci-fi trope, and I love how it integrated with the rest of the universe we're building. In particular, I love the idea of gate travel (*Stargate*, anyone?), so I'm especially excited that there's a new interstellar travel method available for our characters to experience.

Since the beginning of writing the Cadicle series and fleshing out the universe, I always knew that the Taran Empire had experienced numerous rises and falls over the millennia. While the Bakzen War was a defining conflict of the modern era, it was only a blip in a much longer history against far more serious foes. Finding remnants of these past eras was inevitable. Whether or not these ancient forces are still around and active today remains to be seen. I'm excited to take readers on the journey of exploring the larger universe.

Many thanks to the amazing beta reader team— John Ashmore, Gil Forbes, Liz Singleton, Kurt Schulenburg, Steve DeBacker, Chris Pattee, Taria Faust, Leo Roars, Robert Benson, and Eric Haneberg. As usual, you were spot on with what needed to be improved from the first draft. Thank you for your candor and great ideas! Special thanks to my great proofers—Bryan Ellis, Charlie Obert, and Crystal Wren—who always manage to find the errors the rest of us miss. You are incredible!

Thank you to my husband Nick for being the best partner I could have during this strange and unprecedented time. Every day with him reaffirms for me that home is more about the people you're with than it is about physical location.

A lot of exciting twists are coming in the next installment of the Verity Chronicles, and I hope you'll come along for the ride! Until next time, happy reading :-)!

ABOUT THE AUTHORS

T.S. VALMOND

T.S. Valmond isn't an author (despite the claims). More like a glorified reporter delivering the news from far away worlds. She'll tell you she doesn't write books she's building a universe but don't believe the hype; she also thinks she's a Jedi. She resides in Canada with her husband and dog in an undisclosed location. One can never be too careful when exposing the secrets of powerful governments, intergalactic worlds, and illegal aliens. (Yes, they're watching.)

www.tsvalmond.com

A.K. DUBOFF

A.K. (Amy) DuBoff has always loved science fiction in all its forms—books, movies, shows and games. If it involves outer space, even better! She is a Nebula Award finalist and USA Today bestselling author most known for her Cadicle Universe, but she's also written a variety of space fantasy and comedic sci-fi. Now a full-time author, Amy can frequently be found traveling the world. When she's not writing, she enjoys wine tasting, binge-watching TV series, and playing epic strategy board games.

www.amyduboff.com